TWO TICKETS TO
WITH THESE
HOLIDAY HONEYMOON STORIES....

🌺 🌺 🌺 🌺 🌺

"How did your daughter find me?" Tony wondered
aloud, staring at the woman he used to love.

"Well, she's very resourceful for a nine-year-old,"
Jess replied.

Nine years old? The offhand reference to the age of
Jess's child came at Tony without warning, and he
found himself stiffening at its ramifications.

"Let's talk about your daughter," Tony announced.
"Your *nine-year-old* daughter."

—from HIS FIRST FATHER'S DAY
by Merline Lovelace

🌺 🌺 🌺 🌺 🌺

Suddenly Maddy's gaze fell on a man standing a few
feet beyond her. And everything seemed to stop.
Including her heart.

No. She began to tremble. *It can't be.*

But it was. With every fiber of her being, she knew
that it was Evan Blake. The rich boy she'd given
herself to, body and soul, on the night of
July Fourth, all those years ago.

—from MARRIED ON THE FOURTH
by Carole Buck

MERLINE LOVELACE

spent twenty-three exciting years as an air force officer, serving tours at the Pentagon and at bases all over the world before she began a new career as a novelist. When she's not tied to her keyboard, she and her own handsome hero, Al, enjoy traveling, golf and long, lively dinners with friends and family.

Merline enjoys hearing from readers and can be reached at P.O. Box 892717, Oklahoma City, OK 73189 or by e-mail via Harlequin's web site at http://www.romance.net.

Look for her next book, *A Man of His Word,* the second in her sexy MEN OF THE BAR H series, coming from Silhouette Intimate Moments in July!

🐸 🐸 🐸 🐸 🐸

CAROLE BUCK

is a television news writer and movie reviewer who lives in Atlanta. She is single, and her hobbies include cake decorating, ballet and traveling. She collects frogs but does not kiss them. Carole says she's in love with life; she hopes the books she writes reflect this. Readers can contact Carole Buck by writing to P.O. Box 78845, Atlanta, GA 30357-2845, or by e-mail via Harlequin's web site at http://www.romance.net.

MERLINE LOVELACE
CAROLE BUCK

HOLIDAY
Honeymoons
Two Tickets to Paradise

Silhouette Books

Published by Silhouette Books

America's Publisher of Contemporary Romance

SILHOUETTE BOOKS

HOLIDAY HONEYMOONS: TWO TICKETS TO PARADISE

Copyright © 1999 by Harlequin Books S.A.

ISBN 0-373-48392-9

The publisher acknowledges the copyright holders
of the individual works as follows:

HIS FIRST FATHER'S DAY
Copyright © 1999 by Merline Lovelace

MARRIED ON THE FOURTH
Copyright © 1999 by Carol Buckland

Visit us at www.romance.net

Printed in U.S.A.

CONTENTS

CONTENTS

HIS FIRST FATHER'S DAY

For Mary Pat—
a loving, generous, always tired and totally
wonderful single mom who truly doesn't have time
to cry. You're incredible, sis!

Prologue

The silver-haired, blue-eyed cherub in pink sneakers, black jeans and a Spice Girls T-shirt walked into the suburban Atlanta office of Gulliver's Travels five minutes after it opened on a hot, muggy June morning.

"I'd like a ticket to Baltimore." She beamed at the employees still clustered around the coffeemaker. "On Delta Airlines. My mom always flies on Delta, 'cause she says it's got the most leg room."

Dick Spivey, former burglar of incredible ineptitude, and recent parolee, blinked at the little girl's dazzling smile. Since he knew even less about the travel business than he did about burglary, he turned to Tiffany Tarrington Toulouse-Huffmeister, recent bride and the agency's senior travel coordinator.

"Can a little kid, like, buy an airline ticket?"

"Technically, anyone with the means to pay for it can purchase a ticket. But…" Tiffany placed her coffee mug on the mahogany server and returned the girl's smile with one of her own. "We'll need to make sure you have your parents' permission."

"My mom says I can do anything if I just set my mind to it."

"I'm sure you can, dear. Still…"

"I went to visit my grandmother last year. All by myself. Now I'm going to Baltimore to visit my dad, 'cause it's Father's Day this weekend," she confided ingenuously.

Tiffany made a mental note to buy a schmaltzy card for Henry, her own precious daddykins and husband of recent vintage.

"And you know what?"

The question drew her gaze back to the girl. "No, what?"

"I saved up all my allowance to pay for my ticket."

While the travel coordinator watched in bemused fascination, the self-possessed youngster placed a plastic turtle bowl on her desk. The bowl's occupant stared at Tiffany with unblinking interest as the little girl shrugged out of a pink Power Rangers backpack. Unzipping the backpack, she pawed through a collection of beanie babies, assorted CDs, clean socks, a ribbon-tied package of yellowed letters, and what looked like a month's supply of candy bars before triumphantly producing a plastic baggie filled with coins and folded bills.

"I was going to buy a summer pass to Water World. I've got almost sixty dollars!"

"Good for you, but I'm afraid sixty dollars won't get you to Baltimore. Not by air, anyway."

"It won't?" She thought about that for a moment, her silvery gold brows slanting. Then she unzipped an inner pocket of the backpack and extracted a gold credit card. "Here's my mom's American 'Spress. She saves it for emergencies. This isn't an emergency, exactly, but she won't mind."

"Well, we'll just give her a call and check, okay?"

Known throughout the office as much for her soft heart as for her bright, purplish-gray curls and predilection for eye shadow in dramatic colors, Tiffany had to steel herself against the appeal in the girl's limpid blue eyes.

"Can't you just write me the ticket? I know how to get to the Atlanta Airport by bus. My class took a field trip out there last month."

"I'm sorry. I can't run a ticket against your mother's credit card without her authorization." The diamond eternity band Henry Huffmeister had placed on his blushing bride's finger just last year flashed as Tiffany reached for the phone. "What's her number?"

The girl's angelic expression got a little mulish around the edges. "She's at work and I'm not 'sposed to bother her."

Oh-oh. Before Tiffany could probe further, her diminutive would-be customer dropped the baggie into her backpack. Slinging the pack over one arm, she wrapped her other around the turtle's bowl.

"I can see I'll have to take my business elsewhere," she sniffed, her stub nose tilting.

"Wait!"

The glass door swished shut behind her. Stiff-backed, she marched down the tree-shaded sidewalk.

Tiffany watched her progress from the door. Gulliver's Travels was situated in a friendly neighborhood of brick-fronted town homes, small businesses, and trendy restaurants, but the idea of an eight- or nine-year-old walking the streets made the elderly travel agent uneasy.

"Do you think we should call the police and report her as a runaway?"

Still smarting from his own past encounters with the fuzz, Dick shook his head emphatically. "The kid ain't done nothing 'cept want to go see her daddy for Father's Day."

"Yes, but…"

"Didn't you get her mother's name off the credit card?"

Tiffany's curls bobbed. "Yes. It was Jessica, Jessica Taylor."

Easygoing and a few bricks short of a full load, Dick didn't get excited often. Anything that involved persons wearing a badge, however, could work him into a fast sweat.

"Call the mother," he urged Tiffany. "She and the kid's old man need to get together. They're the ones should handle this, not the cops."

Chapter 1

The sun had started to sink behind Baltimore's skyline when a checker cab drew up outside a long stretch of recently renovated row houses just off Harbor Place.

"Here y'are, lady. Tony Paretti's is the one on the end. Number Fourteen."

"Thanks." Her heart hammering with fear, with hope, with a mother's frantic worry, Jessica Taylor shoved a thick wad of bills at the cabby and grabbed for the door handle.

"Paretti's a good guy," the garrulous driver volunteered as she shouldered open the door. He'd been talking nonstop since he picked Jessica up an hour ago at the Amtrak station in Washington, D.C. "I see him on TV all the time, ya know. Brought him home after a fund-raiser at the armory. Good tipper."

Already halfway up the brick walkway, Jess paid scant attention to the rambling discourse or to the snick of a nail-studded tire hitting the cobblestones as the cab pulled away. Her every thought, her entire being, was focused on the door to the end unit. She had lifted her hand to pound on the polished-oak panel before the significance of the brass numerals tacked below the door's etched-glass panels sank in.

Fourteen.

The same number as Tony's race car.

Oh, God!

She closed her eyes, fighting the wave of memories she'd kept at bay since the phone call from Gulliver's Travels this morning…memories she'd refused to let surface, refused to even give shape to during her frenzied search for her daughter Alyxandra at Atlanta's airport, at the bus stations, and finally, at the Amtrak train depot. All Jess could think of then, all she would allow herself to think about, was the fact that a young girl with a collection of beanie babies had reportedly boarded the high-speed Atlanta-Washington Express earlier this morning.

After a frantic call to a neighbor to watch the house in case Alyx returned, Jess had jumped the next plane to Washington and was waiting on the platform when the express pulled into the Amtrak station. To her crushing dismay, the little girl who stepped off the train, her hand tucked securely in her mother's, wasn't Alyx.

Jess had come close to breaking down, right there on the Amtrak platform. Only the bone-deep knowledge that her nine-year-old daughter was more resourceful, more intrepid, than any three kids her age had kept her from falling completely apart. That…and the note Alyx had left propped on the kitchen table.

She was going to Baltimore, her daughter had scribbled. To find Tony Paretti. She'd read his letters to her mother and decided he would make the perfect father.

Dragging in a shaky breath, Jess pounded on the door so hard the etched glass rattled. Let him be home! she prayed. Please, let him be home, and let Alyx be here with him.

She hammered again, harder.

He didn't answer. He hadn't answered any of the phone calls Jess had made after getting his number from Baltimore information. He hadn't returned any of the calls, either, despite the increasingly desperate messages she'd left on his answering machine since early this morning. Maybe he was out of town. Maybe off on one of his many public appearances the cabby had gone on and on about.

So what did she do now?

Catch her breath, then go to the police, which is what she should have done in Atlanta. What she would have done, if Alyx hadn't left her the note saying she was on her way to Baltimore. With the face of an angel, the fearlessness of a pint-size pit bull and the stubbornness of Atlanta's famous Stone Mountain, her daughter could climb Mt. Everest in the middle of winter if she set her mind to it.

Her heart twisting with anxiety and the fervent prayer that Alyxandra would come strolling around the corner in the next sixty seconds or so, Jess sank onto the brick steps. Her feathery blond hair, so like her daughter's in its silky fineness, felt as limp as the rest of her body. The parchment-linen walking shorts, navy tank top and matching blazer, so crisp when she'd pulled them on this morning, were now a mass of wrinkles.

Her round sunglasses slid down her nose. She didn't really need them, now that the sun was a ball of red behind the roofs of the row houses opposite, but was too distraught to take them off. The glasses were still sitting on the end of her nose when a shiny red Corvette, right out of the fifties, muscled around the corner a few moments later.

Even without the well-mannered growl of an engine tuned by a master's hand, Jess would have recognized the lovingly restored classic...and its driver.

Tony.

Her breath got lost somewhere between her lungs and her throat. With one hand on the iron railing, she pulled herself to her feet. She started to shake even before he parked the Corvette at the curb and killed the engine. He looked her over as he climbed out, his eyes shielded behind mirrored, aviator sunglasses.

She did some looking, as well. He hadn't changed. She felt a hundred years older and infinitely wiser, and no doubt looked it after her frantic dash up the coast in the sweltering June heat, but Tony could have stepped right out of her dreams. His black hair still curled with a life all its own. His skin still had a deep, healthy tan, courtesy of his Italian heritage and so many years spent in the heat and the sun of the NASCAR racing circuit. In jeans and a red knit shirt that stretched across his shoulders, he could still cause her stomach to go hollow and tight.

Only when he stepped away from the car did she notice the differences. He walked with a slight limp, she saw, her heart thumping painfully against her ribs. And he was thinner than she remembered. Leaner. Those deep grooves carved on either side of his mouth had no doubt resulted from the pain he'd suffered after the spectacular crash that had ended his racing career.

Jess had ached for him then. She aches now. For him, for herself, for their long-ago love and the barely disguised impatience in his eyes when he peeled off his sunglasses and surveyed the woman on his doorstep.

"Can I help you?"

She deserved that, she supposed. Deserved worse. The fact that he didn't recognize her didn't matter. Nothing mattered except Alyx.

"Yes. I'm—" She gulped, took off her own sunglasses. "Tony, it's Jessica. Jessica Taylor."

At first she thought he hadn't heard her. He didn't move, didn't react at all.

"I—" She swallowed, her throat raw with hurting. "I was Jess Summerville when I knew you."

A muscle ticked on the side of his jaw. Aside from that, he showed no emotion. Certainly no welcome. Those sexy, bedroom-brown eyes that had once looked at her with such laughter and love now held nothing but polite inquiry.

"It's been a long time, Jess."

She could only nod.

"What can I do for you?"

The cool, distant inquiry told her more clearly than words that Alyx hadn't found him. Even after what Jess had done to him all those years ago, Tony wouldn't play games with her, wouldn't hold back the information that a strange little girl had tracked him down and informed him that she wanted him for a father.

Her heart sinking, Jess tried to ask permission to use his phone. "You can…" She gulped, tried again. "You can let me—"

"Yes?"

At that point Jess did what any woman whose nine-year-old daughter had been missing for eight hours would do. She burst into tears. Not demure, ladylike tears. Great, gulping, noisy sobs. Her shoulders shook.

Her chest squeezed. Her cries poured out the cumulative effect of long hours of stress and fear.

Tony stood on the sidewalk, his hands curling into fists. Emotions he hadn't suspected were still alive inside him jumped up to grab him by the throat. Blindly, instinctively, he wanted to reach out to her, to soothe her, to let the sunshine of her hair fill his senses the way she'd once filled his arms.

Rigidly he suppressed the absurd need. It had taken him a long time, but he'd finally understood that all he'd felt for Jess that long-ago summer was lust. The hot, heady, throat-closing kind of lust a man who didn't know any better could easily confuse with love.

He certainly knew better now...so why in blazes was he standing here, feeling guilty as sin for making Jess cry? Why *was* she crying, anyway? And what was she doing here?

Despite the old hurt and the anger he'd thought long gone, Tony couldn't let her sob out the reason for her sudden reappearance in his life on the front stoop. Aside from the fact that her tears made him acutely uncomfortable, Mrs. Genovese next door was already peering through the lace curtains of her front window. The way things worked around this predominantly Italian neighborhood, she'd be on the phone to Tony's mother within the next fifteen to twenty seconds.

"Why don't we go inside?" he suggested, his voice stiff, as his in-bred courtesy warred with other, less-polite emotions.

She clung to the iron railing, her aquamarine eyes swimming with tears. "I...just...need...to use your... phone."

"Okay."

He took a step forward, his door key in hand. She

didn't move, or couldn't move. Tony told himself not to let those huge, frightened eyes get to him. Reminded himself what had happened the last time he let this woman touch his heart. Even with those dire reminders ringing in his head, he couldn't keep his voice from gentling.

"Come on, Jess." He took her arm, edged her aside so he could put the key in the lock. "Let's go inside."

Sniffling noisily, she preceded him into the long, narrow corridor. Resolutely, Tony kept his eyes from the slender legs displayed beneath the hem of her linen shorts. It didn't matter to him that Jess had kept herself in excellent shape all these years, or that her short, feathery bob made her seem at once sophisticated and all too vulnerable.

"You can use the phone in here," he said, sliding back a pair of wooden doors to reveal the big, sunny front room.

His mother and his sister, Angela, had gone to work on the renovated town house when Tony first purchased it a year ago. The restored hardwood floors gleamed. The kitchen included appliances Tony had neither the time nor the inclination to turn on. Even the upstairs bedroom bore traces of Angela's extravagant touch in its thick down comforter and the massive fern he never remembered to water. Good thing the monster seemed to thrive on neglect.

The front room retained Tony's stamp, however. Using a sledgehammer and sheer muscle power, he'd knocked out the wall between the old living and dining rooms, opening both to the sunlight that streamed in through the front bay window. The massive fireplace he'd left intact, as well as the dark oak paneling that gave the room a rich, lived-in feeling. An entertainment center took up one whole wall. Bookshelves filled another. The furniture was leather, man-size and comfortable.

His only concession to the career that had consumed his youth and almost cost him his life was the original Niemans that hung over the fireplace. The brilliant wash of oils depicted Number Fourteen flashing across the finish line at Daytona. Tony's sponsor had commissioned the painting and presented it to him when he'd captured his second NASCAR Grand National Championship.

He'd resisted every attempt by his mother and determined sister to display all the other trophies and memorabilia he'd collected over the years. His racing career was over, he'd reminded them firmly. He wasn't the kind of man to live in the past.

Which was exactly what he told himself when he flipped the switch and caught Jess in the soft glow of the incandescent lights. Even wind tangled, her hair gleamed with the silvery-gold sheen he remembered, and her mouth...

Her mouth still trembled. Soft. Full. Naked of all color except its own pale rose tint.

Damn!

Forgetting the innate courtesy that had prompted him to invite her inside, Tony snapped out the question he'd sworn he wasn't going to ask.

"What's this about, Jess? What the hell do you want from me after all these years?"

She spun around, her back stiffening. "I don't want anything from you."

He folded his arms. He was damned if he was going to make this any easier for her. She hadn't exactly made things easy for him ten years ago.

Her chin came up. The tip of her nose still glowed a bright red from her weeping, but her eyes lost their anguished look.

"I came here to find my daughter."

Tony's eyes narrowed. Across the room Jess swallowed and tipped her chin another notch.

"Alyxandra has decided that she needs a father and that I—" the rest of her face reddened to match her nose "—that I need a husband."

Tony waited, his jaw tight, until he could trust himself to speak. "Last I heard, you had a husband."

"I did," she said quietly. "He died three months after Alyx was born."

The irony of it ate at Jess's soul. She'd loved Frank almost all her life…or thought she had. They'd grown up next door to each other, squabbled and fought all through elementary school, ignored each other in junior high. Without either quite knowing how it happened, they'd become a couple in high school. Maybe because they made the perfect pair. Frank so handsome and outgoing, Jess so willing to follow where he led.

Except that one summer…the summer after her sophomore year at college, when she'd taken a job working at the Talledega Speedway, ninety miles east of Atlanta and just a few miles from her hometown. She'd needed time, she'd told Frank. Needed to think before she married him, as he kept begging her to do. She'd never really dated anyone else. Never even kissed anyone but Frank. Certainly never burned with hot, scorching desire.

Until Tony.

Oh, God! She'd been so young then. So stupid. She had no idea that the acrid sting of motor oil, the roar of the crowds, the pulsing excitement of the races could

get to her like that. No idea that what she'd felt for
Frank came far closer to friendship than love.

Until Tony.

She'd met him during the heady, exciting weeks before the Talledega 500. He'd flashed that cocky grin at
her. Invited her to the pit to meet his crew. Described
in loving detail every modification he'd made to the
Chevy Monte Carlo chassis to transform it into Number
Fourteen. That same evening he'd taken her out for dinner and charmed her with his old-fashioned manners.

She hadn't meant to fall in love with him. Hadn't
intended to be disloyal to Frank, even though they'd
agreed to take the summer to see other people, to test
their relationship. She certainly hadn't planned on falling under the spell of Tony Paretti's hands and mouth
and dark, laughing eyes.

She'd tumbled into love *so* hard and so fast, Jess
remembered bleakly. She couldn't get enough of his
company, couldn't wait until her work shift ended so
she could join him and his crew at the pit.

Then, midway through the final qualifiers, Jess realized that it wasn't the excitement of the races or the
summer heat or being in love that made her feel so
dizzy. She was pregnant with Frank's child. She'd left
Talledega the next day, telling Tony only that she
couldn't risk losing her heart to a man who lived his
life at speeds in excess of two hundred miles per hour.

Once home, she'd told Frank about the baby. Told
him, too, about Tony. In his eagerness to have her and
his child, Frank brushed aside what he termed her summer fling. They were married a week later.

Tony had called, of course. And written. Several im-
passioned letters. Once, he'd driven over to her home-

town to see her. Her father had told him then that she
was married. She hadn't heard from him since.

In her heart of hearts, Jess never regretted her choice.
She wouldn't have denied Frank his child. Nor, in ret-
rospect, could she have taken sitting in the stands race
after race, her heart in her throat, while the man she
loved thundered around the track and courted death with
every turn.

It was one of life's bitter ironies that Frank died in a
car accident just a year after their marriage. By then
Jess had Alyx to take care of. Her grief had faded
slowly over the years. So had her secret aching desire
for Tony Paretti.

Now, in another of those ironic twists of fate, Alyx
had found Tony's letters. Jess had forgotten all about
them. If asked, she couldn't even say why she'd kept
them. Somehow, they'd gotten stashed in a box of childhood keepsakes she never bothered to unpack. Losing
a husband, raising a baby, finishing college part-time
and working full-time made unpacking boxes a pretty
low priority.

None of which was easy to explain to the man watching her from across the room.

"I'm sorry you lost your husband."

He was sincere, she saw. The tight knot around her
chest eased a bit. She'd find Alyx. Take her home. Put
this whole embarrassing business behind them both.

"Me, too," she said simply. "He was a good man."

"I'm not sure I understand how the fact that your
daughter has decided she needs a father...or you need
a husband...concerns me."

"It doesn't. Not really. It's just that— Well, Alyx
found your letters."

"What letters?"

A tinge of heat crept up Jess's cheeks. "The ones you wrote after I left Talledega."

He frowned. "Did I write you?"

He honestly didn't remember. Jess didn't blame him. She hadn't remembered the blasted letters, either.

"Look, I'll explain everything later. Right now I need to call home and see if my daughter's shown up."

He nodded to the end table beside a massive leather sofa. "There's the phone."

Riddled with anxiety, she reached for the cordless. It rang in her hands, startling her so much she almost dropped it. The instant, flaring hope that it might be Alyx had her punching the talk button before she remembered this wasn't her phone or her home.

"Hello!"

A small silence ensued before a woman's voice came over the line. "Who's this?"

Jess shoved her hand through her hair. Maybe it was the police. Her neighbor. Alyx's grandparents. Jess had called everyone she knew and left Tony's number as a contact point.

"This is Jessica Taylor. Are you calling for me?"

Another silence. "No, actually. I was calling for my son, Anthony."

"Hold on." Chewing on her lower lip, she held out the phone. "It's your mother."

Tony took it, his brown eyes following Jess as she paced the floor. "I'll call you back in a few minutes, Mom. No. No. Yes." He blew out a long breath. "No. A few minutes, I promise."

He handed the instrument back. Jess's fingers shook as she punched in her home number. She prayed Alyx would answer. When the recorder clicked on, she closed her eyes against a wave of swamping disappointment. Swallowing, she hit the code to retrieve her messages.

One from her sister, saying anxiously that she hadn't heard from Jess yet. One from Frank's father. One from Mrs. Carruthers. One from...

She bit down on her lower lip, straining to hear the soft, unfamiliar voice. Jess missed the caller's name but heard the blessed news that Alyx was safe!

Limp-kneed, she gave a little moan of relief. She didn't see Tony take a quick step toward her, his face all sharp angles and hard worry. Jess pressed the phone to her ear, listening to the soft voice.

Alyx had taken a bus after all. A Trailways. She'd made it as far as Rocky Point, North Carolina, before she ran out of money and candy bars. The little girl was with her and her husband, the woman assured Jess. She gave her number, repeated it slowly, before the message beeped off.

Jess closed her eyes. When she opened them again, she did what any woman would do who'd just learned that her nine-year-old daughter was safe. She burst into tears.

"Oh, God!" He took another step, concern carving sharp creases in his face. "Jess! Is your daughter okay?"

"She's...fine. She's with...a family in North Carolina."

Afterward Jess could never remember if he gathered her in his arms or she fell into them. Somehow she just sort of ended up there. She *would* remember drenching his red knit shirt, however...and how good it felt to lay her head against his chest. How incredibly, wonderfully good.

Chapter 2

She felt so good in his arms. So damned good. If he closed his eyes, Tony would swear that ten years hadn't passed, that he was twenty-three again, just edging toward his first racing championship, brimming with energy and confidence and the swagger that comes with knowing you're good. Brimming, too, with the utter male certainty that he'd found the one woman he didn't even know he'd been looking for.

Yeah, sure. He'd found her, all right. And she'd left a gaping hole in his heart when she'd walked out on him just a few weeks later.

The hole had healed. Slowly. He'd gotten over Jess, gotten over his bitterness, too. He'd had his racing to occupy his mind and his energies until the spectacular crash than ended his career. Even then he hadn't thought of Jess. Much. Four months in intensive care and almost a year in rehab put things in perspective.

So he didn't understand why the hell his muscles now

quivered with the urge to mold her body to his, or why her scent teased him with every breath he took.

Steeling himself against her assault on his senses, Tony waited until her sobs had dwindled to sniffles before easing her out of his arms. He used the excuse of getting her some tissues to put a safe distance between them.

She took the tissues with a murmured word of thanks. "I need to call North Carolina. Do you mind?"

"Of course not."

She had the phone in hand before he answered. Her teeth worried her lower lip until someone at the other end answered.

"Hello!" Her entire body went taut. "This is Jessica Taylor. You left a message on my recorder about my daughter, Alyxandra. She's all right, isn't she? You're sure? Absolutely sure? Can I talk to her?"

Tony dropped into his chair and listened to the one-sided conversation. A hundred questions whirled in his mind, not the least of which was why Jess had kept the letters he now vaguely recalled writing.

"Hello, sweetie!"

Her face softened into an expression that was at once rueful, relieved and exasperated.

"You're in trouble, Alyxandra. You know that, don't you?"

Motherhood suited her, Tony decided. He remembered a younger Jess, more slender, less...defined. That was the only word he could think of. Even with tear tracks streaking her cheeks, she gave the impression of a woman used to handling whatever life threw at her.

Like the loss of a spouse. Tony wouldn't wish that on anyone, much less the woman he'd once loved. Briefly he wondered how long ago Jess's husband had died. A few months after their daughter was born, she'd said.

"I don't care. You just stay put until I get there, okay? Promise me, Alyx. Cross your heart. Again! One more time!"

She lifted a hand to push it through her silky hair and threw Tony a smile. It was a distracted one, not really for him as much as for the girl on the other end of the line, but it carried more than enough wattage to make his stomach clench.

"I'll see you soon, sweetie. As soon as I can get there. Be good, okay? Promise! Cross your heart!" She listened a moment, then shook her head. "No! No way! Alyx..." She closed her eyes and pushed out a long breath. "We'll talk about it later. Let me talk to Mrs. Stewart now."

Tony waited with her in a small, charged silence. He still couldn't quite believe she sat just a few yards away, a ghost from his youth. The ghost *of* his youth, he reflected wryly. She'd certainly haunted his dreams for longer than he was willing to admit.

"I can't thank you enough for taking her in," she told the woman on the other line. "And for calling me. I'll call you back as soon as I check on airline connections and know when I'll be there. Yes. Yes, I will. Thank you. Thank you so much."

She hung up with a sniffle and used the wadded tissues to blow away the last of her distress.

"Is she okay?" Tony asked.

"She's fine." Her mouth curved in a wry twist. "Better than fine, actually. The little stinker made it as far as Rocky Point, North Carolina, wherever that is, before her money ran out. Wouldn't you know the couple who took her in have a farm...and a new litter of kittens? Alyx has already picked out the one she wants."

She was quiet for a moment, the tension draining visibly from her shoulders. Tony waited until she slumped back against the sofa before asking for an explanation.

"Okay, Jess, what's this all about?"

"I told you. My daughter's taken it into her head that she needs a father and I need a husband. And when Alyx gets something into her head," she said with a grimace, "it's almost impossible to get it out."

"Why me? I don't remember what I said in those letters, but considering how I felt after you walked out on me, I doubt that I came across as prime husband or father material."

"I don't remember the exact wording, either. The last one was pretty angry, but…" She played with the tissues, not quite meeting his eyes. "I think there were a few lines in one of them about, uh, always loving me, or something to that effect."

He let that pass. "She decided a perfect stranger would make a good father based on a few ten-year-old letters?"

"Not just the letters," Jess admitted ruefully. "She said in her note that she saw you on TV. In a promo for Big Brothers, I think. According to Alyx, you looked nice."

"Nice?"

Tony thought of all the adjectives sportscasters had used to describe him during his career. *Fast* came to mind immediately. *Hell on wheels* was a favorite. And in recent years, they'd taken to calling him a shrewd businessman and entrepreneur. To everyone's surprise, his own included, he'd parlayed his racing experience into a multimillion-dollar car parts business. He'd had to, to cover his medical bills and repay his parents and sister for the financial sacrifices they'd made on his behalf. Desperation had driven him, along with the grim knowledge he'd never race again. Nice hadn't figured in there anywhere.

True, he sponsored a number of charities. He was careful which ones he gave his name and support to, though. He made it a point to check the ratio of organizational overhead to moneys distributed before participating in any fund-raisers. Strange that the one charity he really believed in and gave most of his time to would bring Jess Summerville…Jess Taylor…back into his life after all these years.

"How did your daughter find me?" he asked curiously.

"I'm only guessing, but I expect she tracked you down using the Internet. She's pretty resourceful for a nine-year-old."

Nine-year-old? The offhand reference to the girl's age came at Tony without warning, like the wall of a speedway. He felt himself stiffening as the ramifications ripped through his mind.

"I use a computer in my business," Jess went on, unaware of his sudden, shoulder-locking tension. "I wanted Alyx to know how to use it, too. We agreed which programs and search engines she'd have access to and blocked the rest. She's a whiz at tracking people through the yellow pages. That's probably how she found you."

She looked up from the tissues she'd been fiddling with and glanced over at him. Tony didn't respond. He couldn't. His face felt as though it was carved from ice.

"Look, I'm sorry we—Alyx and I—involved you in

this. I'll just call the airlines and check the flights to North Carolina, then I'll be out of your life." She gave an embarrassed smile and reached for the phone. "Again."

"The hell you will."

Startled, she froze with her hand outstretched. Tony pushed out of the leather chair, anger building in him with every breath he pulled into his lungs.

"Let's start over, Jess."

Her eyes widening at the unmistakable menace in his voice, she, too, pushed to her feet.

"What are you talking about?"

"I'm talking about your daughter. Your *nine-year-old* daughter."

The blood drained slowly from her face. For a moment the girl Tony had loved so many years ago stared at him, her face stark, her eyes haunted. She drew in a deep breath, then another, and the girl became the woman.

"Yes, Alyx turned nine a few months ago. And yes, she's the reason I left Talledega."

Fury welled in Tony's chest. All those nights he'd played and replayed her final words to him in his mind. Racing was too dangerous. She couldn't watch him risking his life day after day. He'd called her, asking her to reconsider. Written her. For almost a month, he'd agonized over whether he should abandon the track, his crew, his sponsors. He'd made the choice, gone after her...only to find her married to another man.

Now he knew the truth. She hadn't left him because she couldn't bear to watch him court death with every race. She'd left him because she was pregnant.

"You didn't think I had a right to know?"

"No." She met his eyes squarely. "The only person I owed an explanation to was Frank."

"Bull!"

Her chin tipped up. "Even if it hadn't worked out between Frank and me, I wouldn't have come back to you, Tony. What I said then was true. I didn't know how much, until after Alyx was born, but it was true. The way you drove, the risks you took in every race…I couldn't have sat in the stands and watched you week after week, year after year. I couldn't have married you, had children with you, knowing that every time you walked out the door you might not come back. A child needs stability, security, not a parent who plays with death with every day."

"Yet Frank was the one who died," he shot back. "You played the odds, Jess, and you lost."

He regretted the cruel reminder as soon as it was out of his mouth. A bleakness settled over her face, stretching the skin tight across her cheekbones.

"Yes, I know." Her throat worked, but she refused to look away. "Given the circumstances, I'd make the same choice again. I did what was right at the time, and what was best for my daughter."

Tony curled his hands into fists. Suspicion wrapped its ugly fingers around his heart and squeezed.

"Is that what you're doing now? After all these years, are you still trying to do what's best for your daughter?"

"Yes, of course."

"Is that why you tracked me down? Are you still playing the odds, Jess?"

She frowned, confused and a little wary of his tight expression. "I don't know what you're talking about."

"Don't you?" His brown eyes burned into hers.

"Maybe you're thinking it's not too late to try again. Maybe you're even considering a paternity suit."

Shock sent her stumbling back. "A paternity suit! I wouldn't... I couldn't! We never..."

"We never made love?" Tony smiled. He suspected it wasn't a pleasant sight. "No, we didn't."

He'd wanted to. God knew, he'd ached with wanting her. Only the remnants of his Italian Catholic upbringing had held him back. She was the one woman he'd ever wanted to marry, had ever thought about marrying. So he'd gone to bed alone night after night, hard and aching, yet determined to wait until she wore his ring.

She'd wanted to wait, too. She'd told him about her high school sweetheart. Told him that they'd agreed to see other people that summer. But she'd fallen for Tony too hard, too fast, to give in to the desire that burned in her veins. She needed time...to be sure.

Then she'd left him. The hurt he'd thought long dead rose up to sear his throat.

"*I* know we never made love," he growled. "*You* know it. But maybe you're betting on the fact that no one else did."

"What?"

"Every man on my crew saw how hungry we were for each other. They were all absolutely convinced we were jumping into the sack every chance we got."

"Why in the world would I care what your crew thought ten years ago?" she cried. "Why would I try to claim you fathered my child when a simple medical test could prove otherwise?"

The possibilities brought a bad taste to Tony's mouth. Before his accident, he'd broken every NASCAR record for his age and his category. Fans mobbed him on and off the track. Sponsors stood in line to get his endorsement for their products. Like all celebrities, he'd also been the target of too many near-libelous headlines and more than a few would-be scams.

Even after his accident, the public's attention never left him. Loyal fans inundated him with cards and letters during his long recovery. Sponsors still wanted his endorsement. Charities asked him to act as their spokesperson. And as his business took off, he found that his slowly accumulating wealth attracted even more dubious offers and phony schemers. He couldn't discount the possibility that Jess's sudden reappearance in his life might have its roots in another scam.

"Maybe you got on the Internet, too," he said slowly, watching her eyes. "Maybe you discovered that the racer you walked out on all those years ago, the racer who lost everything after the crash, started a company that just made the Fortune 500. Maybe you figured the sucker would be willing to settle for a hefty sum instead of going through the embarrassment of being slapped with a phony suit."

Her jaw sagged. She stared at him in shock, in disbelief, in sudden, blazing fury. Her mouth went hard and tight. Her fists balled.

"If I hadn't spent the past nine years teaching my daughter that the violence she sees on TV every day isn't the answer to anything," she said through gritted teeth, "I'd haul off and slug you."

Tony hooked his thumbs in the waistband of his jeans. "You're welcome to try."

She declined his invitation. Flinging her head back, she looked him up and down with the same disgust she would an oversize rodent. "You, Mr. Paretti, can go straight to hell!"

She spun around, her fine hair whirling in a silvery

arc. The bad taste in Tony's mouth grew even more bitter as she snatched up her purse. She strode out of the room without a backward glance.

He didn't try to stop her. He'd tried once and failed. He was damned if he'd try again. And he sure as hell wasn't going to apologize for his suspicions. He wasn't the one who'd shown up on her doorstep without warning. He didn't—

The front door slammed with a force that rattled the etched-glass panes. Tony winced, called himself ten kinds of an ass and started for the hallway. The phone shrilled before he'd taken two steps.

He hesitated. It could be for Jess, another call about her daughter. Frowning, he strode back and snatched up the phone.

"Paretti."

"All right, big brother, 'fess up. Who is she?"

Tony rolled his eyes. His mother operated an information and communications network the Pentagon would envy. He might have known she'd get on the line to his sister. Probably his aunt Helen and cousin Guido, too. The damned phone would be ringing all night long.

"I'll call you back, Angela."

"Wait!" she squawked. "I promised Mother I'd get all the details."

"Later."

"Tony...!"

With brotherly ruthlessness, he hit the off button and dropped the cordless phone onto the coffee table. He'd started for the hallway again when someone leaned on the front doorbell.

The opaque glass panels in the door were designed for privacy but didn't disguise the shape on the other side of the door. Tony recognized Jess's outline and

cursed again as a wild relief shot through him. Damn
the woman! She was tying him in knots...again!

He opened the door to her, disgusted by the uninhib-
ited response she could raise in him after all these years.

"I used all my cash getting here," she said stiffly.
"Alyx has my credit card with her."

A tide of red washed up her neck. Clearly mortified
at having to make a request of him after the accusations
he'd just laid on her, she tilted her chin.

"Would you lend me enough for a cab to the airport?
I can use my bank card at an automatic teller there to
pay for my ticket. I'd rather eat dirt than ask, you understand, but my daughter means a lot more to me than
my pride."

Tony believed it. He felt as though he'd swallowed
a shovelful of mud himself. He couldn't remember the
last time he'd acted like such a jerk...or been thrown
so off balance. He could only ascribe his suspicions to
the shock of finding Jess Summerville Taylor on his
doorstep after all these years.

"I'll sign an IOU," she added icily. "I wouldn't
want you to think I was trying to pull some kind of a
scam."

Tony flushed. He warranted that, he supposed. He
stood back, holding the door open. "I'll give you whatever you need, Jess. But you'd better come in and call
the airlines before you head back out to the airport. I'm
not sure where Rocky Point, North Carolina is either,
but I suspect you're not going to get there tonight. Not
by air, anyway."

She didn't budge. "They'll have something heading
that general direction. If you'll just call a cab and lend
me the fare, I'll take my chances at the airport."

"Oh, for—" He stepped out, slamming the door behind him. It didn't make him feel any better when she jumped back, her eyes wary.

"I'll drive you to the airport."

"That's not necessary."

Her icy disdain was starting to grate. The fact that he deserved it grated even more.

"I'll drive you to the airport," he growled.

He strode down the steps to the gleaming red Corvette he'd left parked at the curb. Snagging the passenger door handle, he yanked it open.

She stood on the brick stoop, obviously unhappy with her choices, which at this point were limited to two. She could ride out to BWI with him or walk.

Yeah, sure. As if he'd let her walk a block through Baltimore's back streets with the summer night fast dropping a blanket of darkness over the city. Tony didn't know why he didn't just give her the money for a cab. Why he couldn't just let her walk out of his life again.

He could. He would. But not like this, he reasoned. Not with anger clouding her eyes and bitterness thick and heavy between them.

"Come on, Jess. You want to get to your daughter. I'll help you." His mouth twisted in what he meant as a smile. "For old-time's sake."

Evidently he didn't quite pull it off. She flinched, and Tony cursed the fact that the searing passion they'd once felt for each other had degenerated into something that could still hurt after all these years.

"For old-time's sake," she repeated after a moment, coming slowly down the stairs.

Jess folded herself into the two-seater sports car, determined to hold on to her anger. Without it she knew she'd start blubbering again. The possibility both

alarmed and mortified her. She never cried! Or not often, anyway. Single moms didn't have the time or the
energy to cry, although they wanted to sometimes.

Yet despite her best effort to hang on to her anger, a
niggle of hurt kept poking through. She still couldn't
quite believe Tony thought she'd targeted him for some
kind of sting. When she'd thought about him at all during the frantic search for Alyx today, she'd imagined
his shock, his surprise at seeing her again. But she'd
never for one minute dreamed that he'd become so cyn-
ical.

Not Tony. For a moment she let herself remember
those long-ago weeks when she'd tumbled into love
with this man. He'd been so young then, so cocky and
sure of himself, so confident of his skills on the track.
And so quick to laugh. His brown eyes had teased her,
delighted her, invited her to share his zest for life. Even
then he'd been generous, always a soft touch for the
panhandlers who hung around the track.

She stole a sideways glance at the man wheeling the
powerful car through the streets. A sadness stole over
her. Had he changed so much from the charmer she'd
loved? Had she?

They were quiet, each lost in their thoughts, as the
Corvette whizzed along the interstate that led south to
Baltimore-Washington International. The summer night
had darkened to a deep, midnight blue when Tony dug
a cell phone out of the console between the bucket seats.

"You'd better call and check on flights. I have a
feeling you'll find you won't get any farther than Raleigh tonight." He slanted her a quick look. "It may be
faster to just drive down to North Carolina."

Chapter 3

Nine calls to 800-information and various airlines later, Jess accepted defeat. Tony had hit it exactly. She could get as far as Raleigh tonight, but she'd have to wait until morning to catch a commuter flight to Winston-Salem. From there she could take a bus to Rocky Point, which, she'd learned from a helpful airline ticket agent, was located in the northwest corner of North Carolina, high in the Blue Ridge Mountains. Even with the best connections, she wouldn't arrive before three or four tomorrow afternoon.

Unless she drove all the way tonight.

Wordlessly Tony reached over to dig a map out of the dash, and handed it to her. Jess unfolded it and tried to follow the squiggly lines in the dim overhead light, punctuated by the intermittent glare of headlights coming at them in the opposite lanes.

"I'd suggest taking I-66 out of D.C. to Front Royal," Tony commented. "From there it's a straight shot down through the Shenandoah Valley. We should be able to make North Carolina in..."

Jess's head whipped around. *"We?"* The refusal came hot and fast. "No, thanks. I'll rent a car at the airport and take it from there."

"Don't be stupid, Jess. You'd be driving all night on unfamiliar roads."

"I've driven all night before."

"Not after a day spent chasing down a missing daughter," he pointed out with biting accuracy. "You're wiped. It shows in your face. You look like you're ready to come apart at the seams."

"Thank you," she said frostily.

She felt like she was ready to come apart, too, but she was darned if she'd admit it. Alyx was her greatest joy in life, and her greatest challenge. This time the little stinker had really put her through the wringer. Still, retrieving her daughter was her problem, not Tony's.

When she informed him of that fact, his jaw tightened. "You made it my problem when you camped out on my doorstep, lady."

"I did *not* camp out on your doorstep. I came looking for... Oh, hell!" She snapped the map into folds. "What's the point of arguing like this? I don't want you to drive me all the way down to North Carolina any more than you want to drive me there. Just drop me at the airport."

"We've already passed the airport."

"What?"

"We went by the turnoff for BWI while you were studying the map."

"You're kidding!"

She twisted around in her seat, squinting at the sign over the opposite side of the interstate. Sure enough, it indicated that BWI was already some miles behind them. Her mouth tightening, she flopped back in the bucket seat.

"Get off at the next exit and go back."

"Jess..."

"Go back, Tony."

He blew out a sharp breath. "Look, I'm sorry about what I said at the house."

"About me having ulterior motives for tracking you down, you mean?" she inquired nastily.

"Yes."

"Apology accepted. Now please take the next— Watch out!"

She slammed a palm hard against the dash as a huge semi cut in front of them. Tony downshifted with a smooth coordination of hand and foot and swerved to the left. He found a hole in the bumper-to-bumper traffic on the busy interstate with the same skill he once used to find an opening in a crowded pack of race cars.

Jess flopped back in the bucket seat and breathed a shaky sigh as they sped past the truck. If Tony's accident had diminished any of the razor's-edge coordination that had once made him NASCAR's rookie of the year, she couldn't see it.

"You haven't lost your touch," she murmured.

"I can't smoke a track the way I used to, but the mechanics are still there."

He waited for a safe opening, then eased back into the travel lane. The oncoming lights etched his profile in stark lines.

"Tony, I—" She hesitated, not sure he wanted or would welcome her sympathy. "I saw the replay of the crash on the nightly news. I'm...I'm sorry."

"Yeah. Well, when you live life in the fast lane, you

have to expect a few fender benders. Isn't that what you once told me?''

His curt response cut off that line of discussion. Even if it hadn't, Jess wouldn't have told him that her heart had stopped when she'd seen Number Fourteen explode into flames.

Alyx had just turned five then, she remembered. They'd moved to Atlanta the year before, and Jess was getting her medical transcription business off the ground. Her life was moving in a new, exciting direction…yet that horrific crash took her back instantly to a dusty racetrack reeking with supercharged fuel fumes and the stink of hot rubber, when Tony was the hottest new star on the circuit, a sure bet to win his first Winston Cup.

Jess had followed his career after their brief romance, not as much by choice as by chance. His photo grinned back at her regularly from the tabloids at the supermarket checkout lines. Every sports magazine seemed eager to feature the handsome, photogenic, bachelor superstar. He'd won race after race, taken home a string of championships that engraved his name permanently in the Racing Hall of Fame before he turned thirty.

And then he'd swerved to avoid another car that had lost a tire. Number Fourteen spun across the track, hit the wall and exploded. Seeing the Chevy go up in flames over and over again on TV, Jess had almost died with him. She'd agonized over the reports of his critical condition, had even reached for the phone one night and called the hospital. His sister, Angela, had answered, had thanked her courteously for her concern and promised to pass Tony the message when he could deal with the outpouring of cards and calls from all his fans.

According to the news stories, he'd spent weeks in

intensive care, months in rehab. Jess wasn't surprised that he never returned or acknowledged her call. After all, she'd never returned his after the first one.

He broke into her thoughts, pulling her from the past to the present. "If I remember correctly, Washington to Roanoke, Virginia, is about two hundred and thirty miles. From Roanoke to the North Carolina border is probably another hundred. That's seven or eight hours of driving, Jess. Think you can handle it by yourself, late at night, on unfamiliar roads?"

A headache started thumping at her temples. She didn't answer for a moment, more daunted by the prospect of the long drive than she wanted to admit.

"You're all your daughter—Alyx, was it?—has," he said quietly. "You sure you want to take the risk of something happening to you?"

"No, of course not."

He was right. She had no business allowing the past to cloud her decisions or affect Alyx's future.

"If you're sure you want to do this..."

"*Want* isn't the operative word," he replied, his eyes on the road. "I made the offer because I don't like the idea of you—of any woman—making a drive like that alone, late at night."

"Then I accept." She tried to sound gracious. "Thank you."

"You're welcome."

They didn't speak for several miles. Jess kept her hands folded tightly in her lap and her legs bent to one side. She felt uncomfortable accepting Tony's help, uncomfortable sitting so close to him in the crowded confines of the Corvette. Every time he shifted, his arm brushed the sleeve of her navy linen jacket. The third time it happened, she wedged closer to the door.

"We've got a long drive ahead," he drawled, his voice coming at her out of the darkness. "Relax."

She was as relaxed as she could get with her daughter hundreds of miles away, bedded down with strangers, and the man she once loved with all the passion of her young heart sitting less than a foot away.

Certain she'd spend the entire drive wound tighter than an alarm clock, Jess slouched down in the seat. Her head dropped back to the headrest. She stared at the oncoming lights, counted the markers between mileposts, reminded herself that she'd have to ask Tony to drive her to an auto teller before he left her tomorrow, wondered how in the world Alyx had gotten on a bus for Rocky Point.

The mile markers started to blur. The oncoming headlights hurt her eyes. Jess lowered her eyelids for a minute. Only a minute.

A loud crack brought her straight up in the seat.

"What? Who?"

She shook her head to clear the fuzziness, then jumped again as a streak of light cut through the inky blackness in front of the windshield.

"What's that?"

"Lightning," Tony replied, his voice steady in the darkness. "We're running into some weather."

"Oh, great!" Shoving her bangs off her forehead, Jess blinked away the last of her muzziness. "Where are we?"

"Just past New Market."

That told her a lot. "Where's New Market?"

"About thirty miles south of Front Royal. Two hours out of D.C.," he added helpfully.

"Two hours! I've been asleep that long?"

"Longer." A smile played at the corners of his mouth. "You zonked out halfway between Baltimore and the Washington Beltway."

Oh, Lord! Jess was just hoping she hadn't totally embarrassed herself by snoring or drooling in her sleep when the first fat splats pinged against the car's roof. Within seconds, the pings deepened to a pounding roar. Tony slowed the Corvette to a crawl.

At any other time the slashing windshield wipers and torrential downpour would have made Jess nervous, very nervous. With Tony at the wheel she felt safe.

Or she did until they topped a rise another ten miles or so down the highway and a flash of red lights had him stomping on the brakes. As slowly as it was going, the Corvette still fishtailed across the wet road. Jess's heart jumped into her throat and stayed there for the three or four seconds it took for Tony to bring the car to a halt.

Even after the sports car slid to a stop, her nerves puddled as fast and hard as the rain drumming down on the roof. Tony, she saw in a quick, sideways glance, hadn't even broken a sweat. Narrowing his eyes, he squinted through the wipers at the stalled cars clogging both lanes of the highway. A brief flash of blue-and-white light caught his attention.

"Looks like a police roadblock up ahead. Hang tight, I'll check it out."

When he shouldered open his door, Jess flung up a hand to keep a whip of rain and wind from her face. A few minutes later he came jogging back through the downpour. She couldn't mistake his silhouette in the headlights...or his uneven gait. The visible legacy of his accident hit her again, even more painfully, right in the chest. The sight of his red knit shirt, now darkly

wet and clinging to his lean, muscled torso, hit slightly
lower. Jess gulped, her stomach clenching at the way
the rain slicked his tanned skin. His black hair, she
noted when he slid into his seat and slammed the door,
curled wildly.

Some things in life just weren't fair, she thought with
wry resignation. If she'd dashed through a storm like
this, she'd have come back looking like a half-drowned
cat. Tony Paretti looked like a Greek god. Correction,
Roman god.

"Bad news," he told her, swiping a hand down his
face. "The storm's been hammering this area for the
past hour. A bridge washed out up ahead."

"Oh, no! Was anyone hurt?"

"No, a trucker spotted it in time and stopped traffic.
The police are setting up roadblocks now and getting
ready to close the interstate."

"Close it?" Jess peered through the rain-blurred
windshield. "All of it?"

"The twenty-mile stretch battered by the storm, anyway. The highway patrol wants to check for possible
damage to other sections."

"How long do you think it will stay closed?"

"I'm guessing until daylight."

"Oh, no!"

She sank back, worrying her lower lip with her teeth.
Seven or eight hours closed up in this car with Tony
was rough enough on her nerves. The prospect of extending that period by another five or six hours raised
a lump in her throat.

His wrist draped over the wheel, Tony studied the
rearview mirror. "The cars behind us are backing up,"
he said after a moment. "There's an exit a hundred or
so yards back."

Jess twisted around in her seat. Sure enough, the lines behind them wavered as one vehicle after another edged onto the shoulder and inched backward to the exit. She swung to face Tony.

"Is there another road south?"

"Check the map. I think Route 11, the old state highway, runs parallel to the interstate."

Eagerly Jess unfolded the map. It was hard to read the fainter lines in the dim light, but she finally found Route 11.

"I've got it!" She traced the route all the way down to Roanoke. "It's just ten or so miles off the interstate. We take—" she squinted at the small connecting spur "—we take a left on 1603 and we should hit it."

Frowning, Tony debated the choices. They could stay here all night and wait for the interstate to reopen or try the slower route through the towns nestled at the base of the Shenandoah Mountains. He didn't like the idea of following those snaking roads in this kind of weather, but he liked the idea of sitting here in the dark with Jess only a breath away even less.

He'd listened to her soft breathing for the past two hours, with only his memories to keep him company. With every passing mile, those memories had crowded in on him, made him edgy and tight. *Jess* made him edgy and tight.

"You'll have to navigate," he warned. "Once we leave the interstate, the roads wind through the foothills of the mountains."

"No sweat. I aced map reading and navigation."

"I'm serious. You'll have to stay awake and watch the road signs."

"I will, I will." She wiggled around again to look over her shoulder. "It's clear. Let's go."

Evidently she felt the same need to keep moving…or the same reluctance to spend several hours of sitting side by side in the car without even the minimal effort of driving to distract them. Stifling the last of his reservations, Tony stretched an arm across the back of her seat and twisted to look out the rear window.

At the same moment Jess swung back to the front…or tried to. The movement brought them cheek to cheek, almost mouth to mouth. If he moved an inch…less…their lips would touch. For a blink or two, Tony's mind went blank. Then pure instinct took over. He wanted to taste her, just taste her. See if there was anything left of the girl he'd once loved in the woman she'd become.

The need pounded into him, hard, fast, urgent. Setting his jaw, Tony mastered it. More or less. To his disgust, his jaw stayed locked when he pulled away enough for Jess to settle back in her seat. Even worse, he squealed the tires like some high school dragster when he put the finely tuned Corvette into reverse. Cursing under his breath, he braked and backed the car more slowly along the shoulder.

For God's sake, he had to get a grip here. He'd spent the past three years pulling himself out of a physical and financial hole. The past ten years forgetting all about Jessica Summerville Taylor. He just got his life running on all eight cylinders. No way he was going to let her walk in and short circuit his entire system again.

Jess didn't need to catch the softly muttered curse to know Tony was regretting his impulsive offer to drive her to North Carolina. He couldn't regret the offer as much as she did the accepting. Now that she was wide awake again, she couldn't seem to shut down the senses he'd tripped with that almost-kiss. Her nerves hummed with an awareness she hadn't felt in more years than she could remember. She drew in his damp, musky scent with every breath. To save her soul, she couldn't seem to tune out the way his wet jeans molded his thigh every time he pushed in the clutch.

As if that weren't enough to make her acutely uncomfortable, her stomach chose that moment to remind her that she hadn't eaten since breakfast. She'd been too frantic over Alyx to think about lunch, and too frazzled by her meeting with Tony to consider dinner. Frantic and frazzled now seemed to have given way to famished. Thankfully the Corvette's well-mannered rumble when Tony put it in drive covered her stomach's considerably less-well-mannered growl.

Hunching over the map, Jess groped around the floor for her purse. She had some sugar-free breath mints in there. They'd have to do until Tony stopped for gas and Jess could buy some munchies. Only then did she discover that Alyx must have lifted more than her credit card from her purse. The mints were gone, as well.

She searched the now-drizzly darkness ahead for signs of human habitation. A gas station, maybe. An all-night shoppette. She didn't hold out much hope for any golden arches this far off the main road. But she saw only the blackness of the night, and the even darker blackness of the mountains looming on their left.

After another embarrassing gurgle, Jess crossed her arms over her middle and stayed hunched over the map. Her bent posture suppressed the rumbling. Unfortunately it also caused her to miss a few road signs. Or so Tony deduced after a half hour on the dark, winding road.

Frowning, he slowed to take a sharp turn. "Are you sure this leads to Route 11?"

Jess tilted the map to the dash light. "Pretty sure."

"Pretty sure?" He shot her a hard look. "What happened to acing map reading and navigation?"

"Hey, in case you haven't noticed, it's raining and just a little dark out there."

He found a small pullout and edged the Corvette off the road. "Let me take a look."

Sliding the map from her fingers, he bent almost double to catch the dash light. Jess squeezed against the door to keep from cradling his head in her lap. If he noticed the way she shied away from him, he didn't comment, but his voice was frosty when he tossed her the map.

"As best I can tell, we're heading up to Skyline Drive."

"Is that good?"

"It is if you like driving a hundred or more miles of hairpin turns in the middle of the night."

Oh-oh. Not good. Definitely not good.

"Should we go back?"

He chewed on that for a moment. "No. I filled up while you were dead to the world. We've got plenty of gas. We might as well go on. This route will take an hour or so longer, but will get us closer to where we want to go."

Resolutely banishing all thought of munchies, Jess sternly ordered her stomach to cease and desist its disorderly conduct. She sank back in her seat, determined to hold out as long as the gas did.

She might even have made it, if not for her kidneys. Independent of her stomach, they began their own campaign to make her miserable. She began to search the darkness ahead in earnest. The idea of asking Tony to pull over so she could use the bushes was *not* an option.

When they rounded a turn and Jess spotted a flickering neon light in the distance, she prayed. Silently. Fervently. Every prayer she knew that might deliver a gas station or mountain shoppette, if there was such a thing. She was almost giddy with relief when the light grew brighter, separated into colors, and spelled Hilltop Haven.

"Tony, I need to stop."

He slowed, peering through the windshield wipers at the dilapidated structure. It was tucked under a stand of pine, its unpainted boards washed gray by the rain. On closer inspection, it appeared to be a combination gas station and beer joint. A popular gas station and beer joint. Even now, close to midnight on an ugly, rainy night, it had attracted a number of customers.

"The place looks pretty rough, Jess. We'd better go on."

"Tony, I *need* to stop."

He slanted her the kind of look she too often gave her daughter. For the first time that day, Jess felt in distinct sympathy with Alyx. How many times had she urged the poor girl to hold it just a little longer?

Never again, she vowed.

She should have known that the rest rooms would be around to the side of the building. At least, she thought the sign swinging from a crossbar pointed to the rest rooms. As soon as the Corvette rolled to a stop, she reached for the door handle and braced herself for a dash through the thick, drizzly rain.

"I'll go in and get some coffee," Tony advised. "Make it quick. I don't like the looks of this place."

Jess didn't particularly like the looks of it, either, especially when she ran through the rain and found only a single door with the sign so rusted she didn't know whether it read Men or Women.

At this point she didn't particularly care. There was no way she was running around the building to the other side to check for another rest room. Drenched and near desperation, she twisted the knob. She practically fell inside and groped for the light switch. As soon as the single bulb came on, she almost wished she'd left the room dark.

"Yuck!"

A speckled mirror, a rust-stained sink and an over-flowing trash barrel greeted her. Graffiti decorated every inch of the walls, some of it so graphic that Jess's eyes widened. If she hadn't been desperate, she would have turned around and walked out. As it was, she tended to matters as quickly as possible. Using the very tips of two fingers, she twisted the tap to wash her hands and dried them on her wrinkled linen shorts. With a disgusted glance in the mirror at her bedraggled image, she reached for the door knob.

It was yanked out of her hand. Startled, Jess backed up a step or two.

Just as startled, the beefy male on the other side of the threshold gaped at her. Ball cap turned back to front, plaid shirt straining over his bulging gut, he stood as if poleaxed.

"Excuse me," she muttered, trying to edge past him.

He took a short step back, then got a look at her bare legs under the shorts. Quick as a snake, his arm shot out. He planted his paw against the doorjamb, bringing Jess up short. A gap-toothed grin split his face.

"Well, well. You don't hafta leave. I don't mind sharing the can with you."

Grimacing at the sour beer breath that washed over her, Jess jerked away from him. "It's all yours."

"Naw." He crowded closer, blocking the door. "It's all ourn', sweetie pie. What say we get a little closer, maybe a little friendlier in here?"

"What say you don't."

Tony's growl came out of the darkness behind the big man. Jess sighed with relief.

Her relief spiraled quickly into consternation as her accoster spun around. When he spotted Tony standing in the rain, a coffee-to-go in each hand, he hooked his thumbs in his pockets and rocked back on his heels.

"'Case you ain't noticed it, pretty boy, this here john's occupied."

"In case you haven't noticed it, the lady behind you wants out."

"What makes you think so? Maybe we were just gettin' on with some business here."

"And maybe you've had too much to drink. Let her out."

"You wanna make me?"

Tony shrugged. "Not particularly, but I will if I have to."

"Oh, yeah?" Grinning, the big man hitched up his trousers. "I guess you're gonna hafta."

Thoroughly alarmed by the stranger's drunken belligerence, Jess tried to stop things before they spun completely out of control.

"Wait a minute here!"

Sucking in her stomach, she attempted once more to edge past the obstacle in the door. When that didn't work, she planted two hands in his back and shoved.

He stumbled forward, right into Tony. The coffee went flying, both men went down cursing, and all hell suddenly broke loose.

Chapter 4

Stunned by the sudden eruption of violence, Jess danced to one side to avoid the flailing combatants.

She couldn't believe it! One minute, her most driving concern was putting as little of her fingertip as possible in contact with the rusted faucet in the rest room. The next, she was in the middle of a melee!

In the darkness and drizzling rain she formed the impression that Tony was giving as good as he got, but the brutal thud of fists pounding into flesh and the repeated, animallike grunts horrified her. She debated for several desperate seconds about what to do, then dashed back into the rest room in search of something, anything, to use to help Tony.

All she could find was a rusted can of toilet bowl cleanser tucked behind the stool. Big and heavy and obviously never used by the proprietor of the establishment, the can just fit her hand. She ran back outside in time to see the big man roll onto his knees, pinning

Tony beneath him. His fist came up. With a grunt, he prepared to smash it down.

Jess let fly with a two-handed swing at the same moment that Tony heaved upward, dislodging his assailant. The can she'd aimed at the man's head thumped into his back instead. The force of the blow popped the top. Cleanser sprayed in a white arc, dousing both Tony and the drunk he demolished with a crushing blow to the jaw.

Covered in a white power that rapidly turned into paste as it mixed with the rain, Tony pushed to his feet. He swiped a hand down his face and stared at the thick goop. His chest heaving, he glared at Jess.

"What the hell is this?"

"Ajax," she replied, her heart still pumping hard and fast. She'd never taken part in a brawl before, and sincerely hoped she never would again.

"Toilet bowl cleanser," she amplified, when Tony stared at her in gathering disbelief. "It was all I could find."

Swearing under his breath, he shook his head. Jess caught the curse and gave a little sniff. He might show a *little* gratitude, for Pete's sake. After all, she had distracted his assailant long enough for Tony to finish him off. More or less.

The big man came to just then. He'd lost his ball cap in the brawl. Reddish hair sprouted like muddy weeds from his head. More mud decorated the shirt stretched across his belly. Groaning, he rolled over on one hip and rubbed a hand across his face. It, too, came away smeared with whitish gunk.

"What the hell is this?"

Jess ignored Tony's snort of derision. "Toilet bowl

cleanser," she said frostily. "You'd better be careful you don't get it in your eyes."

He spat out an oath that made her wish the scouring powder had made it into his mouth.

"*You'd* better be careful," he snarled. "Folks up here in the hills don't take kindly to smart-ass tourists."

Dusting his hands on his jeans, Tony walked over to the fallen combatant and tried to negotiate a truce. "Look, the name's Paretti. Tony Paretti. What do you say we call this a draw?"

He reached down a hand to help the other man up. The redhaired ruffian swatted it away.

"What do you say you go to hell," he sneered, staggering to his feet. "I don't need no help, 'specially from a has-been racer who couldn't keep his car on the track."

Jess gasped at the vicious insult. Tony didn't reply, but the sudden narrowing of his eyes had the drunk backing off. Swiping the back of his hand across his bloodied nose, he lurched around the corner of the building. A few moments later Jess and Tony heard the sound of a truck engine kicking over. Tires spit gravel, then a pickup tore out of the parking lot.

"Good riddance," Jess muttered.

"We'd better get out of here," Tony said, his jaw tight. "Your friend may decide to gather his buddies—"

"He's not my friend!"

"—and come back for a second round," he finished on a grim note.

The thought made Jess shiver. One brawl a night was her limit.

"I'll wash this stuff off," Tony said shortly, "then we'll hit the road."

He made for the dingy bathroom. Jess followed, hovering under the overhang beside the open door as he splashed sticky white paste off his face and hands.

"What in blue blazes were you doing playing games with a bonehead like that?" he asked between splashes.

"I wasn't playing games," she protested indignantly. "I just used the rest room."

"Right." He speared a disgusted glance at the grimy towel and dragged up his shirttail to wipe his hands and face. "The *men's* rest room."

Jess didn't answer for a moment, her gaze riveted on Tony's flat belly and broad chest. An old, familiar ache arrowed into her. How many times had she seen Tony Paretti stripped to the waist and bent over the fender of Number Fourteen? How many times had she run her hands down those washboard ribs and combed her fingers through the dark hair that swirled across his chest? How many times had she teetered on the brink and almost, almost, lost herself in the heat of his kisses?

She shook her head, willing the ache away. All that was in the past. The present was giving her more than enough problems to deal with.

"I didn't know this was the men's room and, quite frankly, didn't care."

"Yeah, well, the next time you march into a men's john and entice the occupant to unbridled lust, you'd better be prepared for the consequences."

"Unbridled lust!" Jess sputtered.

She couldn't remember the last time she'd put on any lipstick; her hair stuck to her head in dripping spikes; her body was a mass of goose bumps under her wet, wrinkled clothes. The idea that she could attract the attention of anyone but a drunk was absurd.

"I couldn't entice anyone right now if I wanted to,

which I don't," she said with a touch of acid. "That guy was blind drunk."

Evidently Tony didn't share her opinion. Snorting, he shoved his shirttail into the waistband of his jeans.

"Are you kidding?"

He ran his eyes down her face, her throat, her body. Jess felt herself stiffening under the intense scrutiny.

"Don't you have any idea how sexy you look?"

"Sexy? You're crazy."

Or still so pumped from the brawl that his hormones had taken over his brain, Jess decided. Still, she couldn't suppress a shiver as he slid a hand around her neck. His thumb tipped her face to the dim light.

"With your hair all wet and sleek like that, you look about as old as that daughter you're chasing. But sexy," he growled. "Sexy as hell."

Suddenly, goose bumps weren't all Jess sported under her wet clothes. The look in Tony's dark eyes tightened her belly and peaked her nipples inside her damp bra.

"I'm not— I don't—"

For the life of her, she couldn't get the words out, didn't even know what she was trying to say. The fact that his thumb was now gliding across her lower lip didn't exactly help matters, either.

"You don't what, Jess?"

Tony told himself he was insane to touch her, that the blood roaring through his ears came from the fight. Yet he couldn't have pulled away if he tried...and this time he didn't try.

The skin of her inner lip was like silk, soft and warm and wet. The urge to taste her grabbed him again, as it had earlier in the car. Just one kiss, he swore. Just one taste. To convince himself once and for all that the girl he'd once loved didn't exist in this sensual, wide-eyed woman.

Tony realized his error the moment his mouth touched hers. The fire he'd doused years ago flickered to life instantly, then sparked. It took only another second, a different angle of his mouth on hers, to fan it to flames. He didn't even realize he'd deepened the kiss and brought her body hard against his until he heard her moan. Or his moan. At that point he couldn't tell who had issued that strangled sound.

When he pulled back, his whole body had gone tight. Wordlessly she stared up at him. Her lips, those full, sensual lips he could still feel imprinted on his mouth, trembled.

Oh, Lord! Now he'd done it! She was going to burst into tears again. And no wonder, for God's sake! Tony had just come on to her with all the finesse of that moron in the ball cap. Feeling like ten kinds of a jerk, he slid his hand from around her neck.

"I'm sorry." The apology came out stiff and gruff. "That was a mistake."

A bad one. This woman had tied him in knots ten years ago, he reminded himself savagely. He had to be nuts to even think about kissing her again. And again. And...

"Yes, it was," she agreed, her tone strained and uneven.

Tony thrust his hand through his wet hair and forced himself to meet her stare. The confusion and near panic in her turquoise eyes stung him. He didn't think he could feel any lower, but he managed it when she stuck her chin in the air and informed him in that same shaky voice that they were wasting time.

"The only reason I agreed to come with you," she

reminded him unnecessarily, "was to reach Alyx as quickly as possible. If you don't mind, I'd like to get this trip over with."

So would he. Still aching from the double whammy of the drunk's hard fists to the stomach and Jess's mouth on his, Tony followed her around the corner of the building. Guilt and a perverse desire he couldn't shake needled him as he splashed through the puddles to the Corvette.

A few yards from the mud-streaked vehicle, he stopped in his tracks. Guilt and desire disappeared in a flash of disgust.

"Dammit!"

Jess jumped. The look she threw him was guarded, defensive. "What now?"

"Your friend left us a parting gift."

"He's *not* my— Oh, no!"

Dismayed, she gaped at the flattened tires. They'd been slashed. All four of them.

"Wait over there, under the overhang," Tony instructed curtly. Thoroughly disgusted with himself for not anticipating this kind of retaliation, he stomped inside to roust the bartender/gas station attendant.

Jess huddled under the eaves and waited for his return. The drizzle let up by the time he reappeared with the owner in tow, but that small blessing was offset almost immediately. Her heart sinking, she saw the owner shake his head.

"Nope, I don't stock any tires that'll fit this baby. Don't see many machines like this one 'round here."

"Great," Tony muttered.

"Got a phone inside you can use to call your road service," the man volunteered. "It'll take 'em a while to get here, but the bar stays open till four. Y'all can wait in there."

Not particularly anxious to experience any more close encounters with the patrons of this particular establishment, Jess pushed away from the wall and walked into the puddle of light.

"Do you have a car we could rent?"

"Hey!" Tony's instinctive protest cut through the night. "I'm not leaving the Corvette sitting here."

"I'm not asking you to leave your baby unprotected," she replied with withering politeness. "You stay with your car. I'll go on on my own."

Only after her airy little speech did she remember that she didn't have the funds to buy a cup of coffee, much less rent a car. The sardonic look Tony shot her indicated that the same thought had just occurred to him. Before he voiced any nasty reminders, though, the station owner scratched his head.

"Y'all can rent Bessie. She doesn't look like much, but she's pretty reliable."

Jess peered in the direction he pointed and discovered that Bessie was a decrepit sedan with three different-colored fenders and no hood.

In any other circumstances, she would have declined the offer graciously. Driven by her need to get to Alyx and a decided aversion to hanging around the bar for several hours, she turned to Tony. She could read his opinion of the car on his face.

"This isn't a good idea."

"I'm not real keen on hanging out with the guys inside," she told him stiffly.

His jaw tight, he turned to the owner. "Are you sure this thing runs?"

"Like a charm. 'Course, if you don't want her..."

"I'll take her," Jess said quickly. "That is, I will if my friend will lend me enough for the car and gas."

"Don't be stupid," her "friend" snapped. He dug into his back pocket for his wallet. "How much for two days?"

"Well, one hundred ought to do it."

"One hundred!"

"Per day," the owner amended with a smug grin. "In advance."

Glowering at the outright extortion, Tony forked over four bills. "I'm surprised you don't want another thousand as a security deposit."

"Seein' as I'll be hanging on to your 'Vette, I figured you'll probably bring ole Bessie back."

"You got that right."

It was a promise and a prayer. Guilt nipped at Jess for tearing Tony away from the gleaming, beautifully restored classic. She was secretly so relieved not to be facing these dark, winding mountain roads by herself, however, that she managed to swallow all traces of the uncomfortable feeling. Nor would she acknowledge the little shiver that darted up her arm when he took her elbow to steer her toward the rented wreck.

With a last, anguished glance at his Corvette, Tony slid into the car and shoved the key in the ignition.

Bessie lived down to Tony's worst expectations before she'd traveled five miles. The '72 Olds might have given other cars on the road a run for their money in her prime, but she should have been stripped down to the frame a decade or more ago. Her engine coughed like a consumptive, her chassis rattled and shook, and the steering wheel had more play in it than a symphony orchestra. Her tires still had some good tread left on them, though, which was the only reason Tony had agreed to continue this seemingly endless journey.

That, and the fact that he wasn't about to expose Jess to the rest of the customers in the Hilltop Haven. He ascribed his protective streak to the ordinary instincts any man would feel for a woman in his company. Tony wouldn't have wanted to expose his sister to that crowd, either, although Angela could more than hold her own in any situation, as her husband Jack had learned the hard way.

With a grimace, Tony thought back to those harrowing days when Angela and Jack were on the run, chased by thugs hired by the pharmaceutical company Jack was about to blow the lid on. Tony had tracked his sister down to their uncle Guido's hideout on Maryland's eastern shore. He could still remember his rage when he realized Jack had tumbled Angela into bed, although in cooler moments he acknowledged that it probably happened the other way around. At the time, though, Tony had seen red. His Italian ancestry had sent fury roiling through him…and later, after seeing the passion in Angela's eyes…an envy that ate into his gut.

He'd loved with that fire and passion once.

Only once.

He wrapped his fists around the cracked plastic steering wheel, unconsciously adjusting for its play, and aimed a sideways glance at the woman next to him on the wide bench seat. She hadn't spoken since they'd left the Hilltop Haven. Had barely glanced his way. Her hands were curled tight in her lap; she strained to follow the narrow, winding road ahead.

Why in hell had he kissed her? Tony thought. Regret and disgust whipped through him, along with a stinging need. Why in hell did he ache with the knowledge that she'd left him to bear another man's child?

He couldn't hate her for that decision. If the situation were reversed he wouldn't have wanted Jess to cheat him of his child. And this fearless little Alyxandra could have been his child. So easily. If he'd pushed Jess a little harder, used more of the skills he'd acquired on the racing circuit that didn't particularly relate to driving, he could have taken her to bed. She'd been so young then, so much in love.

Memories bombarded him. Tony couldn't stop them, couldn't turn them off. Through the dark windshield he saw a young, laughing Jess. The dusty Talledega track. His crew up to their elbows in grease and grins as they watched him making a fool of himself over Jessica Summerville. She'd loved him. Tony had never doubted that. He couldn't doubt it now. She'd loved him with a breathless passion that could still make him hurt with regret. He'd been the one who pulled back at the last moment. He'd been the one who insisted that they wait for their wedding night.

Damn his old-fashioned upbringing! If he ever got Jess anywhere near a bed again, he sure as hell wouldn't make the same mistake.

The thought came zinging out of the darkness. Shocked by its savagery, Tony gripped the wheel so hard he was sure the plastic would give.

"There's a sign up ahead," Jess murmured, breaking into his turbulent thoughts. "Slow down and let me read it."

Tony pressed down on the break pedal. Going uphill at a cautious speed, he hadn't needed to rely on Bessie's brakes to finesse the dark, twisting curves. Going down, the brake shoes emitted a high-pitched screech that came through the cracked windows and grated against his ears. He'd been riding the damned things for almost a mile now and didn't like the way they smoked.

"Slow down," Jess instructed again. "I can't read the—"

"Hell!"

At Tony's vicious curse, she broke off and swung sideways in her seat. Her breath caught as she saw him standing on the brakes.

"What's the matter? Tony! What's the matter?"

He locked his jaw, fighting the wheel as the car picked up speed. "We've got a problem here, Jess."

She gulped. "A problem?"

"I just lost the brakes."

"You lost them?" she squeaked.

"The brake line must have cracked."

The line was rubber. In a car as ancient as this one, weather cracks could rupture it like a tired vein. Dammit, he should have guessed that the old buzzard at the Hilltop Haven wouldn't have replaced the line.

She shot a frightened glance at the road. "You mean you can't stop this thing?"

"I'm trying."

He downshifted, forcing the gears into second. They screeched a loud, agonized protest. His jaw tight, Tony ignored their pain and downshifted again, this time into low. With a rending shriek that tore at his gut, Bessie slowed a fraction, only a fraction.

"Hang on, I'm going to hit the emergency brake."

His left foot shoved the smaller brake pedal to the floor. Almost instantly, noxious fumes filled the interior. Eyes stinging, mouth tight, Tony rode both brakes and fought to keep the car on the road. Choking, Jess fumbled for the handle for the window. The cracked glass would only go down a few inches.

"We're not stopping." He ground out the obvious fact through tight teeth. "I can't control her on this slick road."

Panic laced Jess's voice. "What are you going to do?"

He'd already considered his options and knew there was only one left. "I'll have to find a spot to swing her around. Get her pointing uphill instead of down."

It was a desperate move. Bessie was gaining more speed by the second. The Olds was heavy, loaded with chrome, a tank by today's standard. With the play in her steering, she might make a tight turn...and she might not. She could career off the road, plunge down the side of the damned mountain.

Alone, Tony wouldn't have hesitated. With Bessie swerving wider and wider on every turn, it was only a matter of moments until she went off the side. He knew that a spin was the only option left.

A cold sweat formed on his palms. The mountain edging the road on their left and the sheer drop-off on the right gave him little room to maneuver. If he spun the car in too wide a turn, the passenger side would slam into the rock. If he spun too tight, he ran the risk of not being able to correct in time, driving back across the road and going over the side.

The thought of taking Jess with him on a wild ride into oblivion put a frozen lump of fear in Tony's stomach. He jerked his eyes from the road for the second it took to spear her a glance.

She must have sensed his desperation. Her face was stark white, her eyes huge. Then, unbelievably, she grinned. Tony blinked, certain he was hallucinating. But there it was. A weak, wobbly attempt, definitely strained around the edges, but so like the young, laughing Jess he used to know that Tony felt his heart slam hard into his sternum.

"If anyone can tame this beast, Paretti, you can."

They almost made it. For a wild instant that would remain burned in Jess's mind forever, she was sure they were going to make it.

Tony kept the Olds on the asphalt through one tight bend in the road, then another. All the while he scanned the darkness on the left for some break in the dense trees that alternated with sheer rock face. Jess felt as though they were riding a runaway roller coaster when Tony finally spotted what looked like a place to pull over on the inside of the road.

"Hold on!"

With the split-second timing that came from years on the track, he spun the wheel while Bessie was still some ten yards or so from the open area. The heavy vehicle swung around, front end in tight, rear end in a wide arc. Trees and sheer granite walls seemed to rush at Jess out of the darkness. She bit down on a scream as the Olds's rear fender scraped rock.

Then they were clear, back on asphalt, pointing up instead of down. Bessie kept rolling like an out-of-control tank, but her speed lessened with every foot.

"You did it!"

Jess's exultant cry had no sooner left her mouth than the right rear tire blew with a loud pop. Poor Bessie bucked like a beestung Percheron. Fighting Tony's iron grip on the wheel, she humped drunkenly across the road.

"Brace yourself!"

She didn't need his shout to know they faced disaster. The headlights sliced wildly through the darkness. Jess saw the thin metal guard rail on the shoulder coming at them, saw the dark pine tips poking up from the slope below. She closed her eyes, thought of Alyx sleeping peacefully at a stranger's house and heard the guard rail crunch as the Olds went over the edge.

Chapter 5

Jess would always consider it a genuine, honest-to-goodness miracle that neither she nor Tony was injured during that terrifying, five-second ride down the mountainside.

Thankfully, Bessie had lost enough forward momentum by the time she went over the side that she slid instead of charged down the steep slope. Brush and rock scratched at her undercarriage. Young trees whipped at the grill and hood before she plowed into a stand of old growth.

Once again Tony spun the wheel. Once again Bessie lurched, this time to the right, just before slamming sideways into a towering oak. She hit in the left front fender, the only one still sporting its original paint. Metal crunched. The fender buckled. The radiator hissed and spit.

Then, incredibly, there was quiet.

Jess stayed braced against the dash. She couldn't be-

lieve the Olds had stopped, couldn't believe she was
hearing only a dense silence over the panic that roared
in her ears.

"Are you okay?"

Tony gripped her upper arm, pried her hand from its
death grip on the dash.

"Jess! Are you okay?"

She couldn't speak. Terror seemed to have squeezed
all the air from her lungs. She didn't have enough left
to force out even a squeak. She could only nod once,
weakly, hoping he could see the movement in the dark.

Groaning, he folded her into his arms. Jess fell
against his chest. His heart thundered under her cheek,
hammering out a wild, erratic beat that matched her
own. She absorbed the pumping rhythm, the dampness
of his shirt, the tangy aroma of toilet bowl cleanser that
clung to him for two, maybe three seconds, before he
groped for the door handle.

"Come on, sweetheart. We'd better get away from
the car."

Metal groaned as he shouldered the door open and
shimmied out, taking Jess with him. She couldn't seem
to find her footing on the steep, sloping ground. With
an arm around her waist, Tony half dragged, half carried
her through trees and prickly brush that scratched at her
legs. Finally he found a massive boulder a safe distance
away from the wreck to prop her against.

They stood shoulder to shoulder, still panting, blood
racing, while the night folded in around them. It could
have been two or five or ten minutes later when Tony
pushed away from the rock.

"She's not going to blow. Stay here."

"Wait!" She grabbed at his shirt, yanking its tail
from his jeans. "Where are you going?"

"My cell phone's in the car, Jess. I need it to call for help."

Reluctantly she released her frantic hold. "Be careful!"

She didn't think about the irony of cautioning a man who'd almost lost his life in a flaming wreck to be careful. If anyone knew about vehicle safety and emergency exit procedures, Tony Paretti did. Still, Jess's heart hammered painfully against her ribs as she listened to his footsteps crunch through the bush. She didn't breathe easy until he returned.

"I can't find it," he told her, his voice tight. "The damned thing must have fallen out when I opened the door. I can't see it in the dark."

She swiped her tongue across her lips. "What do we do now?"

He was quiet a moment. "We could try to work our way up the slope to the road and walk back to the Hilltop Haven."

From the hesitation in his voice, Jess gathered that a climb up a steep slope and five-mile walk in pitch-blackness didn't appeal to him any more than it did to her.

"And the second choice?"

"We could stay in the car until morning. The Olds is wedged tight against that tree. It's not going anywhere."

Jess wrapped her arms around her waist. The night pressed in on her from all sides, dark, intense, still drizzly moist. Briefly, she wondered if there were grizzlies in these mountains.

"Is there a third choice?"

"Not that I can see."

"Then I opt for the Olds."

Tony nodded, reaching out to take her arm and help her back across the steep, angled ground. Before either of them climbed inside, he tested the vehicle once again by planting his heels against the slope and shoving first against the front, and then the rear bumper. The heavy Olds didn't budge.

"We'd better take the back seat," he said after the second, grunting try. "There's more room there. I'll go first."

It wasn't until Jess ducked down to enter the car that she appreciated how steeply the car tilted. Tony stretched out on the seat and braced his back against the opposite door. Jess crawled in after him, clinging to the door frame with one hand to keep from tumbling against him.

"You might as well get comfortable," he said after a moment of awkward repositioning. "Rest your back against my chest."

She hung onto the door, not wanting the intimacy, not knowing how to avoid it. A small silence spun out, broken by Tony's gruff voice.

"I won't try to jump your bones, if that's what's worrying you."

Jess's face heated. That's exactly what was worrying her. With the terror and adrenaline rush of the slide down the mountain still searing her veins, she had the feeling that the mere touch of Tony's body against hers would ignite the same sparks that had flickered to life at the Hilltop Haven.

"I've already apologized for that incident in the rest room," he said stiffly, reading her thoughts with disconcerting accuracy. "It won't happen again."

The steely promise left a tiny ache in Jess's chest. She didn't want him to jump her bones, for heaven's sake! They were both too old, too different from the people they once were to experience again the kind of passion that used to steam the windows of Number Fourteen late at night, after the pit crew had left.

Which didn't explain why her hip burned where his thigh cradled it when she nestled between his legs. Or why the soft wash of his breath against her temple set her nerves dancing under her skin. Or why her stomach hollowed when Tony looped his arm loosely over it. He didn't have any place else to put the thing, she told herself sternly. It was either rest it atop her or let it dangle at his side for what was left of the night.

How long would she have to endure the scorching feel of her body pressed against his?

"Any idea what time it is?" she murmured.

He lifted his arm, glanced at the illuminated dial on his watch. "Two-twenty."

Two-twenty.

She'd climbed out of the cab and pounded on his door in Baltimore when? Seven-thirty? Eight o'clock? She counted backward. She and Tony had been in each other's company for only six and a half hours. It felt longer, as though days or even weeks had passed.

It felt right.

His arms around her felt even righter.

The traitorous thoughts sneaked right past the mental barriers Jess had erected to ward off the effects of their enforced intimacy. She didn't know where they came from. Even worse, she couldn't seem to banish them despite all attempts to focus her thoughts on Alyx, on the intense silence that surrounded them, on the string of disasters that had led them to a precarious perch on the side of a mountain. Desperate for distraction, she searched for a topic, any topic, that wouldn't lead back to old memories and hurts.

"Alyx said in her note that she saw you on TV," she ventured. "In an ad for Big Brothers or something."

"I do some spots for them occasionally," he replied, his voice a deep rumble in the dark. "It's a good organization, helps kids who really need it."

He was quiet for a moment, then picked up on her conversational lead. "I work with a couple of boys in Baltimore. They're good kids right on the edge of going bad. They don't have an adult male they can turn to for advice. Not that their mothers aren't there for them," he added hastily. "Some kids...boys...just seem to need a father figure to relate to, even the once-a-week kind."

Jess let out a sigh. "All kids need that. Alyx didn't seem to feel any particular void in her life until she turned five or six and began to notice other kids' daddies. After that, she latched on to every male who showed even a flicker of interest in me."

"Did you date a lot?"

She tested the question for hidden barbs, found none.

"No, not a lot. With college and work and raising Alyx, I didn't have the time or the energy."

The quiet darkness gave her the courage to turn the question around. "What about you, Tony? Wasn't there anyone after...after Talledega?"

"Anyone I loved enough to marry, you mean? No, Jess, there wasn't anyone."

The admission should have flooded her with guilt, with stinging regret. But Jess knew Tony too well to believe she'd destroyed his life along with their love. He'd been waiting for another woman, the *right* woman, one he could love with all the passion he'd held in check during those tumultuous weeks with Jess.

The thought filled her with a gentle sadness. She wished Tony had found a wife. For his sake, she wished he'd found love.

"Tell me about Alyx," he said, breaking the quiet that settled around them like a fuzzy blanket. "She sounds like a firecracker."

"She is, believe me! She could charm a panhandler into giving *her* his last dollar with one of her angelic little smiles. It's no act, either. She has the sunniest disposition in the world...most of the time. Occasionally, however, she can dig in her heels, puff out her lower lip and pout with the best of them."

"In other words, she's your everyday, average kid."

"I don't know about the average part," Jess said ruefully. "She was the only four-year-old I know who was expelled from preschool. The final incident, as I recall, had to do with showing the other kids how to flick green beans from their forks to the ceiling. That's when I decided to work at home."

"What do you do?"

"I own and operate a medical transcription service." A little ping of pride crept into her voice. "I started off as a typist, transcribing files to help cover living expenses while I finished my business management degree. I began to see the possibilities for work-at-home moms almost immediately."

Looking back, Jess wondered where in the world she'd found the nerve to apply for a small business loan and invest in a half dozen used computers. She'd recruited other moms she'd met at the local community college, and soon had more business than they could collectively handle. Within a year, she'd incorporated.

Within two, she'd hired another twenty transcribers and won contracts servicing several of Atlanta's major medical consortiums. She'd left Alyx with their neighbor and gone to a meeting with one of her clients to talk about expanding her services yet again when her incorrigible daughter had slipped away and begun her journey north.

"I'm going to ground her for the rest of her natural life," Jess promised fervently, returning to the subject of Alyx. "She'll turn sixty before she sees the inside of another Trailways bus."

A chuckle rumbled in the chest behind her back. "You have to admit, she showed considerable resourcefulness in getting as far as she did."

"Don't take her side on this," Jess begged. "If she senses the least bit of sympathy in you, she'll play you like a violin."

"I don't think so," Tony replied with the utterly misplaced confidence of a man who'd never raised a daughter.

He shifted, bringing the woman in his arms into a more comfortable slouch against him. In a voice full of love, pride, and a touch of exasperation, she recounted more of Alyx's exploits. With picture-perfect clarity, Tony envisioned a miniature version of Jess in a ponytail and freckles. The image was so clear, so poignant, that he half expected bitterness to rise in his throat again at the thought of the girl who could so easily have been his daughter. The bitterness didn't come. All that invaded him was a quiet gladness that Jess had had Alyx to help her through the loss of a husband.

The minutes passed. Jess's chatter slowed, dropped to a sleepy mumble. The darkness around them took on its own life. Insects whirred and chirped. A breeze rustled through the oaks. The clouds broke, allowing slivers of moonlight to slant through the trees.

Tony should have focused on all he needed to do come the dawn. Like find the damned phone. Call for help. Get him and Jess back to civilization. Retrieve his 'Vette. Strangely, he was content to just lean back against the door and breathe in Jess's scent as she drifted into sleep against him. A peace he hadn't experienced in years settled over him.

His last thought before he, too, dropped into sleep, was that he wouldn't mind if they never got down off this mountain.

"Hey! Y'all alive in there?"

The shout and an accompanying rap on the window right next to Tony's ear jerked him awake. He bolted upright, almost dumping Jess on the floor in the process.

"What...?"

As startled as Tony, Jess flailed her arms and grabbed him to keep from tumbling off the seat. Their combined weight took them both over the edge. They landed in the narrow space between the front seat and the back, Tony on top, Jess bent at odd angles over the hump in the floor, both wedged tight.

Cursing, he levered himself up and stared back at the red-faced individual peering through the window. The man looked vaguely familiar, but before Tony could make a connection, his gaze caught on his uniform accouterments. Relief speared through him. Help had arrived.

"It's the sheriff."

"Thank God!"

"Come on, Jess, get up."

"I'm *trying* to." She scrambled awkwardly onto the

seat and put up a hand to shove her flyaway bangs out
of her eyes. She, like Tony, let out a sigh of relief when
she saw the tan and gray uniform.

When he could untangle his legs, Tony hit the door
handle and climbed out, blinking in the hazy dawn. All
signs of the previous night's storm had vanished. Daylight, he saw, had brought with it the kind of morning
that only the Blue Ridge Mountains could produce.

The air was crisp for June, and tangy with the scent
of bark and moss. Mist rose like witch's breath from
the oaks and dogwoods and rhododendrons that grew in
wild abandon all up and down the steep slope. Glossy
green, the bushes formed a startling contrast to the gray
mist. Craning his neck to peer through the canopy of
trees, Tony spotted a sky so blue the poets would be
hard-pressed to describe it.

A downward glance, however, pushed all thoughts of
sky and poetry from his mind. In the light of day, he
saw for the first time how close they'd come to sailing
into oblivion. The mountain plunged straight down for
a thousand feet or more.

God! Cold sweat pooled at the base of his spine. If
the Olds hadn't lodged against that oak...

The sound of Jess scrambling out of the car calmed
his shakes at their near miss. Taking her hand, Tony
helped her find her footing on the angled slope. Together they faced the officer, still red-faced and puffing
slightly from his descent. His plastic name badge identified him as S. Bennett.

"Anyone hurt here?"

"No," Tony answered, "we're all right."

The officer hitched his Sam Browne belt, giving them
a thorough once-over. "Y'all been down here all
night?"

"Most of it."

His glance went from Tony to Jess and back again.

"Helluva a spot to go neckin'," he drawled. "The way you two were tangled up in there, I 'spect you didn't even notice you drove clear off the road."

A flush heated Jess's skin to a rosy pink. Avoiding Tony's eye, she essayed a smile. "We noticed. Believe me, we noticed. How did you find us down here?"

She shot a look up the slope to the road above and answered her own question. "The guard rail, right?"

"That was my first clue," Bennett agreed.

Something about the man's demeanor struck Tony as a little off. His smile didn't quite reach his eyes, for one thing. For another, Tony was sure he'd seen him before, but he was damned if he could remember where. Frowning, he tried to place the man's voice. It carried a thick mountain drawl, a good part of which, Tony suspected, was put on for the benefit of the outsiders.

"Y'all want to tell me what happened?"

"The brakes on that wreck failed," Jess replied with a touch of acid. "The owner tried to tell us it was reliable."

"You don't say."

Tony felt himself stiffening. A dark suspicion grabbed at his mind. He had an inkling of what was coming even before the officer rocked back on his heels.

"Seems Joe's vehicle came up missing sometime after midnight last night. He called to report it stolen."

"What!"

Jess's screech echoed down the mountain and startled a flock of starlings. They rose with a flutter of wings from the nearby trees.

Incensed, Jess grabbed Tony's arm to keep her footing on the slope and sputtered a protest. "He rented it to us! We paid two hundred dollars for that piece of junk. Well, Tony paid it, but I was the one who talked him into it, so I take full responsibility."

"Jess…"

Furious, she ignored the quiet warning. "I can't believe anyone would try to claim we stole this bucket of bolts. How does he explain the Corvette we left as insurance?"

Tony's stomach curled in on itself. He had a feeling he wouldn't see the vehicle he'd spent hundreds of hours restoring anytime soon. Not in one piece, anyway.

Sure enough, the sheriff shook his head. "I don't know anything about a Corvette. Sure wasn't one parked at the Hilltop Haven when I went by to take Joe's report."

"There had to be! A restored red '58 convertible. We just left it there a few hours ago. The tires were slashed."

"Well, I guess it'll be your word against Joe's 'bout that, ma'am."

It took a moment for Jess to grasp the full impact of Joe's perfidity. When she did, she groaned in dismay.

"Oh, Tony! Your baby! I'm…I'm sorry."

He kept his eyes on S. Bennett. "I'm beginning to suspect a missing Corvette may be the least of our worries," he said quietly.

His cordiality unimpaired, the sheriff nodded. "You got that right."

Dismayed and now so angry she almost danced with it, Jess dug her fingers into Tony's arm to keep her balance and swung back to the officer.

"I don't believe this! Do we look like car thieves, for heaven's sake?"

"You learn early in this line of business not to go by appearances, ma'am."

"Well, we didn't steal anything. We rented this car."

"Y'all got any proof of that? A rental agreement, maybe? Something in writing?"

"No! It was late. And raining."

Even Jess realized how lame that sounded. Still disbelieving, still angry, but a little desperate now, she tried one more time.

"Look, my name's Jessica Taylor. This is Tony Paretti. We—"

"I know who he is." The sheriff pushed his Smoky the Bear hat to the back of his head, revealing a thatch of thinning red hair. "The race car driver."

Suddenly it clicked. Tony finally figured out why S. Bennett looked so familiar. The sheriff had to be related to the drunk who'd come on to Jess last night. Without the hat shielding his face, the resemblance between the two was unmistakable.

With a sense of impending doom, he heard the police officer confirm his guess. "My brother said he'd bumped into you in the men's room. You and the lady. That's how I knew what name to put on the arrest warrant."

Chapter 6

"Alyx?" Jess jammed the phone to her ear. "Baby, it's mom."

"Hi, Mom. Where are you?"

She glanced over her shoulder at the holding pens of the Greene County jail. Tony paced like a caged lion in one cell. Jess had just been let out of the other to make her one phone call.

There was no way, however, she was going to tell her intrepid, impetuous nine-year-old that she was in jail. Alyx would hop the next truck or train or plane, a pint-size public defender beating a path to rescue her wrongly accused mother.

"I'm in a town up in the Blue Ridge Mountains, sweetheart. I've, er, been detained. I'll get to Rocky Point as soon as I can."

"Okay."

Okay? Holding back a sigh, Jess leaned her forehead against the cinder-block wall. Things were about as far

from okay as they could get right now. She'd just spent
the night in a car perched on the side of the mountain.
During those dark hours, Tony's Corvette had vanished
into thin air. Twenty minutes ago a female deputy sheriff had relieved them both of their personal belongings
and escorted them to side-by-side cells.

She and Tony were being held on suspicion of car
theft, for goodness sakes! They'd have to cool their
heels in jail until either a judge set their bail, the lawyer
Tony had called arrived on the scene to sort this mess
out or the sheriff admitted he didn't have enough to
hold them, which Jess fervently hoped he'd soon do.

In the meantime, she didn't have any idea of how or
when she'd make it to Rocky Point to reclaim her
daughter. That didn't seem to worry Alyx, however.
Jess understood why in the girl's next breezy remark.

"I'll just play with my kittens until you get here."

"The Stewarts' kittens, you mean."

"No, mine. Mrs. Stewart said I could take two home
with me. Cats like to have company."

"Now, Alyx, remember our agreement? Only a turtle
for a pet until we move out of the apartment into our
own house."

"But, Mom, they're all fuzzy, with little pink noses.
You're gonna love them. I'll let you name one," she
offered on a burst of generosity.

"No, sweetheart. We can't—"

With a keen sense of timing, the daughter changed
the subject before the mother could lock her refusal in
concrete.

"Is Mr. Paretti still with you."

"Yes."

"I can't wait to meet him. Is he as handsome as he
looks on TV? Really, truly, totally awesome?"

Jess shot another glance over her shoulder at the man in the cage. His black hair stuck up in spikes where he'd thrust his hand through it. Streaks of white powder decorated his muddy, rumpled shirt. A night's growth shadowed his chin and cheeks, adding to the fierceness of his expression. He wasn't happy about their incarceration. At all.

Just then his glance met hers through the bars. His expression softened, and he aimed a smile her way that made Jess's heart skip a few erratic beats.

"Yes," she murmured, "he's really, truly, totally awesome."

"I can't wait to meet him," Alyx said again before a touch of uncharacteristic doubt crept into her voice. "Do you think he'll like me?"

A small ache pierced Jess's chest. She couldn't encourage her daughter's ridiculous fixation on Tony as potential father material. It wasn't fair to him. Or to Alyx.

"Of course he'd like you…if he met you. But he won't, sweetie. Not this time, anyway."

Not ever, Jess thought bleakly. If—*when!* they got out of this jail, she and Tony would have to part company. The prospect took the ache in her chest and tripled it.

"But, Mom…"

Hiding her hurt, Jess forced a note of brisk cheerfulness into her response. "Mr. Paretti was kind enough to drive this far with me, but I can't impose on him any longer."

"Mommmmm!"

"No arguments, Alyxandra," she said sharply. "Not this time. Now let me speak to Mrs. Stewart."

After repeated assurances from the kindly woman

that she'd keep an eye on Alyx, Jess hung up and was escorted back to her cell. The door clanged shut behind her. The lock fell into place with an audible click. A moment later the deputy left the holding area, and the outer door thudded behind her.

The sounds raised a lump in Jess's throat. She'd never felt claustrophobic before, but the idea of being penned in like this got to her. Sinking down on the lower of the two metal bunks attached to the wall, she caught Tony's glance. His encouraging smile had disappeared. The fierce expression was back, his brown eyes almost unfriendly.

Jess supposed she couldn't blame him. After all, she'd embroiled him in everything from a fist fight to a wild ride down a mountain, not to mention a phony arrest.

"How long do you think we'll be here?"

"Another couple hours. They'll have to formally charge us and take us before a judge or let us go."

"I don't understand how the sheriff can seriously believe we stole that wreck!"

His shoulders rolled in a small, tight shrug. "I'm guessing this is just payback for roughing up his brother. As your friend informed us last night, they don't take kindly to smart-ass tourists in these parts."

Deciding not to stress yet again that the drunk was *not* her friend, Jess crossed her legs under her and leaned back against the concrete wall. She chewed on her lower lip for a few moments before broaching what she knew was a painful subject.

"I'm sorry about your Corvette."

Scowling, he resumed his pacing. "Me, too."

He was taking the loss hard. Not an unexpected reaction for a man with a bone-deep passion for anything and everything automotive. Jess tried to make amends.

"I was the one who talked you into leaving your baby at the Hilltop Haven. I'll certainly reimburse you for the loss."

"That's what insurance is for."

The terse reply didn't ease her conscience. "Yes, well, insurance doesn't always cover the total cost of replacement."

"Replacement?" He stopped pacing to eye her in disbelief. "That machine can't be replaced. She's an original. I personally reconditioned every moving part in her, from her rings to her exhaust manifold."

Oh, right! Nothing like making her feel even worse.

"I'm sorry," Jess said again, a little stiffly this time. She decided not to remind him that he was the one who insisted on driving her down to North Carolina in the first place. If he'd just loaned her the money for the cab to take her to the airport last night, as she'd requested, he wouldn't have lost his precious car.

And Jess wouldn't have spent the night in his arms.

She buried that thought, fast, before the ache still wiggling around in her chest could spread to other parts of her anatomy.

"Just add any loss from the Corvette to what I already owe you," she said coolly. "Let me know the total."

"Yeah, sure," he growled. "I'll send you a bill."

"You don't have to get nasty about it."

His jaw worked for a moment. "You're right. I don't. Sorry."

She accepted the curt apology with a nod and considered the matter closed. Tony, however, apparently had more to say. Shoving his hands in his jeans pockets, he glowered at her through the bars.

"I guess it just rubbed me the wrong way to get the brush-off like that."

"Like what?"

He jerked his chin toward the phone. Jess's stomach sank as enlightenment dawned.

"Oh. You heard what I said to Alyx?"

"I heard." Pique and something that looked like hurt sparked in his brown eyes. "You don't want me to meet your daughter."

Jess bit her lip. After all Tony had done to help her, she must have sounded like a total ingrate during her brief phone conversation.

"You've got it backward," she said quietly. "I don't want Alyx to meet *you*. She's so impressionable and...and so darned determined to find herself a father. The last thing I want after all you've done for me is to put you in the embarrassing position of having to—"

"I got the picture," he interrupted brusquely. "We'll go our separate ways from here."

As miserable now as she was irritated a moment ago, Jess nodded. "I think it's best."

"Fine," he snapped.

"Fine," she echoed.

Wheeling away from her, Tony dropped onto his own bunk, folded his arms and contemplated the cracks in the ceiling. For the life of him, he couldn't understand why Jess's decision to go it alone scratched such a raw spot inside him. Or why he should feel so damned disappointed that he wouldn't meet her daughter. He had a busy life in Baltimore. A business he had to get back to. A large, lively family of his own that...

Oh, hell! He'd forgotten to instruct his lawyer, who

also happened to be his cousin-in-law, not to mention the fact that he was in jail to his mother, his sister, or any other of their assorted relatives. Lawyer-client privilege didn't stand a chance against Maria Paretti if and when she discovered that one of her chicks was in trouble. Hopefully, Larry got out of his house and on the road without mentioning where he was going to his wife. If not, the Paretti network was probably already on red alert.

That's all he needed, Tony thought with a wry twist of his lips. The whole Paretti clan descending on the Greene County Courthouse. Sheriff Bennett wouldn't know what hit him.

As it turned out, Bennett released his suspects well before Tony's lawyer or any of the other Paretti clan arrived on the scene.

A little before noon the deputy sheriff announced that Jess and Tony were free to go. Escorting them into the outer offices, she asked them to wait while she retrieved their personal belongings. Her boss strolled out of his office just as she dumped the contents of two manila envelopes on the counter for them to inventory.

"Seems Joe got things a little mixed up last night," S. Bennett told his two former suspects imperturbably. "He does that occasionally, ever since he sucked in some Agent Orange or something in 'Nam. He called a while ago to say he's pretty sure he remembers you givin' him cash to rent ole Bessie."

"He does, huh?" Tony shoved his wallet into his back pocket. "Does he remember anything about a '58 Corvette?"

"Well, now that you mention it, he does. Says he's

got it parked in the shed behind Hilltop Haven. Wanted to keep it clean."

Yeah, right, Tony thought as he strapped on his watch. Joe had probably planned to dispose of the car first thing this morning. Sheriff Bennett, for all he gave the impression of being one of the good-ole boys, had probably put the skids on that bit of grand larceny. In the process, however, he'd decided to teach the guy who beat up on his brother a lesson by letting him stew in a cell for a few hours.

Sure enough, the sheriff nodded toward the door. "You folks can get on your way now. Just don't go hasslin' any more of our local residents. The next time, you might find yourselves facin' assault and battery charges."

"Assault and battery!" Jess sniffed. "If anyone was hassled last night, I was. Tell your brother he's lucky *we* don't press charges."

"Yes, ma'am, I surely will."

With another sniff, Jess spun around and marched out of the office. Tony followed her down the hall, their footsteps echoing in the cavernous marble hallway that led to massive wooden doors. Eagerly, Jess pushed through the doors and stepped outside. Tony's gut tightened at the sight of her silvery blond hair haloed in the bright noon sunshine. Tousled and untamed, it fluttered like tangled silk in the mountain breeze.

She paused on the steps to breathe in the crisp air. After the starkness of the jail, the scene that greeted them outside was summer lush and sleepy tranquil. The Greene County Courthouse faced a tree-shaded square with Civil War era cannons pointing from each corner. In the center of the square, an officer on a rearing stallion pointed his sword at the blue sky. Two elderly men occupied a shaded park bench, bent over a checkerboard. A mother pushed a stroller along the sidewalk.

Businesses lined the square...including, Tony saw, the two-story Blue Ridge Mountain Inn. Its white-painted facade peeled in a few places, but the sign hanging above the pillared entrance proclaimed it had earned a three-star rating from a reputable travel service.

"I need to find a phone," Jess murmured, conducting her own survey of the storefronts. "And a bank or an ATM that will take my bank card."

Tony's jaw tightened. She wanted him to butt out. Okay. He'd butt.

"I'm sure there's a bank on the square." Forcing a smile, he held out his hand. "So long, Jess. It's been...interesting."

"Yes, it has." She mirrored the same strained smile. "Goodbye, Tony. Thank you."

He refused to think about the way her hand fit in his, or those turquoise eyes that reminded him of the sparkling water off the Alabama gulf shores. Telling himself to get this over with, he let her hand slide from his.

"Anytime."

He started down the steps, got as far as the sidewalk, stopped. He couldn't do it. He couldn't just walk away with a flippant remark like that. He turned to find her staring down at him, the skin stretched tight across her cheekbones and her eyes stark. She recovered instantly and smiled at him, but not before the knot in Tony's gut had tightened another notch or two.

He knew he was ten kinds of a fool for opening himself up again, but the words came out, anyway.

"Look, we both need to make some calls and clean up before we hit the road again. A decent lunch wouldn't hurt, either. I'm going to rent a room at the inn across the street. You're welcome to use the phone and/or the shower before you head on down to Rocky Point.''

She hesitated for so long that Tony was ready with another goodbye when she agreed.

"I'd kill for a shower and some real food," she admitted. "But you have to let me share the cost of the room."

"I'll add it to your bill."

Jess let the sarcasm roll off her. She wasn't about to take a pass on the chance to clean up and put something other than coffee into her stomach. Or the chance of another stolen hour with Tony.

One hour, she promised fiercely. Sixty minutes max. Then she'd hit the road, reclaim her daughter and put the past behind her once and for all.

"Let me find a bank and meet you at the inn."

"I'll leave a key at the desk for you."

Jess bit her lip as he strode off, a slight hitch in his long-legged stride. Briefly, she wondered if the clerk at the hotel would let him in the front door, much less rent him a room. He looked as disreputable as she felt. Dark bristles shadowed his face, and his clothes showed the effects of both the brawl and the long night in the Olds.

Hers weren't any better, she acknowledged ruefully, glancing down at her once-smart navy blazer and linen shorts. She'd better find a bank *and* something decent to wear. She couldn't show up at the Stewarts' looking like a refugee from the last war.

For a change, Jess's luck held. The bank at the south corner of the square honored her bank card. She walked out with five hundred dollars in cash, sixty of which she spent at a combination gift shop and dime-store. The local crafts section offered a selection of long, crinkle-wrap skirts and matching sleeveless vests. Jess usually preferred plain and tailored over long and flowery, but the one-size-fits-all skirts and lace-trimmed vests promised comfort as well as the convenience of a quick buy. Before checking out, she added two toothbrushes, toothpaste, a plastic razor, a travel-size can of shaving cream and a collared T-shirt with a mountain logo to her purchases.

With the help of the Blue Mountain Inn's desk clerk, she made arrangement for a rental car—from a legitimate agency, this time! A few minutes later she knocked on the door of Room 216. As promised, Tony had left a key for her at the desk, but Jess didn't want to walk in on him unannounced. The door swung open, and Jess crunched the paper bag she was holding to her chest.

Tony in a scruffy beard and a rumpled shirt could make her heart skip a few beats. Tony in no shirt at all stopped it dead.

She tried not to stare, refused to let her gaze linger on the wide expanse of bare chest below his jaw. Still, she couldn't miss the glistening swirls of black hair, the slick, corded muscles, the damp towel draped around his neck. Her heart restarted with a painful lurch as she held up the paper bag.

"I bought you a razor."

"Thanks! I was just about to call the desk to see if they could send one up."

He stood aside to give her access to the sun-filled bed-sitting room overlooking the square. Any other time, the floral chintzes and reproduction antique poster bed would have delighted Jess. At the moment, she was far too conscious of the half-naked man whose presence filled the room to appreciate its furnishings. Fumbling through the purchases in the bag, she produced the T-shirt and toiletries.

"I thought you might want a clean shirt." She shook it out and apologized for the startling purple color. "This was the only one in your size. It's a bit gaudy, but what the heck. You might as well have a souvenir to remind you of your drive through the Blue Ridge Mountains."

"Somehow I suspect I won't need any reminders."

The grin that accompanied his dry response did a number on Jess's respiratory system. She sucked in a swift breath as he started for the bathroom, shirt and toiletries in hand.

"I'll shave, then turn the bathroom over to you. Why don't you call down to room service and order us something to eat?" He stopped, a question in his dark eyes. "Unless you'd rather go down to the dining room?"

She'd allowed herself an hour, Jess reminded herself. Only an hour. With a dart of pure selfishness, she refused to share those sixty minutes with anyone, even the anonymous patrons of a dining room.

"Room service will be quicker." She reached for the menu card tucked under the phone. "They can prepare our order while I take my turn in the bathroom." A quick scan of the hand-printed menu gave her the options. "Would you like soup and salad, a sandwich, or today's special, whatever that is?"

That throat-closing grin flashed again. "All of the above. I'm starved."

Leaving her to make the choices, Tony disappeared. The sound of splashing water punctuated Jess's short conversation with the inn's kitchen. By the time she finished ordering two garden salads, two bowls of corn chowder, a sugar-cured ham sandwich with home fries, and the daily special, Tony had reemerged. The purple shirt clung faithfully to his muscles and, surprisingly, complemented his dark, Italian looks. He surrendered the bathroom with a bow and a flourish.

"It's all yours."

"Lunch is on the way. I'll be out before it arrives."

And be gone as soon as it was eaten.

The thought followed Jess into the bathroom. Resolutely she banished it and closed the door behind her. Tony had swiped down the shower and the sink after he'd used them, she noted with approval. If only she could teach Alyx to be as considerate and neat.

She stepped out of her clothes and into the shower. Allowing herself five minutes of pure bliss, Jess closed her eyes and turned her face up to the stream. Slowly, the stress of the past twenty-four hours washed away with her accumulated grime. When she toweled herself off and donned her hasty purchases, she felt like a different person.

A quick look in the mirror showed that the sleeveless, lace-trimmed vest and long, twirly skirt gave her a different look, too. Softer. More feminine than she normally went for. The delicate lilac tones brought out the silvery sheen of her hair. Sensing the minutes ticking away, she attacked the wet tangles with the brush she carried in her purse, and swiped a little color on her lips.

Tony and their lunch were both waiting for her when she walked back into the sitting room. The heavenly scents started her mouth watering as she crossed the room to join him at the table set in front of the windows. Covered dishes were heaped three high on the tray.

"I see you took me at my word," he said, eyeing the

array of food she uncovered. "There's enough here for an army."

"Good! My stomach's been rumbling since early last night."

A corner of his mouth kicked up. "I know. For a while there, I wasn't sure if that was you or poor old Bessie grinding her cylinders."

Seduced by the twin delights of his teasing smile and thick, creamy corn chowder, Jess didn't respond. She spent the next few moments spooning up her soup and memorizing the way Tony's dark hair curled when it was damp.

An hour, she reminded herself. Less, now. Forty minutes, perhaps, to store up a whole new set of memories.

She might even have stuck to that schedule if she hadn't made a pig of herself by scarfing down a slice of caramel pecan pie at the end of the sumptuous feast...or if Tony hadn't pointed out that she had caramel on her chin. Grabbing her used napkin, she swiped at the corners.

"You missed it. No, lower," he said after a second swipe. Rising, he came around the table. "Here, I'll get it."

Unthinking, he curled a knuckle under her chin.

Unthinking, Jess tipped her face to his.

The napkin brushed the curve of her lower cheek, followed the line of her lips, stopped somewhere in the middle of her chin. She didn't feel it, didn't notice when the linen caught on a drop of stickiness. The heat of Tony's hand on her chin blocked every other sensation. Slowly she rose.

He didn't move, didn't give her the breathing room she suddenly, desperately needed.

"I've—" she wet her lips "—I've got to go."

"I know."

"Alyx is waiting for me."

He nodded.

She hesitated, then said simply, "Thank you...for everything."

"You're welcome."

She rose up on tiptoe. Brushed a kiss across his lips. She meant it as a farewell. A thank-you. A last memory of her young love to take with her and tuck away with all the others.

Except they weren't young, and Tony wanted more than a thank-you. She read it in the sudden narrowing of his eyes. Heard it in his indrawn sharp breath. She wanted more, too. With a sudden, piercing need, Jess knew she wanted more than she could ever have.

She should have broken the contact then, should have backed away and left. But she didn't. She couldn't. A single heartbeat later, Tony had bent his head and covered her mouth with his.

Just a few more minutes, a greedy voice cried inside her. *Only a few.*

With a wild singing in her veins, Jess gave in to the clamoring, clawing greed. Her arms slid around his neck. Her mouth opened under the hard pressure of his. Her body fit his with the same ease, the same perfection she remembered.

Chapter 7

"Jess. Sweetheart."

Tony broke the kiss and dragged his head up. Eyes fierce, breath harsh, he fought the desire that slammed through him. He might as well have tried to hold back the wind or the roaring, rushing tides.

The woman in his arms felt the same need, the same urgency he did. He saw it in her trembling mouth, in the aqua flames that lit her eyes. Battling the urge to crush her against him, he dug his hands into her hair, tipped her head back.

"We can't do this, Jess."

"Why not?"

The question rushed out on a whisper, surprising her as much as it did him. She looked as though she wanted to take the words back, but she didn't.

"We drove down this road once," Tony said savagely. "I can't guarantee what will happen if we go down it again."

She answered slowly, painfully, as if she pulled the words from somewhere deep inside. "I'm not asking for any guarantees. We've both learned the hard way that there are none in life. Your racing career ended just as you were reaching your peak. Frank died three months after his daughter was born. And I..."

"You what?"

She gathered her courage with a visible effort. "I haven't thought about us much in the past ten years, Tony. I wouldn't let myself think about us. It hurt too much. But when I did, when I couldn't stop the memories from sneaking in, I always wondered—" she shook her head "—no, I always wished we'd made love. Just once."

"Jess...!"

"But now I'm glad we didn't." Her palms came up, her fingertips traced his mouth, his smooth-shaven cheeks, his chin. "Now I can feel again exactly what I felt ten years ago. Trembly. Nervous. Excited. On fire with need."

And desperately in love.

The realization knifed into Jess's heart. She'd never stopped loving Tony Paretti. She'd buried the truth deep inside her, but it had always been there, just below the surface of her busy life. Now it came rushing back, bringing with it all the excitement, all the passion of those weeks at Talledega. With everything in her, Jess wanted to consummate the love she'd once given and then wrenched away from this man.

He didn't love her. He couldn't, after the way she'd walked out on him all those years ago. But he wanted her. Wanted the woman she was now. The desire in his eyes stirred a need so great in Jess, she wanted to weep with it.

Tony didn't give her the chance. His mouth came down on hers, harder, fiercer, even more demanding than before. Jess felt an instant of shock, of doubt, of wild, soaring delight, before the liquid heat that swept through her veins consumed her.

Then there was only Tony. His still-damp hair thick and curly under her fingers. His skin rough-smooth and smelling of shaving cream. His hands wicked on her body. They shaped her waist, her hips, her bottom, canted her hips into his. She felt him against her, hard and rampant. Felt him put just enough space between them to work the buttons on her vest with one hand.

Suddenly and ridiculously shy, she buried her face in his neck. The air-conditioned air kissed her skin as he peeled back the lilac vest and unhooked her bra. Time and a nine-year-old had wrought inevitable changes in her body as well as her life. She wasn't as slender or as firm as she'd once been. Not that she was ashamed of the woman she'd become. But this was Tony, who'd known her in those long-ago days of thin thighs and tight bottom.

"You're beautiful."

The murmur carried more than enough husky masculine lust to banish Jess's shyness. The pinpricks of sensation his exploring hands raised in her breasts certainly helped, too.

"Even more beautiful than I remember."

And he was even more skilled at lovemaking than she remembered! When he dipped his head to drop a kiss on the swell of her breast, Jess gasped in delight.

And when he swept her into his arms, delight melted into aching need. Three strides took them to the high, canopied bed. He stopped beside it, his arms tight around her, his eyes questioning.

"You're sure?"

She'd never been more sure of anything in her life. Whatever happened, whatever came, she'd always have this time with him to remember.

"Yes."

He'd take it slow, Tony vowed. Savor every second. Measure the reality of loving Jess against the mountain of what-ifs that had built in his mind over the years.

What if he slid her skirt and panties down, as he'd wanted to do all those years ago? What if he bent and kissed her navel? Skimmed his tongue along the silken skin of her belly? What if she gasped and arched under him, the way she did now?

Afterward Tony would never remember when he abandoned his plan to take it slow or who pulled who into the whirling, roaring vortex or even when he shed his clothes. All he knew was that the living, breathing Jess was so much more than his collective memories of the girl he'd once loved. More sensual, more arousing, more woman.

He couldn't get enough of her mouth. Of her body soft and straining and urgent beneath his. Of the gasping little sounds she made far back in her throat when his fingers found the heat between her legs. She was ready, more than ready, as frantic as he for the joining they'd denied themselves so long ago. His muscles burning with the strain of holding back, he primed her even more.

She did the same, her hands and her mouth eager on his body. He was rock hard and aching when her womb tightened around his fingers, her whole body convulsing with her need.

"Tony! Please. Now!"

He took only the few seconds necessary to protect

her before he kneed her legs apart. With a mewling cry of eagerness, she wrapped her legs around his and welcomed him into her satiny wetness.

Even ready and dying for him, Jess gulped when he lodged inside her. He stretched and filled her in a way she'd never experienced before. It wasn't physical. Some distant corner of her brain not yet lost to passion sensed that. Tony filled a void, that tiny, empty part of her heart she'd always refused to acknowledge.

She'd loved Frank in those short months they'd had together, tried with everything in her to be an eager, responsive wife. Yet a hidden, secret part of her had always, *always,* ached for Tony's touch, Tony's kiss, Tony's...

"Open your eyes."

The fierce command brought her lids flying up.

"I want to watch pleasure take you. I want you to know who..."

"Who's giving me this pleasure?" she finished on a rasping breath, when he didn't, or couldn't. "I know, Tony. I know."

When he thrust into her, once, twice, again, Jess didn't even try to fight the waves that rushed in, receded, rushed in again, each faster, sweeter, higher than the last. The dizzying sensations built with each grind of hips against hips, each greedy kiss and frantic slide of hands and legs and bodies.

Moments, or maybe hours, later Jess felt her climax rushing at her. She couldn't stop it, didn't try. She went up in a flash of white heat, a groan ripping out of her throat. Her body was still singing when Tony buried his face in her neck, gave a muffled shout and dived into the maelstrom with her.

* * *

The shrilling phone pulled them both from the aftermath of passion. Jess lifted her head from Tony's damp shoulder as he rolled to one side and snatched at the receiver.

"Paretti."

He listened, shot her a quick frown.

Alyx! Jess held her breath, sure that her daughter had plunged into some new disaster or adventure.

"There's an agent downstairs with your rental car," Tony said, his brows slashing down into a frown.

Relief washed through her. Regret followed on the next wave. She'd known this moment would come, known she and Tony had only a short time together. Resolutely she pushed the regret aside. She couldn't, *wouldn't,* remember this stolen hour with anything but joy.

"Tell him I'll be right there."

Scrambling off the bed, Jess snatched up her clothes and retreated to the bathroom. Once inside, she leaned against the door. She'd never imagined that one day she would leave Tony Paretti for the second time. If she had, she would have bet everything she owned that the experience would tear her apart...again.

She was amazed that she felt only a silent, shimmering happiness. It didn't take a genius to figure out the source. She'd never loved the way she loved Tony. Never *been* loved like that. The guilt and aching sense of loss from those days after Talledega were finally, irrevocably buried.

Evidently Tony didn't consider anything buried. When Jess came out of the bathroom a few minutes later, he was zipping up his jeans. He glanced over at her, his eyes hooded and just a bit wary.

"I think we need to talk about this, Jess."

She shook her head. "The last thing we need to do right now is talk. I've got to get to Alyx and you've got to reclaim your baby."

He pulled on his shirt, still frowning. Jess tucked her purse under her arm and crossed the room to stand beside him. The tangled sheets still bore the scent of their loving. So did Tony. She breathed him in, a small, selfish whiff to take away with her.

"Call me. If you want to. If not…"

She rose up on tiptoe to brush his mouth with hers, understanding his frozen silence and not hurt by it. He needed time and distance to put what had just happened in perspective. So did she.

"If not," she murmured with a smile that came from her heart, "I'll never forget our ride through the Blue Ridge Mountains. 'Bye, Tony."

She left him standing in the middle of the room, his brows a dark slash and his jaw tight. Downstairs she signed the rental agreement and walked out of the inn into the bright afternoon sunlight. She'd carried too many regrets away from Talledega with her, too much hurt. Now she took with her only that strange, quiet joy and the lingering taste of Tony on her lips.

She paused on the sagging wooden steps, letting her eyes grow accustomed to the afternoon sun. Its warmth felt wonderful on her bare arms, filtered as it was through the tall shade trees lining the courthouse square.

Her daughter waited for her just across the North Carolina state line. It was time to go. Sliding into the driver's seat, Jess keyed the ignition and pulled out of the parking space in front of the inn. Halfway around the square, she found the road the clerk had advised her to take. She flicked a last glance at the inn in the rearview mirror and hung a right.

* * *

Not five minutes after the rental car disappeared around the turn, a dusty Mercedes turned onto the square and pulled into the parking space Jess had vacated. Its occupants piled out, one after another, and headed for the steps. Scant moments later the driver raised his fist to pound on the door to Room 216.

Tony yanked the door open after the first rap. "Jess! I was just coming after—"

He broke off, groaning when he saw who faced him.

Ignoring his instant and instinctive protest, his mother, sister and cousin swept past him, leaving only his shamefaced cousin-in-law in the corridor.

"I tried to convince them not to make the trip, Tony, but when your mother heard you were in jail…"

"Some lawyer you are," his ungrateful client groused. "Why the hell didn't you have your cell phone on or check your call notes? I left three separate messages saying that your services weren't needed."

"I got them, but by then we were three-quarters of the way here."

"So of course you came the rest of the way."

"It was either that or get dumped beside the road to find my own way back to Baltimore. You know how your mother is, especially since the accident."

Tony blew out a long breath. "Yeah, I know. Come on in, Larry. I might need some legal advice after I strangle her and my loving sister."

His loving sister anticipated just such a possibility. Folding her arms across her high, protruding stomach, she flashed him a grin that was all Angela.

"Think of your unborn niece."

"My unborn niece is all that stands between you and

an instant, painful death," he retorted before turning to face his cousin.

"And as for you…"

Eileen held up both hands, palms out, to ward off the stinging rebuke she guessed was headed her way. "Go easy here, Tony. I only told Angela because I knew neither she nor your mother would ever forgive me if we let you serve time."

"That doesn't say a whole lot for either my innocence or your husband's skills as an attorney," he returned. Still, he knew Eileen hadn't formed up the troops and charged to his rescue on her own. Only one woman wielded that kind of absolute power.

Outsiders often marveled that a single phone call or piercing stare from tiny, delicate-boned Maria Paretti of the olive skin and the Mona Lisa smile could make grown men tremble. She exuded all the warmth of her northern Italian ancestors, all the passion for life that she showered indiscriminately upon her boisterous, extended family. Along with her warmth and joy, however, came a fierce protectiveness for her cubs and kin that rivaled any jungle beast's.

Angie's husband, Jack, had served an extended probationary period until he'd won Maria's conditional approval by transferring from Atlanta to D.C., only a few hours from Baltimore, where his mother-in-law could keep an eye on her daughter. Six months ago Jack had finally sealed his acceptance into the family by fathering Maria's first grandchild.

Angie's blossoming pregnancy hadn't diverted her mother's attention or let Tony off the hook, however. If anything, his sister's wedded bliss and impending motherhood had convinced Maria Paretti to redouble her efforts on her son's behalf. He braced himself, knowing it wouldn't take her all of thirty seconds to pick up on the evidence presented by the tangled sheets and the remains of a dinner for two, still sitting on the table by the window.

Sure enough, her luminous brown eyes fixed first on the bed, then on the tray. When they turned to Tony, he knew he wouldn't get away unscathed.

"Who is she, Anthony?" She glanced pointedly around the room. "Where is she?"

Over the years Tony had learned just how much of his life he could and couldn't share with his mother...for her peace of mind as much as his own. He'd never told her about Jess, or Talledega, or the hurt he'd carried around until it got buried beneath the layers of his life. Now that old hurt didn't seem to matter.

"Her name is Jessica. Jessica Summerville Taylor."

"Jessica?" Maria lifted a brow. "Is she the same Jessica who answered your phone yesterday?"

"She is. She flew to Baltimore to ask me to help her find her daughter. I drove her down here last night."

"She has a daughter?" Dismay rippled across his mother's Madonnalike face. "She's not married, is she? Or divorced?"

Tony knew darn well that adultery ranked right up there among the worst offenses against God and man, in his mother's considered opinion. Divorce ran a close second. That didn't mean Maria would encourage a friend or relative to remain in an abusive relationship. She worked several days a month in a women's shelter and saw the brutal effects of marriages gone bad. Still, divorce was a last, desperate resort for those of the Catholic persuasion.

"She's a widow," Tony replied, hiding a grin at the relief that spread across his mother's face.

"Where did you meet her?" his sister asked, joining in the inquisition.

"In Alabama, ten years ago...not that it's anyone's business," he added in a pointed but futile attempt to terminate the interrogation.

Angela threw her mother one of those *where*-do-they-come-from looks before turning back to her brother.

"You disappear without a word to anyone. The next we hear, you're sitting in a jail cell. We dash to your rescue—"

"Did I ask you to dash anywhere?"

She waved aside that minor point. "The least you can do is tell us about this mysterious Jessica Taylor who shared, uh, your lunch."

"She asked me to help her find her daughter," Tony repeated. "I drove her part of the way to North Carolina."

Angela snorted. It was a delicate snort, the kind a generous, warm-hearted sister might make, but definitely a snort. "You were good, brother of mine. The best on the racing circuit. But even you can't pass this off as 'driving.'"

At that point Tony decided that retreat was the better part of valor. Besides, he'd wasted enough time already. The decision he'd made just before his mother appeared on the scene now burned like a brand in his gut.

"Look, I'd stay and tell you folks all about Jess, but I lost her once, ten years ago. I almost lost her again last night, when we drove off the side of that mountain, and I'm damned if—"

"Anthony!" Paling, his mother made a quick sign of the cross. "You drove off a mountain?"

Tony cursed his slip under his breath and tried to

recover. "We only went a little way down. A tree stopped us."

"A tree," Maria echoed faintly, crossing herself again. "Were you hurt? Did you see a doctor?"

"No, only the sheriff."

"He arrested you for driving off a mountain?"

"It's a long story. I don't have time to explain now." Wrapping his arm around his mother's shoulders, he dropped a quick kiss on her cheek. "I'll see you back in Baltimore."

"Tony!" She grabbed at his purple T-shirt. "Where are you going?"

"After Jess. Again." His mouth curved in a self-deprecating smile. "The last time she walked out on me, I stewed about it for too long before deciding to follow her. By the time I got to her, she'd already married someone else."

Angela's brows soared. "The woman doesn't believe in wasting time, does she?"

"No, which is why I'm not taking any chances this time. Come on, Larry. I need to buy some tires, then grab a ride to the Hilltop Haven."

"Where?"

"It's a beer joint about fifteen miles from here," Tony explained impatiently. "I left my car there last night."

It was his cousin-in-law's turn to pale. "You left the 'Vette at a beer joint? All night?"

Grabbing the attorney's elbow, Tony hustled him out the door. "It's a long story," he said again.

"Yeah, but a beer joint?" Anguish painted across Larry's face. "Your Corvette?"

"I'll tell you about it on the way."

Impatience grew like a living thing inside Tony. He

wanted out of the inn, wanted his hands on a steering wheel. He had to get to Jess. The moment the door had closed behind her, he knew instinctively he'd follow her. For five, ten minutes, he'd fought the crazy urge, argued against it, told himself he was a fool to set himself up for a second fall.

He had no idea what made him decide to take the risk. Maybe it was the memory of her hair spread across the pillow. Or her desperate, determined grin during their out-of-control plunge down the dark mountain road last night. Or the ache in his gut when he thought of another ten years—hell, another ten minutes—without her.

All he knew was that he had to get to her, fast, before she slipped out of his life for the second time. Plucking the keys from Larry's hands, he strode around the hood of the dusty Mercedes.

"I'll drive."

Chapter 8

Tony had claimed his first Winston Cup championship at the ripe old age of twenty. At thirty-four, he hadn't forgotten the skills that had propelled him into one of racing's most popular heroes.

Those skills came into play during the swift ascent to the Hilltop Haven. With the scent of rubber wafting from the new tires loaded in the trunk and the back seat, he wheeled Larry's Mercedes around the hairpin turns of the mountain he'd half driven, half rolled down last night. As anticipated, the import took the steep, winding roads like a Thoroughbred ridden by a jockey who knew just how to put her through her paces. The engine emitted only well-mannered growls as it gobbled up the miles.

Even the weather cooperated today. Sunlight slanted through the thick stands of hickory and oak, weaving a dappled pattern across the road. Occasional breaks in the trees gave spectacular views of the mountains.

From the corner of his eye, Tony saw Larry clutch the armrest once or twice. On a particularly sharp turn, his foot stomped the floor in search of the brake. But it wasn't until Tony pointed out the twisted remains of the metal guard rail the Olds had plowed through last night that his lawyer/cousin-in-law turned green around the gills. Gulping, he tore his gaze from the gaping hole.

"How far is it to this Hilltop place?"

"Another five or so miles."

Larry didn't breathe easy until the combination gas station and bar came into view. He almost choked, however, when he got a closer look at the ramshackle structure.

"Good Lord! You left your Corvette here?"

"Not by choice."

Tony had to admit the place looked even worse in the daylight than it had in the rainy dark. The neon sign that had flashed like a beacon of hope in the night now showed itself to be all fly-blown and speckled. Rusted motor oil cans overflowed the trash can beside the pump. Even this early in the afternoon a couple of cars were parked in front of the bar attached to the station.

Eyes narrowed, he swept the dusty parking lot with a swift glance. To his intense relief, he spotted gleaming grillwork through the half-open doors of the shed behind the bar. Joe had jacked the 'Vette up onto blocks, probably in anticipation of putting new tires on her...tires he claimed he didn't stock, Tony remembered wryly.

Parking the Mercedes beside the shed, he dragged the replacement Uniroyals out of the back seat.

"My pit crew could change a tire in twenty-seven seconds flat," he stated, bouncing a tire at Larry. "Think we can beat their record?"

To his credit, the attorney didn't even blink at the fact that he'd driven all the way down from Baltimore to perform pit duties, not to bail a client out of jail. Leaning the tire against the Mercedes's fender, he shrugged off his suit coat, laid the hand-tailored summer worsted across the back seat and rolled up his monogrammed cuffs.

"We can sure as hell try."

"I knew there was a reason Eileen married you," Tony replied with a flashing grin. "Other than the fact that you keep her in diamonds and fresh-baked cannoli. Let's get with it!"

They had three tires in place and were lifting the last onto the axle mount when the station owner ambled over to the shed.

"The sheriff told me you took ole Bessie down the side of the mountain," he said by way of greeting.

"Ole Bessie took us down the side of the mountain," Tony retorted, torquing a lug nut.

"That right? Heard you wrapped her clear around a tree."

Tony knew where this was going. He had no intention of forking over any more cash to this character, however.

"My insurance will cover it."

He had a good idea of the claim Joe would try to submit for his rusted heap of tin. Ruthlessly he thrust his cousin-in-law into the fray.

"This is my attorney, Larry Trent. He'll get the necessary information from you on the Olds before he leaves."

Joe ran an eye over Larry's grease-streaked face and now wilted shirt. Shooting a stream of brown tobacco juice into the dirt, he nodded.

"Good enough."

"Any reason why you can't take care of that bit of business yourself?" Larry muttered as the owner strolled away.

"Yes." Tony tossed the lug wrench back into the tool bag and reached for the jack handle. "Jess has an hour start on me already. I'll have to make tracks to catch her before she leaves Rocky Point. Come on, let's get this baby off the blocks."

A look of genuine alarm crossed the lawyer's face. "You're taking off from here?"

"I am."

"You can't just drive off and leave me with your mother and sister and Eileen!"

"You hauled them down here," Tony replied with callous cheerfulness. "You haul 'em home."

He left Larry standing in the parking lot, swiping at his cheeks with a paper towel and muttering about ungrateful clients and hot-blooded Italians.

Smaller, faster, and tuned by a master's hand, the Corvette took the roads like the superbly crafted machine she was. Luckily Tony didn't have to retrace his route all the way back to the county seat. The road forked several miles outside of town. A quick glance at the map showed an alternative direction to Sparta, with a direct drop down to Rocky Point. Anticipation singing in his veins, Tony cut to the left.

Thirty minutes later, he crossed the North Carolina state line. An hour and fifteen minutes after that, he turned onto an unpaved road just outside Rocky Point. The single-lane dirt track led to a white clapboard house set under a stand of towering oaks. Tony's stomach clenched when he spotted a dusty sedan with Virginia plates parked in front of the farm house.

Unless the Stewarts drove a vehicle with out-of-state plates, he'd caught up with Jess. He eased up on the accelerator to give himself time to rehearse yet again the words he wanted to say to her. He'd tried them out in his head for the past hour, practiced them aloud to hear how they sounded.

He loved her. He'd always loved her, even during those first, angry days when he'd come close to hating her. He'd lost her once. He didn't want to lose her again. Not now. Not after what they'd shared this afternoon at the Blue Ridge Mountain Inn.

Not ever.

Bringing the 'Vette to a stop beside the sedan, he dragged in a deep breath and reached for the door handle. He didn't have any reason to believe Jess felt this same rush of need, this same panicky feeling in the pit of her stomach. When she'd raised up on tiptoe to kiss him goodbye, she'd looked so serene, so damned calm. He was still reeling from the passion she'd unleashed in him, and she'd just kissed him gently and invited him to call her sometime...if he wanted to.

Right. As if he could say all he needed to over the phone. He had to see Jess's eyes when he tried to explain why he couldn't let her out of his sight. Had to hear her reply firsthand, not through a phone.

Sweating a little under the purple shirt, he climbed out of the Corvette. The car door slammed shut a second or two before the farmhouse screen door opened. Tony froze, his gaze riveted on the curly-haired little girl who backed out, a knapsack looped over her shoulders and a plastic bowl in her hands.

She was halfway across the porch before she spotted Tony. Like him, she stopped. Her head tilted. Curiosity filled her eyes, so similar to her mother's that his throat closed.

This was Alyx. Alyxandra the imp, the angel, the fearless adventurer.

Alyxandra…who might have been his daughter if he'd met Jess a few weeks sooner that long-ago summer.

The realization caused a tight, hard feeling in the middle of Tony's chest. Suddenly all his mother's lectures about settling down, about having a family, about viewing the world through the joyful eyes of a child came crashing in on him.

"I know you!" the girl exclaimed. "You're Mr. Paretti! I saw you on TV."

Delight flooded her face and generated a smile that lit up the front porch. "I *knew* you would come! Mom told me you couldn't, but I *knew* you would."

Tony blinked. The last time he'd been exposed to that much brilliance was during his last victory lap at Daytona, when the track officials threw every one of the switches and lit up half the Florida night sky.

She skipped across the porch, both arms wrapped around the plastic bowl. "You know what?"

Bemused, Tony shook his head. "No, what?"

"Mrs. Stewart gave me two kittens to take home! I picked them out, but I told Mom she could name one. I hope they get along with Tomasina. Tomasina's my turtle. She goes everywhere with me."

She came down the stairs, chattering nonstop. Pink sneakers flashed under her black jeans. Like Tony, she wore a souvenir T-shirt no doubt purchased by the kindly couple who'd taken her in.

"The people at the store called all their turtles 'Tommy,'" she confided with another of those thousand mega-watt smiles. "Isn't that silly? But she sorta got used to it, so I had to name her Tomasina. You can pet her if you want."

Bemused, Tony hunkered down on one heel to get to eye level with the occupant of the plastic bowl. Tomasina stared back at him unblinkingly. He reached out a tentative finger, not really into turtles, particularly turtles the size of this one. Tomasina looked as if she could swallow a frog whole. For all Tony knew, the store where Alyx had purchased her pet replenished its stock by raiding a nearby swamp for snappers.

"Go on. Pet her. She likes it. Here, I'll show you."

Placing her hand atop his, Alyx guided his finger along the bumpy shell toward the green-and-yellow-striped head. Contrary to his expectations, Tomasina didn't retreat into her shell. She fixed her beady eyes on Tony and worked those jaws, as if in anticipation of a finger lunch. Steeling himself, he let Alyx's small hand urge his into a slow, stroking tickle along her neck.

Surprisingly, the reptile did like being petted. Its head nodded up and down. Its scaly lids dropped. She leaned sideways against Tony's finger.

"How do you know she's a she?" he asked curiously.

"You can tell by those little yellow spots beside her eyes." Alyx's bright smile dimmed for a second. Her thoughts took a lightninglike change of direction. "The kittens won't eat her, will they?"

Tony suspected it might be the other way around. He wasn't about to say so, however. "Maybe you could attach a plastic lid to the bowl," he suggested. "Just to be on the safe side."

"But how would she breathe? Turtles need air *and* water, you know. They're amphobus."

He decided she meant amphibious but let it pass.

"Well, let's see. You could punch holes in the lid. You'd better use a heavy piece of plastic, though, so it stays down."

Beseeching azure eyes lifted to his. "Would you help me?"

Tony felt the impact of that limpid gaze all the way to his toes. Swallowing a lump the size of a turtle egg, he nodded.

"Sure."

Her smile grew positively radiant. "I *told* mom you looked nice, and you know what?"

"No, what?"

"You are."

Tony felt his bones melting, one after another. He was lost from that moment on and knew it. Draping an arm over his bent knee, he basked in the little girl's shining approval.

"What do you say we put a hinge on the plastic, so you could lift it to clean the bowl."

"But then the kittens could push it up," Alyx pointed out.

"We'll add a hasp. And a little lock." Warming to his task, he sketched the proposed modifications in the dirt. "Look, here's how we'll do it."

Her arms clasped around Tomasina's bowl, Alyx leaned her shoulder against his and contributed her ideas to his. The proposed modifications soon took on the proportions and complexity of a multistory condo. Alyx's infectious giggles rippled through the afternoon air as Tony added first a deck, then a carport to the schematic.

That was how Jess found them when she pushed open the screen door to check on her daughter. Shoulder to shoulder. Dark hair almost brushing pale blond. Alyx laughing in delight and Tony chuckling as they peered at something he was drawing in the dirt.

"Oh, God," Jess whispered.

A trembling hand came up to press against her mouth. For the third time in less than twenty-four hours the mom who never had either the time or the energy to cry felt tears sting her eyelids.

How could she love them both so passionately? Alyx with the soul-deep attachment that had formed between them well before her birth. Tony with a searing, soaring joy that seemed to have replaced all the old guilts and regret.

That love burned like a brand in her chest when he rose, dusting his hands on his jeans. Alyx fairly danced with excitement when she spotted her mother.

"Mom! Mr. Paretti's here. You said he wasn't coming, but he did."

"So I see."

"And guess what?"

"What?"

"He's going to help me make a lid for Tomasina's bowl so the kittens won't eat her."

Over her daughter's head, Jess met Tony's eyes. "He is?"

"Yes, and he didn't even jerk his hand away when he petted Tomasina, the way you always do. Tomasina likes him," Alyx pronounced, beaming. "*I* like him. We think you should marry him."

Jess didn't groan, but she wanted to. Badly.

Alyx took advantage of her mother's silence to press

her point. "He's just the kind of dad I want. He likes turtles. And kittens."

Her face brightening, she turned a radiant smile on him. "Hey! I bet Mrs. Stewart would give you one, too! She's got five more to find homes for."

"Alyx…"

"I'll go ask her!"

Whirling, she deposited turtle and bowl on the back seat of the sedan and dashed for the porch. Jess caught her on the fly.

"Hold on a minute."

"What?"

"Mr. Paretti might like kittens, but that doesn't mean he wants to take one home with him."

Alyx turned to him, all injured innocence and hopeful blue eyes. "You do, don't you?"

He tore his gaze from Jess. "Well, uh, I…"

"If you take one," Alyx explained earnestly, "then your kitten can play with ours. They won't be lonely, like Tomasina. And if you marry mom," she added on an afterthought, "she won't be lonely anymore, either."

This time Jess didn't even try to hold back her groan. "Go inside and get your kittens, Alyx."

"But…"

"Now, please. I want to talk to Mr. Paretti."

Opening the screen door, she urged her reluctant daughter inside. Alyx threw an anxious look at Tony over her shoulder.

"You won't go away, will you?"

The tremor in her voice twisted Jess's heart. Tony's quiet reply twisted it even more.

"No, I won't go away." His brown eyes locked on Jess. "Not this time."

The screen door bounced against the door frame.

Alyx darted into the house, calling for Mrs. Stewart. Silence enveloped the two people outside.

Jess's heart beat so hard and so fast her chest hurt. She couldn't move, could barely breathe. She'd half expected Tony would come after her. If he hadn't, she'd already decided on another trip to Baltimore...after he'd had time to think and she'd had time to savor her joy. She just hadn't expected him to follow this soon or this fast.

The silence stretched another moment or two, then they both moved at once. Jess came halfway down the porch steps, Tony halfway up. She stopped one step above him, her eyes level with his. The intensity in their brown depths cut straight to her soul.

"I can't let you leave me, Jess," he said in that same quiet voice. "Not again."

With a tremulous smile, she lifted a hand to stroke his cheek. "I don't want to leave you. Not again."

His hand covered hers, gripping hard. "Then don't."

She gulped. "Everything happened so fast this afternoon. I just thought we needed time to think about where we go from here."

"We've had ten years to think."

He turned his head and planted a kiss in her palm. Jess felt the heat of his lips burn into her skin. She was trembling all over when he lifted his head once more.

"No more thinking, Jess. No more waiting. Marry me. Today. Tomorrow. As soon as we can get a blood test and license."

His expression was so fierce, so determined and so achingly tender that Jess felt her knees go wobbly.

"I love you," he said, coming up to join her on her step. His hands tunneled into her hair and tipped her face to his. "I've loved you since the first time you climbed into Number Fourteen and asked me where the heck the key went.''

She gave a little huff of laughter. ''How was I supposed to know race cars started with a flick of an ignition switch, not a key?''

The laughter lingered in her voice, but the question she whispered next came straight from her heart. ''How can you be so sure it's me you love, Tony, and not the girl you once knew?''

It was his turn to smile. Sliding his hands down her back, he pulled her close, cradling her against his thighs.

''None of the memories I carried around of Jess Summerville came even close to the Jess Taylor I held in my arms last night on that mountainside...or the one who wrapped herself around my heart at the inn. You're the woman I want, Jess. The woman I can't live without.''

Happiness tumbled through her in bright, shining waves. Her arms locked around his neck. Her heart thumped against his.

''Well, in that case, I think you should know that I love you, too. I suspected it the first time you climbed out of Number Fourteen and flashed that cocky Paretti grin at me. I suspected it again last night, on the mountainside. I knew it for sure the afternoon at the inn. And you know what?'' she asked, appropriating Alyx's favorite expression.

''No,'' he said with another of his trademark grins. ''What?''

''You're right,'' she said on a note of breathless joy. ''We've had plenty of time to think these past ten years. I'll marry you. Today. Tomorrow. As soon as we can get a blood test and license.''

With a sound halfway between a groan and a whoop, Tony crushed her against him. His mouth came down on hers, hard and hot. Jess strained upward with a wild joy singing in her blood.

She felt as though she'd returned from a long, long journey. Here, on a stranger's front steps, in a town she'd never even passed through before, she'd come home.

"Mom! Are you and Mr. Paretti *kissing?*" The screen door banged. "You are! You're *kissing!*"

Alyx pranced onto the porch, her face suffused with delight. Jess turned in Tony's loose hold to smile ruefully at her daughter.

"You were right, Alyx. Mr. Paretti…Tony…is nice. I like him, too."

She glanced from one to the other, her eyes round. "Are you going to get married?"

"Yes."

"Right away."

Tony and Jess answered at the same time, glanced at each, shared a smile.

"Good!" Gleefully, Alyx clapped her hands. "Now I get a dad, and he gets his very own kitten, and we can all drive home together."

"Sounds good to me." Without a moment's hesitation, Tony abandoned his Corvette for the second time in less than twenty-four hours. "Let's go pick out my cat."

"Kitten," she giggled. "It's only a kitten."

"Whatever."

Epilogue

The silver-haired, blue-eyed cherub in a pink blouse with a ruffled collar and a jean jumper bounced into the offices of Gulliver's Travels just after it opened on Thursday morning. A slender woman, obviously her mother, came in behind her, followed by a tall, dark-haired Adonis so handsome that even the recently married Tiffany Tarrington Toulouse-Huffmeister's heart bumped.

"Hello." Smiling, she went to greet the little girl who'd flounced out of the travel agency less than a week before. "Did you decide to go to Baltimore after all?"

"Yes." She beamed at Tiffany. "We're getting married there."

"You are?"

"Yes, and you know what?"

"What?"

"The wedding's on Saturday!"

She made the announcement joyously, as if the day held special meaning. Tiffany searched her mind for a moment until she remembered that Sunday was Father's Day! And she still hadn't bought a card for Henry.

"Tony has a cousin who's a bishop or a pope or something. He's going to marry us. Mom said we should ask you to make the airline arrangements 'cause you told on me. That wasn't very nice of you, but I forgive you," she said magnanimously, "'cause if you hadn't, my mom wouldn't have come after me and driven off a mountain and decided to marry Tony."

"Oh, dear." Tiffany lifted merry eyes to the girl's mother. "Did I do all that?"

"More or less." A smile spread across her as she held out her hand. "I'm Jess Taylor. I had to come in and thank you for letting me know about Alyx's visit."

"You're welcome." She cocked her head of blue-gray curls. "Do you really want me to get you on a flight to Baltimore tomorrow?"

"Yes."

"The fares will be expensive on this short notice," she warned.

"They'll be cheaper than a funeral," the dark-haired hunk put in with a wry smile. "My mother informed me that I'm a dead man if I don't bring Jess and Alyx home to meet the family. When Jess got on the phone with her, the threat somehow got translated into a short-notice wedding of gargantuan proportions."

Tiffany might have sympathized with the poor man if she hadn't seen the laughter that danced between him and his bride. Wherever and whenever the wedding, these two had already begun their honeymoon.

Sighing, she wished that Lucy or Dick Spivey or any of her co-workers would stroll over and catch this moment. They, like Tiffany, had worried about the little girl who'd stuck her nose in the air and informed them that she was taking her business elsewhere. And now she was back to arrange her family's collective honeymoon.

Tiffany had to admit that her record when it came to arranging honeymoons was spotty at best. She'd sent one couple to the Caribbean on a luxury honeymoon cruise that got hijacked, another to an inn north of Atlanta just before an ice storm closed the whole area down. She didn't even want to *think* about a Valentine's Day trip she'd arranged a few years ago.

But this… This was perfect. Two people so much in love they lit up the room. A little girl who was going to get a daddy for Father's Day.

And next month, she thought with a happy smile, was the Fourth of July. Her lively imagination alight with sparklers and bright-colored starbursts and lovers entwined on blankets in the park, she smiled at her customers.

"All right, let's check out the fares for two adults and one child."

"Better make that four adults, one child, one turtle, and three cats," the girl's soon-to-be father said dryly.

"Four adults?"

"Mr. and Mrs. Stewart of Rocky Point, North Carolina, will be our special guests at the wedding."

"But a turtle and two cats?" Tiffany said faintly.

"Three," he corrected.

Alyx slipped her hand in his. Small and white, it got lost in his big, tanned grip.

"We're a family," she declared happily. "We all hafta go together. And you know what?"

Tiffany's eyes twinkled. "What?"

"There's going to be more of us. Tomasina just laid some eggs! Mom says she got pregnant up at the Stewart's farm, but I think it happened that time she got loose in the backyard. And mom's gonna get pregnant, too."

"Alyx!"

"Well, you are! You and Tony kiss *all* the time. It gets kinda mushy," she confided to Tiffany, "but I don't mind."

"Good thing," her prospective father declared with a grin as he caught Jess's hand and lifted it to his lips. "Because I intend to spend the rest of my life kissing your mother."

The light that gleamed in his brown eyes had Tiffany sighing once more.

* * * * *

MARRIED ON THE FOURTH

To Mom, Dad & Eric:
You've always made my July Fourths special!

Chapter 1

Although Evan Blake could have settled into his new home in Atlanta without assistance, he was thankful that he hadn't been required to. When it came to unpacking, three sets of hands definitely were better than one. And when two of those three sets belonged to good friends, what would have been a tedious chore became an enjoyable experience.

The "good friends" were Chris and Lucy—nee Falco—Banks. Evan's ties to Chris dated from nursery school. The two of them had grown up in the same social circle in Chicago and shared an apartment in Cambridge, Massachusetts, while attending Harvard. Had he been able to choose a brother, Chris would have been his unequivocal pick.

He'd gotten to know Lucy during her first marriage to Chris. Although he couldn't claim that they'd become particularly close during that short period, his liking for her had increased each time they'd met. He'd been both surprised and distressed when she and his long-time pal had split up less than a year after they'd traded *I do*'s.

As for his reaction to the out-of-the-blue news that the two of them had reunited...

Evan had been deeply pleased to hear it. Despite their very real differences in background and temperament, he'd always sensed that there was a special connection between Christopher Dodson Banks and Lucia Annette Falco. That they'd made their ways back to each other after a decade of traveling on separate paths had struck him as right. *Very* right.

Which wasn't to say that he wasn't bemused by the rather bizarre set of circumstances that had precipitated their happily-ever-after reconciliation. Because he was. He still vividly recalled his response to Chris's initial recounting of what had transpired nearly five months earlier, on New Year's Eve.

"Okay," he'd said after his buddy had finished relating what could only be described as an extremely screwball tale. "Now tell me what *really* happened."

He'd eventually been persuaded that even though it sounded farfetched, what Chris had told him *had* been a fairly accurate summation of what had occurred. In a nutshell: Chris had found himself stranded in Atlanta on the final day of the year and, having recently learned that his former wife lived in the city, had decided to seek her out. One thing had led to another...then another and another...and Chris and Lucy had ended up spending what would have been their tenth wedding anniversary being held captive by an extraordinarily inept trio of would-be robbers.

It could have been a disaster, for a whole lot of different reasons. Tying ex-spouses together and sticking them in a supply room during the attempted commission of a crime probably would not strike anybody—except, perhaps, a TV sitcom writer with a seriously warped sense of humor—as a felicitous idea. Yet Chris and Lucy had transformed their enforced proximity into an opportunity to talk through the painful misunderstandings that had driven them apart. They'd rediscovered each other. And in doing so, they'd begun rebuilding the shattered foundation of their mutual love. They'd taken the first crucial steps toward constructing a relationship far stronger than the one they'd had during their initial whirl on the marriage-go-round.

Watching them interact as they helped him unpack had affected Evan in ways he wasn't prepared to explore. While Chris wasn't as touchy-feely demonstrative as Lucy, Evan could tell that he was absolutely nuts about his second-time wife. This knowledge moved him at a very basic level. It also suffused him with an uncharacteristic and uncomfortable sense of envy. Given how badly he'd messed up his own relations with the opposite sex, he felt a touch of envy as he realized that someone he considered a peer had been able to—

"I really appreciate all you two have done for me," he said, abruptly deciding that this was not the time to start wallowing in his personal failures. He had a new home in a new city and he was poised to begin a new job that promised to be a lot more satisfying than his previous one as the top portfolio manager for a prestigious brokerage firm. While he realized that at age thirty-five he was beyond the wiping-the-slate-completely-clean-and-starting-all-over stage, the book of life had presented him with a fresh page upon which to write. He was *not* going to blot it by dwelling on the past.

"Glad to pitch in, Ev," Chris returned easily. "That's what friends are for."

"Besides," Lucy said with a humorous lilt, her dark eyes sparkling. "This has given me a perfect excuse to check out all your belongings without seeming nosy." She paused a moment, glancing consideringly about the carton-strewn living room of Evan's high-rise condo. Then she added, "And you *do* have an awful lot of stuff to go through. Chris sometimes accuses me of being a pack rat, you know. But compared to you—" she gestured with graceful expansiveness "—I'm a minimalist."

"But *only* compared to him," her husband inserted dryly, earning himself a reproachful look. He responded with a quick wink and a grin. Lucy sustained her mock-injured expression for a moment or two more, then acknowledged his point with a rueful smile.

"I had things pretty winnowed down after the divorce," Evan commented, watching the affectionate byplay with a pang. He lifted his right hand to the back of his neck and began massaging an all-too-familiar knot of tension. His ex-wife, Barbara, had come out of their marriage a wealthy woman, much to the disgust of his lawyer. But what neither she nor his attorney had realized was that he'd been willing to shell out a lot more than he'd had to, in order to secure his freedom. "Then my mother sold the house in Chicago last month. She called me and said she had a few mementos she thought I'd like to have. What she *didn't* mention was that these 'few mementos' filled nearly two dozen cardboard crates."

He shook his head, remembering the shock he'd gotten when his coolly elegant mother had taken him up to the attic and displayed the hoard of things she had wanted to bestow upon him. He'd been speechless. He'd had no idea that she'd squirreled away so many pieces of his childhood and adolescence. Although his mother had never treated him badly, she'd always been a little…standoffish. And she'd distanced herself even further following the sudden death of his father, the summer before his senior year in high school.

"I was pressed for time at that point," he concluded with a shrug. "So, I decided to ship the boxes down here unopened and cull through them as I got moved in."

"Why didn't you just chuck the stuff out?" Chris inquired, closing the plastic drawstring on a trash-crammed garbage bag and securing it with a double knot.

Evan thought that this was a very reasonable question. In point of fact he'd raised it with himself more than a couple of times. Unfortunately he'd been unable to come up with any reasonable answers. "Well—"

"Chris!" Lucy preemptively exclaimed, brushing a lock of dark brown hair away from her face. "How can you even ask that? This 'stuff' is Evan's *past*. He's not going to toss it away, sight unseen. He needs to sort through it. To *savor* the memories."

"It's mostly junk, Lucy," Evan felt compelled to say. Sure, he'd gotten a kick out of discovering that his mother had saved his first baseball glove. And it had been kind of cool to find that he was the owner of some highly collectible, mint-condition *Spiderman* comic books. But ninety-nine and nine-tenths of the rest of the items she'd kept…

Junk. Total junk.

His gaze strayed to the cluster of bulked-up garbage

bags sitting in the middle of the living room. It was time for another dumpster run, he decided.

"Maybe so," Lucy replied. "But 'junk' can have great sentimental value." She slanted a look at her husband, her lips starting to curve. "To say nothing of outstanding blackmail potential. Take, for instance, that photograph I discovered a couple hours ago. You know, the one of a certain supposedly respectable individual—"

"I repeat my question, Ev," Chris said. Although his voice was mild, Evan was intrigued to note that the color in his cheeks was a bit higher than usual. Chris's latent tendencies toward taking himself too seriously were no match for his wife's penchant for puncturing pomposities. It was one of many, many reasons they were so well matched. "Why didn't you just chuck the stuff out?"

"Because even though he isn't a lawyer, Evan knows it's wrong to destroy evidence of a felony," came his wife's irrepressible response.

"Felony?" Chris grimaced and shook his head. "Give me a break, Lucy. It was a misdemeanor. The statute of limitations expired years ago. Besides. I was in the *sixth* grade!"

"Which makes it all the more shocking," his wife declared sweetly, crossing to a stack of still-unopened cartons. "I wonder what Tom, Dick and Butch would say if they found out that 'Mr. Harvard Law School' is a former juvenile delinquent. It would shake their faith in the legal system clear down to the ground."

Evan swallowed a laugh, knowing that Lucy was referring to the three men who'd held her and Chris captive on New Year's Eve. Tom and Butch were behind bars for their lamebrained foray into crime and likely to remain there for several more years. Dick—a first-time offender—was out on some kind of parole deal and working at the travel agency Lucy managed. Although he had yet to meet the guy, Evan had heard enough about him to figure that he could, er, finger him in a lineup should the need ever arise.

Not that such an eventuality seemed likely. He'd also heard that Dick had been assigned to a female parole officer, who apparently was more than capable of keeping him on the straight and narrow.

"You...*wouldn't*," Chris said.

"Maybe. Maybe not." Lucy flashed a smile and picked up a box, clearly relishing her husband's discomfort. "But I *am* going to have to fill Maddy in on your sordid past. Consorting with unsavory characters, even ones with Ivy League law degrees, is probably a violation of Dick's parole. And given all the trouble we went to get him out of prison—"

"Lucy!" Evan interrupted sharply, suddenly noticing an ominous bulge in the underside of the carton she'd just lifted. "Watch the—"

Too late. The bottom of the box gave way, releasing a cascade of papers and other items on to the living room's wooden floor.

"Damn!" Lucy discarded the ruined carton and dropped to her knees. She looked genuinely upset. "Oh, Evan. I'm sorry. Of all the stupid things to do!"

"No need to apologize," he quickly assured her, bending over to retrieve a small, hoop-shaped object that had come rolling across the polished parquet and stopped a few inches from his left foot. What the heck...?

He inhaled on a short, sharp breath as he realized what he'd just picked up. He straightened, staring at the item he was holding. His pulse stuttered. He couldn't believe it.

Sunny's bracelet, he thought, buffing the pad of his thumb gently over the gleaming surface of the first and only gift he'd purchased for the first and only girl he'd ever loved. The delicately etched gold seemed to warm in his hand, as though welcoming his attention.

Evan expelled the air from his lungs in a hiss, struggling against a sudden surge of memories. Time cartwheeled backwards, transporting him out of the present and into the past. He felt the sultry heat of a summer night. Heard the distant thunder of holiday fireworks and the much louder *boom, boom, boom* of his frantically beating heart. He smelled the intoxicating scent of flowers and aroused femininity. Tasted the honeyed hunger of a soft, seeking—

"Hey, Ev, who's this?"

Evan started. He blinked several times in rapid succession. Then he looked at Chris, who was now hunkered down beside Lucy, helping her gather up the stuff that had spilled out of the box.

"H-huh?" he stammered blankly, feeling very off balance.

"The girl in this photo," Chris elaborated, holding up a snapshot. "I was wondering who she is. Or…was."

Evan closed his fingers around the bracelet, then crossed slowly to Chris and Lucy. He stepped carefully, as though edging along the brink of a precipice. One false move, and he'd plunge into the abyss.

His mouth was dry; his palms, slightly sweaty.

He didn't need to look at the picture. Didn't…want to.

But he couldn't stop himself from doing so.

The chestnut-haired girl in the photo had neither classic beauty nor pampered prettiness. Her fine-boned, sungilded face was too full of contradictions for easy categorization. The expression in her wide-set hazel eyes was surprisingly intense, boring through the camera lens with very adult intelligence. Yet the smile blossoming on her lush, dimple-bracketed mouth was as innocent as a child's—full of tender expectations and heartfelt hopes.

Evan had thought her rather plain the first time he'd seen her. Plain, yet not at all commonplace. Something about her had caught and held his interest. And at the moment he'd snapped this photo of her, he'd believed her to be the most lovely—

"She looks familiar," Lucy observed, tilting her head to one side and narrowing her eyes.

"You don't know her."

Lucy glanced at him, plainly startled by his curt, leave-it-alone tone. "I might," she countered evenly. "I meet a lot of people in my line of work, Evan. What's her name?"

Evan swallowed, ordering himself to relax. He was getting all bent out of shape over nothing.

No, he corrected a moment later, his stomach tightening. Not "nothing." As miserably as it had ended, what had happened between him and Sunny had *not* been nothing. It had been one of the pivotal episodes of his life.

"Kincaid," he answered quietly. "Her name's Sunny Kincaid."

"Sunny Kincaid," Lucy repeated, furrowing her brow. "Kincaid. Kincaid. Mmm..." She shook her head after a few seconds, clearly frustrated by her inability to place the name. "Nope. It doesn't ring a bell. Still. I *know* I've seen her before."

"It's an old photo." Evan paused, not really wanting to continue. But something overrode his reluctance. "Sunny and I hung out together one summer on St. Simons."

"The island where your family has the cottage?"

Evan nodded. Deciding whether to sell 'the cottage' in question was one of many items on his current To-Do list.

"Yes," he affirmed, then began to temporize. "Actually...it wasn't even the whole summer. The time Sunny and I spent together, I mean. It was more like five, maybe six weeks. We were kids. Still in high school." He shifted his weight from one foot to the other, trying to resist the powerful tug of memory. "I—I haven't thought about her in a long time."

He hadn't intended to lie to his friends. In all honesty, he didn't even realize that he *was* lying until he heard the words coming out of his mouth. That's when Evan Blake slammed into a truth about himself that he'd managed to evade for most of his adult life.

For better or worse, he'd been thinking about Sunny Kincaid for nearly eighteen years.

Where was she? he wondered, his fingers tightening on the dainty gold bangle he'd bought with such blissfully naive intentions.

What has she been doing?

Whom was she doing it with?

And when she was doing whatever it was with whomever it might be...did she ever think about him?

Chapter 2

Madison "Maddy" Malone had a lot on her mind as she walked briskly toward Gulliver's Travels two days later. But her brain wasn't quite as jammed up as it usually was at the start of a work week.

This was because she was on vacation. For the next fourteen days she was a free woman. Her time was her own. She could do anything she wanted.

Well, no, Maddy amended with a characteristic respect for the realities of life. Not *anything*. "Anything" implied that she had the wherewithal to…oh, say, impulsively jet off for a five-star holiday on some fabulously exclusive Greek island. She didn't. Heck. Her fiscal situation was such that she'd be hard-pressed to eke out the price of a ticket to the Six Flags Over Georgia Amusement Park!

She could have adopted the pay-with-plastic approach to vacationing, of course. When she'd mentioned her impending time off to the folks at Gulliver's Travels a while back, they'd been quick to offer their professional expertise. They'd even come up with some pretty incredible go now, pay later, vacation bargains.

Take that Caribbean getaway package Tiffany Tarrington Toulouse-Huffmeister had found, for example. Lord, had Maddy been sorely tempted by *that!* But she'd resisted. She'd spent a significant chunk of the past three years clawing her way out of debt. She couldn't justify plunging herself back into the hole for a self-indulgent week of lolling around on white-sand beaches and gorging on all-you-can-eat buffet meals.

Dream about doing so, sure. But justify it? Unfortunately, no.

Maddy Malone was a firm believer in the importance of being able to justify one's actions. She was an ardent advocate of accepting personal responsibility as well. So...

So, she'd take a vacation next year, she told herself firmly.

Except *next* year she intended to devote all her free time to studying for the state bar exam.

Okay. Okay. Make it the year after next. She'd treat herself to an honest-to-gosh vacation once she graduated from law school and earned the right to hang out her shingle. She'd celebrate the new millennium while she was at it. And if she started saving right now, she'd have enough cash salted away to pay as she went rather than rack up a bunch of charges at some usurious interest rate.

Sounds like a plan, Maddy decided as she turned north onto Peachtree Street. A balmy spring breeze ruffled her thick, reddish-brown hair. She swatted a few stray strands off her right cheek with a careless swipe of her hand. She knew that she needed a cut. While judicious snipping with her manicure scissors had kept her casual coiffure fairly presentable for the past month, the reflection she'd seen in her bathroom mirror that morning had been a shock. Despite her pruning, she was looking downright shaggy. It was time to visit a professional stylist.

Maddy had chopped off most of her hair nearly five years ago in a time-honored gesture of mourning. Except she hadn't been thinking about tradition when she'd grabbed a pair of shears and started hacking away. She hadn't been thinking, period. She'd been pretty much out of her mind with grief and anger over the in-the-line-of-duty killing of her policeman husband.

Detective Keith Malone had been one of the finest men she'd ever had the privilege of knowing. A better man than she'd deserved, she'd often thought in her heart of hearts. That he'd been snatched from her with such savage suddenness—

Maddy shook her head, pushing the pain away. It served no purpose to reopen old wounds. Keith would have been the first to counsel her to put the past behind her. Not to forget him. Heavens, no. He would want her to cherish the wonderful times they'd had together and the love they'd shared. But he'd want her to move on with her life, too, now that he was gone.

Which she was, to the very best of her ability. Lord knew, she'd experienced plenty of problems—more than a few of them, self-created—in learning to cope with widowhood. She was a far cry from being a perfect person. But she firmly believed that she was improving.

She credited her personal growth to a lot of different things. Included among them was the unanticipated blossoming of her friendship with Lucia Annette—nee Falco—Banks.

Maddy had never had much of a knack for making friends. Especially not *female* ones. The whole giggle-giggle, just-between-us-girls stuff had always seemed rather alien to her. But with Lucy...

The source of the affection that she felt for the other woman was difficult to put into words. She'd certainly never expected to like her. In all honesty, she'd had Lucy pigeonholed as a bleeding-heart Yankee nutcase before their first encounter.

Unjust? No doubt about it. But, geez! What else *could* she have thought once she'd read the case file? Not only had Lucy talked her husband, an Ivy League attorney, into defending the three scuzzballs who'd held them captive during some outlandish, New Year's Eve robbery attempt, but she'd also volunteered to be a character witness on their behalf! And no sooner had the assistant D.A.—who'd apparently developed a very healthy respect for Mrs. Banks's persuasive abilities—opted to make a plea deal, than she'd started agitating to get one of the trio—a none-too-bright first-time offender named Dick Spivey—released from prison. She'd succeeded, too.

To say that Maddy had been less than enthusiastic going into her initial meeting with Lucy was akin to claiming that skunks weren't very welcome at formal garden parties. But she'd swiftly realized that her stereotyping of the other woman as a cluelessly liberal kook had been way off the mark.

Lucia Annette Banks was a very savvy lady, with a deep reservoir of street smarts. Despite her unabashed sympathy for Dick Spivey, she plainly understood that he needed to be booted in the butt on a regular basis. What's more, she clearly was willing to personally ap-

ply *her* tootsies to *his* tush if circumstances required her
to do so.

To put it simply, Lucy didn't just talk the talk when
it came to trying to help rehabilitate her ex-captor. She
walked the walk all the way down the line, which
earned her major points as far as Maddy was concerned.

First and foremost, she'd found a job for Dick at the
travel agency she managed. And not some goofball
make-work slot, either. She'd provided the guy with
meaningful employment at an adequate wage. She'd
also helped him find a decent place to live. She'd gotten
him enrolled in night school as well.

"'Cept for my darlin' Dora-Jean, there isn't a woman
in the world who's been better for me than Lucy," Dick
had informed Maddy with great sincerity during one of
their regular parole check-ins.

"Mmm," she'd grunted.

It had afforded her no pleasure to be so noncommittal
in her response. But there was no way she could have
endorsed her parolee's mush-minded sentimentality!
Given that the aforementioned "darlin'" had married
and divorced Dick twice—*and* done a brief stint as his
brother Tom's wife in between—Maddy harbored some
serious doubts about how good an influence she was.

She knew that Lucy shared many of her concerns.
That Lucy's inherent romanticism inclined her to root
for a fairy-tale-style resolution rather than resigning herself to a probable crash-and-burn break-up was beside
the point.

It wasn't that Dora-Jean Purvis Spivey Spivey Spivey
was deliberately nasty or naturally wicked. If truth be
told, Lucy thought she was kind of sweet. But she was
also a few cupcakes short of a tea party. Dora-Jean had
the attention span of a fruit fly. She was impulsive in

the extreme, as well. She was given to leaping before she looked—never mind checking to make sure that her parachute was properly packed or that there was a cushy piece of ground on which to land. And when her feck-lessness was combined with Dick's, uh, well, lack of intellectual prowess...

Maddy grimaced inwardly.

Still, she reflected a moment later, there was no dis-puting that Dora-Jean *had* demonstrated remarkable loyalty in recent times. The busty, dyed-by-her-own-hand blonde had surfaced shortly after Dick's arrest and stuck by him with leechlike tenacity through all that had followed.

So maybe, just *maybe,* the third time 'round would prove a charm.

Either that, or it would be strike three and *O-U-T* for Dick Spivey's twice-ex'd wife.

Maddy reached the impressive looking building in which Gulliver's Travels was located. A quick glance at her watch informed her that she was about fifteen minutes early for her lunch date with Lucy. No big deal. If her friend couldn't slip away ahead of schedule, she'd spend the time chatting with Dick. And if her parolee was otherwise occupied, she'd leaf through travel bro-chures and fantasize about exotic vacations.

She pulled open one of the heavy glass doors and entered, shivering slightly at the transition from sun-shine warmth to air-conditioned coolness. The soles of her shoes squeaked softly against the lobby's marble floor.

"Hey there, Maddy," the beige-uniformed man be-hind the guard's desk hailed her with a wave of his ham-size hand.

"Hey, George," she responded. George was a retired cop. He'd worked with her late husband.

"What brings you 'round? Don't tell me you're here to haul Dick Spivey in for violatin' parole."

"Not today." Not *ever* if she had anything to do with it. She had absolutely no qualms about busting ex-cons for cause and putting them back behind bars. Frankly, she thought a lot of her "clients" belonged in the slammer, not walking the streets. But in Dick's case...

Put it this way. Dick Spivey had a shot at shoring up Madison Malone's sagging faith in the notion of post-incarceration rehabilitation. She would be mightily PO'd if he messed up.

"Glad to hear it, sugar," George declared. "He may be dumber than a box of rocks and have a criminal record, but he don't mean no harm. Dick's a good ol' boy."

"Amen to that," Maddy said feelingly, and moved on.

She headed toward the bank of elevators in the rear of the lobby, then hung a right. Gulliver's Travels was at the end of the hallway.

A forty-something man bobbed up from behind his cluttered desk almost as soon as she entered the agency. Jimmy Burns, his name was. Maddy had discovered that he'd held a wide variety of jobs, including short-order cook and used-car salesman, before finding his niche as one of Gulliver's Travels' top agents.

"Maddy!" He gave her a beaming grin and hearty handshake. Like a politician, only sincerely sincere. "What brings you here?"

Maddy tried not to stare at Jimmy's attire. The pink-and-yellow-dotted tie he was wearing was gaudy enough. But when teamed with a blue-and-orange plaid shirt...

"Well—"

Her scrutiny apparently unnerved Jimmy. His expression changed from enthusiastic to anxious in the blink of an eye.

"Dick called you, didn't he?" he asked, lowering his voice. "He said he was going to. I told him I didn't think he—uh—I mean, I certainly don't *condone* what he did. But it's just one little infraction. He feels awful about it, Maddy. Dora-Jean let him have it with both barrels when she found out. Lucy, too. There's *no way* he's going to do it again."

"Do—"

"Maddy!" The explosive invocation of her name came from the door of the agency's supply room. Its source was Wayne Dweck, a lanky young man whose platinum punk hair and pierced nose were in remarkable contrast to his starched white shirt, neatly pressed khakis and Hush Puppies. A bona fide cyber-whiz, he'd volunteered to do some tinkering on her home computer system a month or so ago. Grateful though she was for his assistance, Maddy couldn't help wondering whether all the upgrades he'd installed were absolutely legal. She had visions of pressing the wrong key and finding herself hacked into an ultraclassified database belonging to the CIA. "Oh, *man*. Don't tell me Dick turned himself in!"

"Uh—"

"Why, Madison Malone," a dulcet female voice cut in. "Aren't you supposed to be on vacation?"

Maddy rolled her eyes, wondering what the heck was going on and whether it had something to do with a plot to prevent her from uttering more than a single syllable at a time. She pivoted to confront the latest entrant in the game, Tiffany Tarrington Toulouse-Huffmeister. The same Tiffany Tarrington Toulouse-Huffmeister who'd nearly lured her into abandoning her fiscal principles and jetting off for a week of fun in the Caribbean sun.

"I—"

"It's Dick, isn't it?" Tiffany interrupted, sashaying out of the agency's conference room in an amethyst knit suit and matching high-heeled pumps. She might be in her mid-sixties, but the recently wed Mrs. Huffmeister had the hip action of a nineteen-year-old supermodel. "We're all distressed as can be about his regrettable lapse in judgment. Of course, none of us would *dream* of suggestin' that you should shirk your sworn duty by lettin' it slide. But if you could see your way clear to considerin' that there were some extremely mitigatin' circumstances..."

"Like, he was only a couple of hundred feet over the border," Wayne picked up.

"And in addition to the drawing being on Dora-Jean's birthday, the projected jackpot matched her age," Jimmy added. "Not the one on her driver's license. Her *real* age. Poor guy felt compelled, you know? Thought he'd been given a sign or something."

Maddy blinked. Comprehension began to dawn. "Are you—"

"*Miz Malone!*"

The shocked exclamation came from behind Maddy. As she turned to face its source, she wryly reflected that she was making progress. She'd actually been allowed to get two whole words out before being cut off.

"Miz Malone," Dick Spivey repeated, staring at her with undisguised dismay. He walked forward slowly, clutching a large brown paper sack bearing the name of a local takeout place. "What are you doing here?"

A pause.

"She's, uh, here because you, uh, called her, Dick," Wayne responded after a few seconds. He punctuated his reply with a nervous laugh.

Dick's mouth twitched beneath his scraggly mustache. His eyes darted back and forth. He tightened his grip on the paper sack.

"No, I didn't," he denied, shaking his head. "Tell them, Miz Malone. Did I call you?"

"Uh-uh." While she knew it probably signified a flaw in her character, Maddy couldn't help being amused by this situation. Now that she finally understood what was going on, that is.

"I was planning to," Dick emphasized earnestly. "But then I remembered you were on vacation. And it didn't seem right to disturb you on your time off, you know? So, I thought about reporting myself to somebody else. Only then I decided that what with all you've done for me, it wouldn't be fair to let some other parole officer get the credit for putting me back behind bars. Finally I made up my mind to wait till our next official appointment and confess then." His lips twitched again. His mustache wriggled like a mangy caterpillar. "Only, I guess I don't have to now...huh?"

There was a stunned silence.

"You mean, you didn't show up here to haul Dick off to the hoosegow?" Jimmy finally asked, turning back toward Maddy.

"Nope," she answered cheerfully. "I showed up because I have a twelve-thirty lunch date with Lucy."

"Then when I said..." Tiffany paused, raising a be-ringed hand to her apparently palpitating bosom. *"You didn't know?"*

"Know what? That Dick violated his parole by leaving the state without permission to buy a Powerball lottery ticket? Or that you've all made yourselves accomplices after the fact?"

The older woman bobbed her silver-haired head, seemingly too upset to speak.

Maddy suppressed a smile. Like Jimmy Burns, she couldn't condone what her parolee had done. But she wasn't about to bust him over it. Throw a little scare into him? Absolutely. Send him back to prison? Definitely not.

"I didn't have a clue," she confirmed, glancing from Tiffany to Wayne to Jimmy. She supposed she'd need to have a few choice words with the three of them, too. While she believed their supportiveness of Dick was a terrific thing, she didn't want them getting the idea that it was okay to cover for him every time he made a boneheaded—much less illegal—move.

"Wow!" Dick exclaimed admiringly, still hugging what probably was his colleagues' lunch orders to his concave chest. "You showed up knowing nothing and now you've got the whole story? That's amazing, Miz Malone."

"Not so amazing," Jimmy muttered unhappily. "All she had to do is stand back and let us rat you out."

"Cold, Maddy," Wayne said. "Really...cold."

"Oh, no," Dick protested. "Miz Malone used her listening skills. Dora-Jean and me went through counseling both times before we were divorced and we heard over and over that good listening is one of the keys to successful interpersonal relationships. Along with sharing, of course. Which reminds me of something my darlin' shared with me this morning after she got done calling me six kinds of fool for violating my—''

But the wit and wisdom of Dick's ''darlin''' would have to wait. At that moment, the door to Lucy Banks's private office swung open.

''Uh-oh,'' Maddy heard the manager of Gulliver's Travels say. ''Chris, I think you'd better put on your legal briefs and get out here. We may be busted.''

Maddy pivoted, experiencing a disconcerting prickle of uneasiness at Lucy's teasing reference to her husband. She had nothing against Chris Banks personally. In point of fact, she'd come to like and respect him. But she had a thing about the privileged, only sons of well-to-do families. *Especially* when those families hailed from Chicago.

Well, no. The word ''thing'' was too benign. What Madison Malone harbored against monied Yankee males of a certain age and background was a flat-out prejudice. She'd been vulnerable to one once. She would never—*ever*—be vulnerable to one again.

Chris Banks—tall, tawny-haired and impeccably turned out—appeared next to Lucy. ''Whatever the charges, my wife takes the Fifth,'' he announced, dead-pan. ''And I'm pleading temporary insanity.''

Maddy started to smile. Then her gaze slid beyond Chris and Lucy, focusing on a man who'd come to stand a few feet behind them.

Everything seemed to stop. Including her heart.

No, she thought desperately, feeling her body go cold, then hot, then cold again. There was a sudden buzzing in her brain, as though it had been invaded by a swarm of killer bees. She began to tremble. *It can't be.*

But it was.

With every fiber of her being, she knew that it was.

Evan Blake. The rich boy to whom she'd given her-self, body and soul, on the night of July Fourth, nearly eighteen years ago. The rich boy who'd used her—once—then strolled away without a word, shattering her fragile sense of self-esteem into a million jagged pieces.

Of course, he wasn't a boy anymore. Oh, no. He was all grown-up now. A rich *man*. Confident. Compelling. Clad in a beautifully tailored gray suit that probably cost more than her entire wardrobe!

He looked...Lord. Like someone had engineered a DNA cross between Harrison Ford and Robert Redford, then added a couple of chromosomes from Brad Pitt for good measure.

The passage of time had burnished his youthful good looks to a classy gloss. His hair was still thick, still all-American sandy blond. But it was elegantly shaped now, not over-the-collar casual. And while his eyes were as intensely blue as ever, they'd acquired a striking depth of expression along with a few faint squint lines at their outer corners.

He was several inches taller than he had been that fateful summer, she estimated, unable to look away. Six foot one, maybe two. Broader through the chest and shoulders, too. The lanky adolescent body had matured into a lithely powerful male physique.

The surge of attraction Maddy felt shocked her. She hated Evan Blake. No. She *despised* him. She wanted to spit in his face. Or slap his smoothly shaved cheek.

She wanted to know why the hell he'd done what he'd done to a seventeen-year-old girl who'd loved him with all her heart.

She watched Evan nudge Chris and Lucy aside and walk toward her. He was staring at her as though he

were seeing a ghost. Most of the color had drained from
his handsome features.

The urge to step back was very strong, but Maddy
resisted it. This was partly because pride demanded that
she stand her ground. It also stemmed from her fear that
her legs would buckle if she tried to move.

He halted just within touching range. While he made
no effort to reach out, his eyes stroked her face like
fingers.

"Sunny?" he asked huskily. "Sunny Kincaid?"

She flinched at the nickname that he and he alone,
had employed. She'd felt so damned *special* when he'd
bestowed it on her. As though he'd glimpsed the person
she aspired to be and found her worthy of loving. Hearing the nickname now made her feel...

Hurt.

Angry.

Like a gullible little fool.

I'm sure he didn't mean to hurt you, one of Evan's
friends had told her. Barbara Wilcox, her name had
been. Also from Chicago. Also summering on St. Simons. Although Maddy had thought Barbara stuck-up,
she'd proven unexpectedly sympathetic after Evan's
precipitious departure from the island. *He was just looking for a little fun. Nothing serious. He—well, let's just
say that Ev's parents have lots of plans for his future.
There are certain things expected of him....*

And none of those things—none of those plans—had
included a teenage waitress whose mother was dead,
whose daddy was an alcoholic, and whose boldest am-
bition centered on saving enough money so that when
she graduated from high school she could move to Atlanta, find a job and start working her way through college.

The former Sunny Kincaid lifted her chin, gazing defiantly into the sky-colored eyes she'd once thought held the offer of true and lasting happiness.

"My last name's Malone now, Evan," she said, exerting every bit of self-discipline she had to keep her voice steady. "And my *friends* call me Maddy."

Chapter 3

Evan took a gulp of Scotch. He didn't have much taste
for alcohol and seldom indulged in it at lunch. But after
what he'd gone through back at Gulliver's Travels...

He needed a drink.

Maybe a couple of them.

Anything to help obliterate the memory of the hostile
expression he'd seen in Sunny's long-lashed, green-gray
eyes.

She loathed him. No ifs, ands or buts. Sunny Kincaid
hated his guts.

He took another gulp. The liquor burned down his
throat, fueling a fire in the pit of his belly. It should
have warmed the rest of him, but it didn't. He felt
chilled to the very core of his soul.

That the one night he and Sunny had shared together
had started out fine but ended up a sexual fumble-fest,
he couldn't deny. The memory of his ineptitude had
gnawed at his psyche for nearly eighteen years. So he

could understand her resenting him for having made her first time a pretty lousy experience. And she had reason to be upset about what had happened afterward, too.

But, dammit! Did she think he'd *wanted* to leave the island under the circumstances he had? He'd been desperate to contact her. To explain. But because she'd been so tight-lipped about where she lived or how she could be reached by phone, he'd had no way to do so. Scrawling a note with his Chicago address and number and asking Barbara to give it to Sunny had been lame, he knew. It had also been his only option in an extremely difficult situation.

Only Sunny had never called.

Never written.

Never really cared.

He'd seen the proof of this last fact with his own two eyes. The disillusionment he'd experienced when he had been so intense, he'd scarcely been able to breathe.

So where in the name of heaven did Sun—no, make that "Maddy Malone"—where did Maddy Malone get off glaring at him as though he were the villain in this piece? Huh? Huh? Where did she find the damned nerve? Within days of his leaving St. Simons, *she'd* moved on to another guy.

He'd wanted to hate her. He'd certainly given it his best shot. But when all was said and done, he hadn't been able to kill the love he felt for her. All he'd been able to do was to hurt and hurt and hurt.

He'd gotten over the pain eventually. Well, no. Not "over" it. But he'd learned to go ahead with his life as though it didn't exist. And as time had passed, he'd shouldered more and more of the blame for what had happened.

If he'd been a better judge of character...

If he'd been a better man in bed…

Evan exhaled in a rush. Raising his glass, he belted back the remainder of the Scotch.

"Feeling better?" Chris asked, spreading mustard on the grilled-chicken sandwich he'd ordered.

"Not yet." Evan caught the attention of a passing waiter. He mimed his desire for another Scotch. The waiter nodded.

"Want a piece of advice?"

"No."

"Tough. I'm giving it to you, anyway. You're not going to feel better after the next drink, either. Or the one after that. And even if you do manage to swill down enough booze to numb the pain for a while, you're going to pay a hell of a price for it tomorrow morning."

Evan regarded his best friend through narrowed eyes. Chris was the straightest arrow he'd ever known. "Two-Beer Banks," he'd been called in college. The closest he'd seen Chris to intoxication was during the reception for his first wedding to Lucy Falco. But his buddy had been drunk on love on that occasion, not alcohol.

"And how would you know?" he asked after a moment. The question had more of an edge than he intended. He owed Chris for hustling him out of Gulliver's Travels after his disastrously unexpected reunion with Sun—*Maddy*. Lord only knew what he would have done if he'd stuck around.

"Been there. Done that."

"*You?*"

Chris took a drink of mineral water. "Me."

"After you and Lucy—?"

"Yep."

Evan frowned, suddenly feeling guilty. He'd never

pushed Chris about his breakup with Lucy. As close as the two of them were, they'd always skated around the serious emotional stuff. It was partly a guy thing. Partly a product of the uptight way they'd both been raised.

"I didn't know," he admitted quietly, hoping that his friend would hear the apology beneath his words.

"No reason you should have." A brief smile said the apology had been understood and accepted. "And no reason you shouldn't learn from my mistakes."

"Going to let me crib from your notes on life experience, huh?" It was an allusion to their shared schooldays.

"Something like that."

The waiter arrived with Evan's scotch. "Anything else?" he inquired as he set it down.

"As a matter of fact…" Evan picked up the just-delivered drink and handed it back. Chris was right. Getting drunk wasn't going to solve anything. "Keep this on our tab, but take it back. I've reached my limit. Sorry for the inconvenience. And if you'll bring me the same thing my friend's having, I'd appreciate it."

"No problem," the waiter replied, then bustled off.

"So," said Chris after a few moments, forking up a chunk of fried potato. "You want to talk about it?"

Evan raked a hand through his hair and leaned back in his seat. "There's nothing to talk about."

"You've got a strange definition of nothing, buddy."

"Meaning?"

"Meaning, you just ran into a woman whose picture you've been carrying around for nearly—"

"I have not been *carrying around* Sunny's picture!" Evan snapped. Not physically, anyway. But the image of her had been with him since the moment he'd peered through the viewfinder and snapped the photo. Unacknowledged, to be sure. But indelibly imprinted on his soul. And his heart. "You saw it fall out of that box this weekend. The damned thing had been stored away for years! I didn't know it still existed."

"And wouldn't have cared if you had."

Evan opened his mouth to retort but shut it again when he realized he was being baited. It had been a long time since anyone had been able to push his buttons as effectively as Chris was doing. He'd built up a lot of barriers during the past eighteen years. Unfortunately, at least some of them had come crashing down the instant he'd seen Sun—

Maddy, he corrected himself.

Her "friends" called her Maddy.

Well, to hell with that, he decided a split second later. Whatever he was to her, it obviously wasn't a friend. So he was going to go on referring to her as Sunny!

"It was a long time ago, Chris," he finally said.

"Mmm." His friend took a bite of grilled-chicken sandwich.

"It's…personal."

Chris chewed and swallowed. Evan knew he'd had the same table-manner training as he had. One did not speak with one's mouth full.

One was not supposed to joke around while eating, either. But he remembered a picnic on a beach on St. Simons when Sunny had gotten him laughing so hard that he'd spewed out a partially-chewed bite of hamburger. At which point, *she'd* started giggling uncontrollably. And the silvery sound of her merriment had—

No, he told himself fiercely. *Do not go there. Not now.*

"Yeah, I noticed," Chris said dryly.

Evan blinked, lurching between past and present. "Huh?"

"I noticed that what's between you and Maddy is 'personal.' Heck. If it were any *more* personal, Lucy'd probably have to have the walls at the agency repainted to cover the scorch marks."

Evan started to groan but swallowed the sound as the waiter returned to their table. Another lesson learned in childhood. One did not emote in front of the help.

"Thank you," he said as the younger man served his sandwich and mineral water.

"Anything else, sir?"

"I think we're fine for now."

"Okay."

"Sharing is good, you know," Chris commented once the waiter had moved out of earshot.

Evan paused in picking up his sandwich, thrown by the seeming non sequitur. "Excuse me?"

"Something I learned from Dick Spivey."

"Dick Spivey." Evan set the sandwich down. He wasn't really hungry. "Would this be the Dick Spivey who tied you and Lucy up and stuck you in a supply room on New Year's Eve?"

"The very same. He said we should look on our captivity as an opportunity."

"To 'share?' "

"Exactly."

"Which you did."

"Oh, yeah."

"And you think I should…share…the story of what happened between Sunny and me with you."

"Uh-huh."

He gave a mirthless laugh. "Why?"

"Because you're my best friend. Because I know

you're hurting. Because, contrary to the keep-it-in code we were both brought up with, talking things out *can* help.''

Evan had a knack for a great many things. Dealing with this kind of emotional directness was not one of them.

"Very persuasive, counselor," he said sardonically, lifting his glass in a mock salute.

"Top five at Harvard Law, what do you expect?" Chris retorted, matching his tone. Then he leaned forward. His gaze was steady, with just a hint of ruefulness. "But as good as those other three reasons are, let me give you the clincher. If you don't tell me what happened so I can tell Lucy, she's going to come after you herself."

Evan took a slow sip of the mineral water, then set the glass down. He considered what he knew of his friend's wife. Lucy Banks was one very determined lady.

"She would, wouldn't she?" he said.

"Bet on it." Chris sat back. He sighed. The sound held a mix of affection and aggravation. "If it's any consolation, she's probably giving Maddy the third-degree right now."

Evan shifted in his seat, unable to prevent himself from wondering whether Lucy would "share" with Chris what she gleaned from Sunny. Perhaps the two of them would end up comparing notes.

Half of him wanted to give in to his friend's probing. To finally get another person's perspective on what he'd gone through the summer before his senior year of high school. To be reassured that despite Sunny's obvious loathing of him, he was not solely at fault for what had happened. But the other half of him...

He shifted again, decidedly uneasy with the idea of offering up such an intimate piece of his life for dissection. Yet he couldn't help acknowledging the validity of his friend's criticism of the emotional constraints that had been imposed on both of them from childhood.

"I was almost eighteen," he began slowly. "We hadn't summered on St. Simons since I was a kid. My mother inherited a place on the island, but she wasn't really fond of it. Basically treated it like a rental property. I'm not absolutely sure why she was so determined to go that particular year. I *think* she and my father were having some serious problems. It was never easy to tell with them, you know? They were always... polite...around me. Around each other, too. Anyway, she decided to go, and insisted I accompany her. My father stayed in Chicago. He promised to come down on alternate weekends, if business allowed."

"Which it never did."

"Which it never did." Evan didn't have to elaborate. He knew that Chris's father had been as distant as his own. Maybe more so. "Which didn't much matter to my mother. Or to me. There were a couple of other families from Chicago there that summer. Chuck Martin and his parents. Terry and Joanne Rayburn and their folks." He hesitated for a beat then noted, "My future ex-wife was staying with them."

"Barbara?"

"Yeah." He took another drink of mineral water, washing a sudden sourness off his tongue. "There was a guy I vaguely knew from prep school, too. Plus a couple of kids Chuck had palled around with the previous summer. We basically hung out together."

"Was Sunny part of the group?"

Evan averted his gaze a bit, staring at a spot over

Chris's left shoulder without registering much. It was strange to hear another man use the nickname he'd devised. He wasn't certain he liked it.

"No," he answered after a moment. "She was a local. She was a waitress at a burger place we went to."

There was a pause. Evan looked back at Chris. His friend said nothing, simply nodded at him to go on.

"I noticed her right off. I still can't say what it was that hooked me. I mean, if I had a 'type' back then, Sunny wasn't it. She was—well, you saw the snapshot."

Maddy Malone was more striking in her thirties than Sunny Kincaid had been at seventeen, Evan reflected, conscious of a sudden stirring in his groin. She'd grown into her intriguingly complicated looks. She'd also acquired some curves. Although her body was still slim, its lines no longer ran straight up and down.

"I was with other people the first few times I saw her. But then one day I came into the burger place by myself. We started talking. She seemed shy. But smart. And she had this…*intensity*…about her. One thing led to another, and I ended up asking if she'd like to go out with me."

"Alone."

Evan knew what Chris was asking. "Yeah," he confirmed. "Just me and her. I…" He hesitated, then opted to be honest. Not just with his friend. With himself, too.

"Okay." He spread his hands. "Okay. I'll admit it. I had some doubts about whether she'd fit in with my friends. I mean, they made—we *all* made jokes about the full-time islanders. Stupid, snotty jokes. But it was more than that, Chris. I wanted to keep Sunny to myself."

"I can relate to the impulse."

He probably could, Evan realized with an odd twist of surprise. He'd only recently learned that the first time his friend had seen his future wife, she'd been working the cash register at her family's pizzeria in downtown Chicago. Chris had gone into the place expecting to meet a friend—namely, him. Only he'd never shown, because his car had broken down.

He'd always wondered why Chris had been so forgiving of his failure to turn up that night. Once he'd heard the story of what had transpired in his absence, he'd had the explanation.

Chris had kept his relationship with Lucy private for quite a long time. While Evan had known that his friend was seeing someone and getting serious about her, he hadn't actually been introduced to the mystery lady until a week or so before she and Chris had gotten engaged.

"Sunny and I started seeing each other," he resumed. "I won't say we snuck around. But we didn't exactly go public, either. She—well, she didn't say very much about her family situation except that her mother was dead. Still, I got the definite impression she didn't think her father would approve of her dating me." He grimaced, a vision of his seventeen-year-old self filling his mind. "I probably gave off the same vibes about how my parents would react if they found out I was dating her."

Another pause. Another nod of encouragement.

"It was pretty hands-off in the beginning. We talked a lot. Then one night I kissed her. And all of a sudden, hormones I didn't even know I had kicked in. Things got more complicated after that. More basic, too. I told Sunny I loved her. She told me she loved me back. And after nearly a month of going right up to the brink, we...did it.''

Evan stopped again, assailed by recollection. For all the locker-room lies he'd told in prep school, he'd never been much of a stud. Still, he'd done a lot more fooling around than Sunny had. He'd tasted innocence the first time he'd touched his mouth to hers.

Or so he'd believed.

Yes, Sunny had been a virgin. As had he. But considering her behavior in the aftermath of their Fourth of July rendezvous in his family's boathouse, she obviously hadn't been the romantic naif he'd thought.

''And?'' Chris prompted.

''And, I screwed things up.'' Evan felt himself flush. Shame suffused him. ''To give you the condensed-but-crude version, I finished before Sunny got started. It was her first time, Chris. I—I *hurt* her.''

He fell silent, reliving the heart-stopping instant when the fragile physical proof of Sunny's lack of sexual experience had yielded to the thrust of his manhood. She'd jolted beneath him, gasping aloud at the pain, her slender fingers digging into his shoulders. Somewhere in the back of his sensation-saturated brain he'd known that he should stop, or at least slow down and give her time to adjust to him. But he'd been too far gone—too caught up in his own clamoring needs—to put the brakes on.

He'd been clumsy.

He'd been selfish.

But he'd loved her, dammit!

Whereas she...

''She pretended I didn't,'' he went on tautly. ''But I know I did. Afterward, I babbled a bunch of stuff about how it would be better the next time. Which must have struck her as arrogant or insensitive or both. I'm sure the last thing she wanted at that point was to have me yammering about our having sex again.''

''Did you?''

''What? Have sex again?''

''Yeah.''

A deep breath. They were cutting down to the bone now.

''No.'' Evan shook his head. ''Sunny had biked over to meet me that night. I wanted to drive her home, but she said no. We…argued about it a little. Finally, she rode off. I took a long walk on the beach, trying to get my head straight. Eventually I went back to the cottage. I found my mother in hysterics because my father had had a heart attack and wasn't expected to make it through till morning.''

''Oh, God, Ev…'' The response was softly horrified.

''We had to go back to Chicago. A friend of a friend of the Rayburns had a private plane, so we didn't need to wait for a commercial flight. Right before we left for the airport, I started panicking about Sunny. Because I realized I didn't know how to get in touch with her. So, I wrote a note with my home number and address and begged Barbara—she'd come over with Mrs. Rayburn to be with my mother—to give it to her. Which she did.''

There was another pause. Finally: ''Sunny never contacted you.'' It was a statement, not a question.

Evan decided he wasn't going to tell Chris about the fruitless call he'd made to the burger place where Sunny worked. Nor the night, one month after his father's funeral, when he'd phoned the two Kincaids that directory assistance had listed for St. Simons. He'd gotten no answer at the first number, although he'd rung it repeatedly. The second number had netted him a useless exchange with an angry-sounding drunk.

"No," he replied without inflection. "She never contacted me. Barbara was evasive when I saw her at the end of the summer and I asked her what had happened. I thought at the time she was trying to spare my feelings. Now I don't know. But she finally told me Sunny had pretty much blown her off when she gave her my note. I couldn't believe that, so I pressed her for details. Eventually, she showed me a photo of Sunny and one of Chuck Martin's buddies. Jack, his name was. Or Jeff. He...he had his arms around Sunny. They were laughing."

Yet another pause. Evan stared down at his barely touched grilled-chicken sandwich. After a moment he shoved the plate away. His hand was shaking and he felt slightly sick. Confession might be good for the soul, but it was hell on the stomach.

"So, what happened today at Gulliver's Travels...?"

Evan raised his gaze to his friend's concerned face. "That was the first time I'd seen Sunny Kin—Maddy Malone—since the night of July Fourth, nearly eighteen years ago."

"What about the snapshot?"

"The one of her and what's-his-name?" Evan slid his hands beneath the table, clenching and unclenching his fingers. "I ripped the damned thing up."

"I meant the one we found in the box at your condo."

Evan winced. His mouth twisted. "You want to know why I didn't trash it, too?"

"Uh-huh."

"I..." He stopped, swallowing hard. Then he shook his head and forced himself to go on. "I couldn't. I remember wanting to get rid of it after I talked with Barbara. But something...God, Chris. I don't know. I just couldn't! I stuck it in a drawer. Or maybe it was a book. I guess I assumed somebody—my mother, the housekeeper, *somebody*—would chuck it out somewhere along the line. I never expected it to turn up the way it did on Saturday.''

A few seconds ticked by. Evan averted his gaze again. He was intensely aware of the beating of his heart. Of the rise and fall of his chest as he drew air into his lungs, then let it out. He felt raw. As though strips of his skin had been peeled away, exposing the nerves beneath.

Scarcely forty-eight hours before, he'd been relishing the promise of his decision to relocate to Atlanta. He'd seen himself making a fresh start. Starting anew. And now...

"So," Chris said quietly. "What did you do with the snapshot after Lucy and I left?"

"What do you think I did with it?"

No answer. None was necessary.

Evan sighed and began kneading the nape of his neck again. His temples were throbbing.

"I'm an idiot, right?" he finally grated.

"Not necessarily." Chris forked up what undoubtedly was a stone-cold cottage fry. He examined the potato chunk thoughtfully for a moment, then transferred his attention back to Evan. "Right now you're a man with unfinished business. Whether you're an idiot depends on how you handle it."

Chapter 4

Deep in a seldom-visited corner of her soul, the woman who'd once been called "Sunny" Kincaid had spent nearly eighteen years wondering how she'd react if she ever met Evan Blake again. Well, now she knew.

Had she achieved what the folks on the TV talk-show circuit called "closure"? Maddy asked herself. No. Definitely not. Seeing Evan had stirred up as much as it had settled. Probably more. Still. She'd survived the encounter with her dignity intact. She could finally stop asking herself, What if? She didn't have to deal in hypothetical scenarios anymore. She'd played out the reunion drama, for real.

Maddy couldn't say that she was proud of the way she'd behaved back at Gulliver's Travels. While she was desperately grateful that she hadn't broken down and cried, she wished she'd been cooler. That she could have found it in herself to brush off the man who'd hurt her like an insignificant bit of lint.

At least she'd been honest in her responses! Evan, on the other hand—

She snapped off this line of thinking as she realized that Lucy was staring at her. She stared back challengingly, using a variation on the don't-mess-with-me expression that she'd cultivated during her career as a parole officer. The brown-haired Mrs. Banks responded with a bland-as-butter smile and returned to perusing the menu she was holding.

Maddy reached for the basket of bread to her right. It had been brought to their table shortly after she and Lucy had been seated. The deliverer had been an eagerly attentive young man who'd introduced himself as Todd, their waitperson.

"Look, Lucy," she said tightly, snagging a hunk of fresh-baked focaccia. "If you dragged me off to lunch, thinking I'd spill my guts about Evan Blake, you can forget it. I'm *not* going to talk about him."

"I'm not expecting you to." Lucy's voice was calm. She didn't even glance up. "Gut spilling is a lousy accompaniment to good food. You're having the grilled vegetable risotto, right? What do you say I get the linguini with seafood and we share?"

"I mean it." Maddy tore the piece of herb-flecked bread she'd picked up in half. She knew she wasn't going to eat it. But the act of ripping something into pieces was soothing. "I'm not saying anything."

"That's fine with me." Lucy peered more closely at her menu. "Yum. The special of the day is cannelloni with prosciutto and artichoke hearts. Maybe I should order that, not the linguini."

Maddy discarded the bread with an under-her-breath expletive. She glared across the linen-draped table at the closest female friend she'd ever had. She knew exactly what the other woman was trying to do, and she wasn't going to fall for it. Frankly she was insulted that Lucy thought she would.

"Then again, the wild-mushroom ravioli was terrific the last time I had it," her luncheon companion went on. "The pasta puttanesca's good, too. Chris swears by spaghetti with clam sauce. But between you and me, I don't think they put enough—"

Something inside Maddy snapped. She decided later that it had been waiting nearly eighteen years to do so.

"Do you want to know what happened or not?" she demanded.

Lucy discarded her menu so quickly that she nearly knocked over the vase of flowers sitting in the middle of their table.

"Are you kidding?" she demanded, scooting to the edge of her chair. Her expressive brown eyes flashed with emotion. "God, Maddy. You are one tough chick. I can't *believe* you held out this long. Are you sure you don't have any Sicilian—"

In an act of incredibly bad timing, Todd, the waitperson, chose this precise moment to make a return appearance.

"So, ladies," he began cheerfully. "What can we get for you today? If I might make a few recommendations—"

Lucy shut him up with a look. He stopped speaking so abruptly Maddy was surprised that he didn't choke on his tongue.

"I'll have the linguini with seafood," Lucy announced decisively. "My friend wants the grilled-vegetable risotto. We'll split the mixed green salad. House dressing. Two glasses of—no, better make that a *bottle* of Chianti. And Todd, don't feel you have to impress us with your personality when you bring our order. Both of us here have waited tables. We appreciate that it's hard work. Can the commentary, serve the food without spilling it on us, and you'll get a good tip. *Capisce?*''

A chill of suspicion skittered up Maddy's spine as she registered the implications of her lunch partner's remark about both of them having waited tables. While she wasn't ashamed of her employment background, she didn't remember having mentioned to Lucy that she'd been a waitress. She certainly hadn't said anything about it to Chris. Nor to Dick Spivey. So how had—

"Huh?" she gulped, suddenly registering that Lucy was speaking to her.

"Do you want fresh ground pepper on the salad?"

"Uh...whatever." She honestly didn't care. She had absolutely no appetite.

Lucy turned to Todd. "Yes to the pepper. And thanks."

"You're welcome." The server beat a hasty retreat.

"Okay," Lucy said, shifting back to Maddy. Her expression was very intent. "I think I know the basics. Local girl has summer romance with out-of-town guy. Summer ends. So does the romance. Or maybe vice versa. Anyway, they split up. And for the next seventeen and a half years, the girl carries some kind of grudge. The guy, on the other hand, carries the girl's picture—"

"W-what?"

"All right, all right," Lucy temporized, apparently oblivious to the true nature of Maddy's distress. "So I'm exaggerating a little. Evan hasn't had your photo tucked away in his wallet since the summer of whatever on St. Simons. But he *has* had a snapshot of you all these years. It turned up Saturday when Chris and I were helping him unpack at his new place.''

Maddy's throat constricted. Her brain began to buzz again.

It had been a setup, she thought numbly. The woman she'd thought was a friend had found out that she and Evan Blake had once been involved and she'd maneuvered to get the two of them in the same place at the same time.

But *why?* What possible purpose could such a manipulation serve? Was it some hideously misguided effort at matchmaking? Or worse, some kind of cruel joke?

''So…he knew?'' Maddy's voice was thready. ''At the travel agency. When I…Evan *knew?*''

Lucy blinked several times, clearly taken aback. Then she started to frown. The expression in her dark eyes went from wary to downright worried.

''Knew?'' she repeated. ''You mean, was Evan expecting to see you at the travel agency today?''

''Y-yes.'' Maddy could barely get the word out.

''No.'' Lucy shook her head. The back-and-forth movement was vehement. ''*No*, Maddy. Of course not. How could you think—''

''He had my picture,'' Maddy said fiercely. She wouldn't allow herself to speculate about the reasons for that particular circumstance. The possibility that Evan had kept the snapshot like some kind of trophy made her sick. ''You saw it!''

''But I didn't *recognize* you!'' Lucy insisted, leaning forward. ''Yes, I thought the girl in the snapshot looked familiar. But I swear, I didn't realize it was you. When I asked for a name, Evan said 'Sunny Kincaid.' I'd never heard of Sunny Kincaid. I only know you as Maddy Malone.''

Maddy stared across the table. Her instincts told her that the other woman was telling the truth. But how could she trust her instincts? She'd trusted Evan, too, once upon a time.

"Maddy," Lucy's complexion was several shades paler than normal. "Look. It's obvious I've misread the situation between you and Evan. Maybe the fact that Chris and I were able to straighten out the mess we made ten years ago and get back together has clouded my brain. Turned me into a driveling romantic. But I figured you and Evan had some kind of, um, thwarted first-love thing going, you know? If you'd seen his expression Saturday when the snapshot of you turned up, you'd understand. And then there was the look on *your* face when you spotted him at the travel agency.''

"My...face?''

A nod. "Yeah. I'm not saying you looked happy to run into him. God, no. To tell the truth, I was afraid you might haul off and belt him across the chops. But underneath—well, I know unalloyed hostility when I see it, sweetie. And that *wasn't* what you were feeling.''

Maddy stiffened, remembering the visceral jolt of attraction she'd experienced when she'd looked at Evan. It had flashed through her like summer lightning, leaving her temporarily dazed.

"I'm not asking for the gory details.'' Lucy's voice was soft, but threaded with steel. She plainly intended to do what it took to get the information she was seeking. "I just want to understand what he did to you.''

The sympathy implicit in the phrasing of this assertion surprised Maddy. It also moved her in a very elemental way. She was not accustomed to people taking her side. Keith had, of course. But that had been different. Besides. She'd never told him about Evan.

She'd never told *anybody* about Evan.

"He's your husband's friend," she pointed out uncomfortably. One of the many things she admired about Lucy was her loyalty. She didn't want to put her in an awkward position.

"True," the brunette agreed. "And you're mine. Please, Maddy. Talk to me. *Tell me what happened.*"

There was a pause. During the course of it, Todd, the waitperson, returned with their order. He'd plainly taken Lucy's instructions to heart. His presentation of their food was as silent as it was swift. Sort of…stealth service.

As he completed his duties and pivoted away from the table, Maddy reached for the glass of Chianti he'd poured for her. She recoiled in self-disgust when she registered what she was on the verge of doing. Her father had drunk to drown his sorrows. She had no intention of following in his staggering footsteps.

"Maddy?" Lucy prompted.

Maddy sighed heavily, fiddling with her silverware. "You had the basics right," she finally admitted. "I met Evan the summer before my senior year of high school. It was on St. Simons Island, off the Georgia coast. I was a native, born and raised. His family had a vacation place there. A 'cottage' he called it. More like a mansion. I mean, even the b-boathouse was fancier than the place I lived."

Her voice snagged slightly during the last comment. Small wonder. The boathouse had been the site of the Fourth of July rendezvous during which she and Evan had finally surrendered to physical passion. Not the most romantic of locations in which to lose one's virginity, perhaps. But for an all-too-brief part of the evening that had changed her life forever, Sunny Kincaid had believed it to be paradise on earth.

"The first time I saw him was when he and some of his friends came into the place I was waitressing," she went on. Her mind's eye filled with details that she'd done her damnedest to suppress. The casual confidence of Evan's movements. The stray lock of sun-bleached hair that had kept falling down onto his tanned forehead. The endearingly irritated way he'd keep brushing it off his brow only to have it flop back, again and again. The contrast between the crispness of his freshly laundered, fashionably logo'd knit shirt and the faded comfort of his snug-fitting denim cutoffs. "I remember, he was the only one who looked me in the eye when he ordered. And he smiled, just a little. Not trying to flirt or anything. But *acknowledging* me, you know? The others, well…"

"They couldn't be bothered," Lucy finished flatly. "Except when they wanted something. I know exactly what you're talking about, honey. Believe me."

Maddy did.

"Anyway," she continued after a moment or two. "One afternoon Evan came in by himself. Things were slow. It was after lunch. Before dinner. He sat at the counter instead of in a booth. We started talking. He seemed really nice. Eventually the boss yelled at me to disengage my mouth and shift my butt into gear. I was so embarrassed. But what could I do? I told Evan I had to get back to work. He said it was okay, he needed to be going anyway. And then—" she moistened her lips with a darting lick of her tongue "—he asked me if I'd like to go out with him the next night."

"And you said yes."

"No. Not right away. At first I thought he was teasing. But he wasn't. Then I was afraid he meant go out with him and his friends. I...I knew I wouldn't feel comfortable doing that. So I started to make up an excuse why I couldn't. But he must have understood what I was thinking, because he said he was talking about just the two of us. He—well, like I said. He seemed *nice*. I'd had a few other summer guys try to date me. But I knew all they wanted was to get in my underpants." She paused, cringing inwardly at how pathetically naive she was about to sound. "I didn't...I didn't think Evan was like that."

"So you went out with him."

"Yeah."

"And...what? He jumped you?"

Maddy almost laughed. It probably was a good thing she didn't. She suspected that the sound she would have made wouldn't have been very pleasant.

"No," she answered. "He was a perfect gentleman. He didn't even try to kiss me that first time."

"But the next time?"

"In the beginning it was just friendship, Lucy. We talked. We made each other laugh. Just the two of us. We didn't sneak around, exactly. But we didn't go very public, either. Finally, one night on the beach, Evan kissed me."

Maddy looked down, acutely conscious of the sudden thrumming of her blood. Nearly eighteen years later, and she could still summon up every nuance of that first kiss. The slow slide of Evan's fingers through her long, breeze-ruffled hair. The teasing eddy of his warm breath as he'd lowered his mouth to hers. The first feathering moment of contact, when every nerve ending in her body had started to tingle. The explosive instant when instinct had overwhelmed inexperience and her lips had parted beneath his.

"We kept seeing each other," she finally continued, her voice throaty. "We still talked. But we were f-fooling around a lot, too. Finally, on the night of the Fourth of July, we...we went all the way."

"Was it your first time?" Lucy asked gently.

"His, too."

"Did he force you?"

Maddy's head came up with a jerk. She stared at the other woman, shocked to the marrow by what she was suggesting.

"No," she denied. A part of her was appalled by how swiftly she leaped to Evan's defense. But she knew she couldn't lie. "It was a mutual choice. I *w-wanted* to make love with him."

Lucy eyed her silently for several seconds. Eventually she heaved a sigh and said, "Okay, then. Let me guess. You didn't exactly set off fireworks together."

Maddy felt herself blush. She glanced away, once again engulfed by memory.

She'd been shy that night in the boathouse. And a little scared. But she'd been intensely excited, as well.

She'd wanted.

Dear Lord, how she'd wanted!

Evan had been tied up in knots, too. His hands had been unsteady as he'd helped her undress. His breathing had been so shaky he'd scarcely been able to speak.

He'd been so...careful. So gentle. At least at first. But the more intimate their kisses and caresses had gotten, the more tenuous his control had become. Goaded by an arousal rhythm more potent than her own, he'd begun to accelerate the pace. And she, desperate to please, yearning to be his, had simply gone along. She'd surrendered. Allowed herself to be taken.

She'd known what to expect. Sort of. True, she'd had no mother to give her the customary birds-and-bees talk. No girlfriends with whom to share sexual confidences. But she had read some books. She'd been inexperienced, not ignorant.

Evan's frantic possession of her had hurt. There was no denying that. She'd anticipated some pain, but she hadn't truly been prepared for it. She certainly couldn't have guessed at the sense of invasion she'd feel.

And it had been over so quickly! She'd tried to get Evan to slow down, to give her a few moments to adapt to him, but he'd been too far gone. A few herky-jerk movements punctuated by an inarticulate cry and the deed had been done. He'd collapsed on top of her, panting like a runner who'd just completed a thousand-yard dash.

She hadn't cried. That was one small consolation. Yes, she'd wept as she'd pedaled home on her bike afterward. But she hadn't shed a tear in front of Evan. A matter of pride, she supposed. And a slight case of shock.

Maddy brought her gaze back to Lucy's face. "No," she replied evenly. "We didn't exactly set off fireworks together."

"Was it...bad?" There was nothing prurient about the inquiry. Quite the contrary. Lucy's concern was a palpable thing.

"It didn't leave me sexually traumatized, if that's what you're asking," Maddy answered. "It just wasn't very good."

Lucy took a moment to digest this. Then she said,

"So—what? You and Evan got into some kind of argument?"

"No." Maddy shook her head. She didn't think it was necessary to mention the disagreement that she and Evan had had about her biking home alone. "Not really. Although Evan was…upset. Embarrassed, I think. He, uh—" she made a face "—told me he'd make it better the next time."

"He just *assumed* there'd be a next time?"

At another time, in another context, the feminine outrage in Lucy's voice might have seemed funny. As it was, Maddy was oddly touched by the other woman's indignation on her behalf.

"Actually, he knew there wouldn't be," she answered with devastating simplicity. "He, uh, was planning to fly back to Chicago the following afternoon."

"What?!"

"We left things kind of vague when I finally left to go home that night. I mean, we didn't make another date. I suppose I figured we'd see each other at the burger shop the next day. But when his friends came in, he wasn't with them. So I waited and waited, thinking he might show up later. Alone. He didn't. Same story the day after that. And the day after the day after. Finally, one of the girls in the group pulled me aside. She said she knew about me and Evan and that she hated to be the one who told me, but he was gone and he wasn't coming back. She said—she said she felt sorry for me because she could tell I really cared about Evan. The thing was, he—uh—he didn't care about me. He'd just been out for some f-fun."

"And that was it?"

"Pretty much." Maddy decided that she wasn't going to recount Barbara's comments about Evan's parents' plans and expectations for their only son.

"You never heard from Evan again?"

"No."

There was a long silence. Maddy watched the woman opposite her closely, trying to gauge her reaction. Lucy frowned, clearly perturbed. Twice she opened her mouth as though to speak. Each time she snapped it closed before uttering a word, apparently changing her mind about whatever she'd been about to say.

"Geez, Maddy," she finally began. She sighed heavily and shook her head. Her expression was extremely conflicted. "I don't—this is really rough. It's hard for me to imagine—I mean, the Evan Blake I know—"

Maddy went rigid, her defenses slamming back into place.

Fool! she berated herself. *What did you expect?*

"I'm sure the Evan Blake you and your husband know is a prince among men, Lucy," she retorted acidly. "But the Evan Blake I knew—or *thought* I knew—did everything I said. Whether or not you believe me is your business."

And with that, she started to get up. Lucy forestalled her by reaching across the table and grabbing her wrist.

"I believe you." Lucy's brown eyes sparked with temper. "From beginning to end. Absolutely! But believing you doesn't preclude me from thinking there's got to be more to this story."

Maddy pulled her hand free of the brunette's grasp, but didn't bolt. "Like what?" she challenged. After a moment she lowered herself carefully back into her seat.

"Like—uh—the girl who pulled you aside and told you about Evan. What was her name?"

Maddy hesitated, having no idea what possible relevance this could have to anything.

"Maddy? Do you remember her name?"

"Barbara. Her name was Barbara."

"Barbara...*Wilcox?*"

Maddy shifted on the edge of her chair. "Yes. Why?"

Lucy didn't answer. She looked away, muttering in what sounded like Italian. Her inflection strongly suggested that she was cursing.

"Lucy?"

"Evan married Barbara Wilcox. About eleven years ago. Around the time he finished business school, I think."

"He m-married...?" Maddy felt the color drain out of her face. She suddenly realized that she'd assumed Evan was single. Because in the midst of the emotional tumult she'd experienced when she'd run into him at Gulliver's Travels, she'd checked his left hand for a wedding band. She hadn't seen one. "Well, what do you know. Evan and Barbara. I...I hope they're very happy together."

"They're divorced."

"Oh." Maddy didn't know what else to say. Which probably was just as well.

"Maddy." Lucy pushed her untouched plate of seafood linguini aside. "This is important. I want you to tell me exactly what Barbara Wilcox said to you, okay? *Every...single...word.*"

"That bitch!"

"Lucy—"

"Tell me you're not thinking exactly the same thing, Chris."

"Well—"

"You're just too well-mannered to say it out loud."

"No, I'm not. Barbara Wilcox is a bitch. Always has been, always will be."

"She ruined everything for Maddy and Evan."

"I don't know that I'd go *that* far."

"I would. The question is, what are we going to do?"

"Well, considering she's in Chicago and we're in Atlanta—"

"I'm not talking about Barbara! She'll get hers one of these days. I'm talking about Maddy and Evan. *Sunny* and Evan. We have to help them understand what really happened between them."

"Lucy—"

"We do, Chris! Other people helped us work through our messed-up past. Now we have a chance to pass on the favor. No. It's more than that. We have an *obligation*."

A long pause. Then Chris said, "Evan's still carrying a torch for her."

"Maddy still cares, too. She doesn't like it, but she does."

"So, what are you suggesting? That we tie them together, shove them in a supply closet and tell them to 'share?'"

"Of course not! I was thinking along the lines of inviting them both over for dinner."

"At the same time?"

"Yes."

"Would Maddy come if she knew Evan was?"

"Uh…"

"That's what I thought."

"Got any better ideas? And don't say 'Leave well enough alone,' because we *both* know this situation isn't remotely 'well.' Two friends of ours are hurting. They've *been* hurting for nearly eighteen years!''

A resigned sigh. ''How about Friday night?''

''You think we should give them a couple of days to stew?''

''I think we should let them have a little time to get their bearings back. Seeing Maddy—'Sunny'—again really knocked Evan for a loop. I don't know how he's going to react when he finds out what Barbara did.''

''Maddy was seriously shaken up, too. I mean, she'd done a good job of convincing herself she'd relegated Evan to the memory trash heap. And then—*wham!* That scene at the agency rocked her down to her socks.''

Another long pause. There was mutual shifting of positions beneath crisp white sheets. Feminine softness curved to fit more closely against hard masculinity. A lean, strong arm circled a slender waist, fingers stroking over sheer cotton. Lips nuzzled gently at the nape of a silken-skinned neck.

''Mmm. Very nice, Mr. Banks.''

''Just wait, Mrs. Banks. It's going to get nicer.''

''I—oh.'' A throaty laugh. ''Definitely…nicer. *Better* than nicer.''

More caressing. More kissing. Pulses sped up. Breathing patterns began to unravel. Then, abruptly, blossoming passion was put on hold.

''Lucy?'' The invocation of the name held both concern and frustration.

''That snapshot Barbara showed Evan. The one of 'Sunny' and the other guy. Whatever the story behind it is, I'll bet my entire collection of Sinatra tapes it's *not* the one Barbara the Bitch was trying to peddle.''

Another sigh. ''I sincerely hope you're right.''

"So, we're agreed? Friday night? You ask Evan. I'll invite Maddy."

"And once we've got them over here?"

"We get them talking to each other."

"What if they won't cooperate?"

"*Then*—" a gasp of surprised pleasure as clever fingers finessed a particularly sensitive bit of flesh "—we try the Dick Spivey approach to reconciliation."

Chapter 5

Evan didn't know which had been more difficult: listening to Sunny offer her version of what had happened in the aftermath of their less-than-satisfying Fourth of July rendezvous, or watching the tumultuous play of emotions over her expressive face as she listened to him recount his....

He had felt as though he was bleeding inside by the time she finished her quiet recitation. The revelation of his ex-wife's treachery had torn at him. But as hurtful as that had been, Sunny's apparent willingness to accept Barbara's lies about his actions had been even worse.

"You honestly believed I was capable of—" he'd demanded when she'd finally stopped speaking.

"Uh-uh," Lucy had swiftly intervened, holding up her right hand like a traffic cop. "There'll be plenty of time for questions and recriminations later on. Maddy's told you what she told me on Monday. Now you need to tell her what you told Chris."

Evan had glanced at his friend at this point, wondering what he was thinking. His initial impression had been that pushing him and Sunny into "sharing" with each other had been Lucy's idea. He'd assumed that she'd engineered the scheme and that Chris had acquiesced to it with great reluctance. He'd soon revised this assumption; it had become clear to him that Chris was solidly behind what Lucy was attempting to do. If she needed him to step in, he was there for her—one hundred percent.

Chris had nodded slightly as their eyes had met. *Go for it,* he'd seemed to be saying.

And so Evan had. He'd fixed his gaze on Sunny's face and he'd poured out *his* version of the "truth." A version he'd already realized had been tainted by another person's deliberate lies. The words had come haltingly at first. Then faster and faster and faster, as though he were trying to purge himself of a soul-killing poison.

Sunny's changeable green-gray eyes had widened with shock as he'd detailed the chaos he'd found when he'd returned to his family's cottage following their awkward liaison in the boathouse. They'd sheened with compassionate tears as he'd explained the reason for the upset. Her lips had moved once or twice, and he'd had the impression that she was murmuring words of condolence without even being aware of it.

Her cheeks had lost some of their color the first time he'd mentioned his ex-wife's name. The rest of it had seeped away—leaving her milky white—as he'd revealed the contents of the note he'd given Barbara to give to her.

She'd flinched violently when he'd described the snapshot that Barbara had showed him, shaking her head in obviously anguished denial of the conclusion he'd drawn from it. But she hadn't tried to interrupt him. If truth be told, he'd had the sense that she'd been too stunned to speak.

She'd been trembling like a leaf in a windstorm by the time the rushing flow of his words had slowed…faltered…and finally trailed off into silence. It was only then that he'd realized the two of them were alone in Lucy and Chris's cozily furnished living room.

At what juncture in his confession their host and hostess had withdrawn, Evan had no idea. His universe had narrowed to exclude everything but Sunny Kincaid as soon as he'd started talking. He suspected that the roof of the Banks's charming Victorian-style house could have come crashing down during his monologue and he wouldn't have noticed.

He took a deep breath, his gaze still riveted on Sunny's pale face. He could only imagine the hurt and humiliation she must have suffered nearly eighteen years ago. Bad enough that she'd had the misfortune to bestow her virginity on a hormone-crazed seventeen-year-old who hadn't had the skill to make her first experience a pleasurable one. She'd also been left to think that she'd been deliberately seduced and indifferently abandoned.

That she'd believed him capable of such callousness was like a knife to his heart. But Evan could understand her loss of faith. He'd told her that he loved her, then he'd taken her physical innocence with all the finesse of a rutting pig. And having had her once, he'd vanished from her life—apparently caring so little that he hadn't even bidden her goodbye.

Listening to Barbara's pseudo-sympathetic words about his intentions—or lack of them—must have been akin to having salt rubbed in an open wound. Although he'd been too buffered by his privileged upbringing to fully understand its implications back on St. Simons, he'd known that Sunny was self-conscious about the differences between what she'd once called "his kind" and "hers."

Barbara obviously had seen that self-consciousness and divined the insecurities beneath it. She'd exploited both to viciously effective advantage under the guise of offering kindness.

"I'm sorry," Evan said after what seemed like a very long pause. "Sunny—" He broke off as he saw her features tighten. He immediately corrected himself. "*Maddy.* Please. I can't—God! I'm sorry. So, so sorry."

Sunny tilted her chin a notch. She was seated in one of the chairs that flanked the living room's fireplace. He was standing by its twin, about five feet away. While part of him desperately wanted to obliterate the distance between them, he remained where he was. This was not the moment to invade Sun—*Maddy's* personal space. He also needed to keep his head clear. Every one of his instincts warned him that the closer he moved to his one-time summer lover, the more difficult it would be to do so.

"Sorry for what?" she asked. Her Dixie drawl was less pronounced than it had been when she'd related her part of "their" story. An indication, Evan thought, that she'd regained a lot of her emotional control.

The temptation to answer Sunny's question with an all-inclusive "everything" was very strong. But he refused to yield to it. For all the angst that it had ended up generating, he could not bring himself to apologize for having wanted to be with her—in every sense— nearly eighteen years ago. *He'd loved her.*

Perhaps his love had been shallower than it should have been. It certainly had been limited by the callowness of youth. But it had also been one of the most potent emotions he'd ever experienced. Even now—

No, he told himself sharply. *This isn't the time for that. You have to get right with the past before you can think about the present…much less the future.*

"I'm sorry I hurt you," he said. "From the bottom of my heart, Su—Maddy. I'm sorry."

She studied him without speaking for ten, perhaps fifteen, seconds. Her expression was impossible to read. That she'd learned to mask her thoughts so completely was disturbing to Evan. Sunny Kincaid's openness, her lack of guile, had been one of the many reasons he'd been drawn to her back on St. Simons. Sure, she'd indulged in a little feminine teasing once she'd gotten to know him, but she hadn't played games. And while she'd kept things to herself—most notably, facts about her family—she'd never closed herself off the way she seemed to be doing at this moment.

"I'm sorry, too," Maddy declared with maddening ambiguity. She held his gaze for another moment or two, then broke the eye contact and rose to her feet.

His heart surging into his throat, Evan took a quick but clumsy step forward. The awkwardness of his movement was in stark contrast to the graceful economy of hers.

"*Maddy…*" he began urgently. He couldn't—wouldn't!—let her go. If she walked out on him now, before they had a chance to—

She wasn't leaving. The realization rushed through Evan like a wave, leaving him feeling a little weak in the knees. Instead of heading for the door, she crossed to one of the windows that dominated the wall to the right of the fireplace.

He watched silently as she fingered the window's sheer underdrape, then twitched it aside. She edged nearer to the glass, nearly pressing her nose against it. She apparently was fascinated by the view.

What kind of view this might be, Evan couldn't say. Frankly, he doubted that she could see much of anything. It was pitch-dark outside.

"Maddy?" he repeated, his voice gentler than it had been.

No answer.

Ignoring a jab of frustration, he kept his gaze locked on Maddy's back. Her posture was more revealing than her expression had been. Her shoulders were tense; her spine, yardstick straight. It was obvious that she was holding herself together by pure force of will.

"Maddy?" he tried a third time.

Her fingers—ringless, tipped with neatly trimmed, unpolished nails—spasmed against the curtain. A tremor ran through her slim body. He heard a shaky intake of breath that sounded like a frantic effort to hold back tears.

Evan forgot his conviction that it would be wiser to keep some distance between Maddy and himself. He crossed the living room in several swift strides, coming to stand about a foot behind the woman he'd wronged. He could see her pale, elegantly angular face reflected in the windowpane. She wasn't weeping, but she was close.

"Please," he said huskily, appalled by the prospect that she was going to cry. It wasn't just that he felt inadequate to the task of dealing with an emotional storm. He also sensed, deep in his gut, that she would

hate breaking down in front of him. Sunny Kincaid—
Maddy Malone—was a proud woman. "Sunny.
Please…"

He touched her then, carefully placing his right hand
on her right shoulder. She shuddered at the contact, but
didn't jerk away. Emboldened, he exerted a little pressure, wordlessly urging her to turn around and face him.

After a moment, she did.

She'd always had to tilt her head up to look him in
the eyes. Somewhere in the back of his brain, Evan
registered that the angling now seemed to be a few degrees sharper than it had been nearly eighteen years ago.
He knew that he'd grown several inches during his final
term in high school. It seemed that Maddy's height was
about the same as it had been during their summer on
St. Simons, hovering a hair or two above five foot six.

Evan's stomach clenched as he watched his companion's wide-set eyes tear up. She blinked rapidly and
sniffed hard, fighting to forestall the inevitable. Finally,
one tear welled over the bottom lashes of her left eye
and trickled down her pallid cheek.

Maddy got rid of the errant moisture with a brusque
swipe of her right hand. "How c-could you believe I'd
be with that b-boy, Evan?" she demanded shakily.
"That—that—Jeff person. Or J-Jack. Whatever his
name was. How could you?"

Evan stared at her, stunned. Of all the things with
which he now believed she had a right to task him, he'd
never expected that this would be the first one she'd
fling in his face.

"I told you," he answered after a moment. "I saw a
snapshot. The two of you. Together. *Laughing.* Barbara
said—"

"Barbara." Maddy spat out the name as though it

were a vile-tasting piece of food. No. As though it were toxic. Which, Evan reflected with a flash of bitter fury, it probably was. "About ten days after you left, what's-his-name sneaked up and grabbed me from behind. A joke, he said afterward. He thought I was somebody else, he claimed. Well, I didn't think it was funny, Evan! In fact, I jerked free, whirled around and slapped him. B-Barbara was there. I don't remember her having a camera. Frankly, I was too upset to notice details like that." She shook her head, glaring up at him. "Maybe what's-his-name was laughing. But no matter what you thought you saw in that photo...*I wasn't!*"

Evan summoned up the snapshot in his mind's eye. Although he'd tried hard to banish the image from his memory, it was crystalline clear.

God, he thought. Dear...God.

That he'd viewed the picture Barbara had showed him through a haze of emotion, he'd always recognized. What he hadn't understood until this instant was how horribly his anger and jealousy and confusion had warped his perceptions. He hadn't really focused on Sunny's expression. He'd seen the hilarity on what's-his-name's face—seen what's-his-name's arms locked possessively around Sunny's body—and he'd leaped to the worst possible conclusion.

"I'm sorry," he whispered.

"You...you believe me?"

"Yes." He gazed down into his companion's overly bright eyes, willing her to accept that he was telling her the absolute truth. "I believe you."

"*Good,*" she said fiercely.

He took a steadying breath, shifting his weight. After a second or two, he returned to the issue he'd tried to broach earlier.

"You honestly thought I'd...*dumped*...you?" he asked, his voice strained. "That all I wanted from you was sex, and that once I got it, I just—just—"

"I...I didn't want to b-believe it." Sunny's breathing hitched audibly. She took a moment to compose herself, then forged on. "I tried not to, Evan. Even after B-Barbara told me what she told me, *I tried not to.* But it got harder and harder, you know? Day after day. Week after week. Not a w-word from you..."

"If only I'd known where you lived." Evan chose his words carefully, not wanting to sound as though he was blaming her for his lack of information. "Or had a phone number. I—God, Sunny! It almost killed me, not being able to get in touch with you. When I called the restaurant where you worked, and the guy who answered blew me off, it was like hitting a brick wall."

Her soft mouth twisted into a sad smile. "I quit the burger place about a week after you l-left. One of the hotels on the island had a job open up. I took it because it meant nicer working conditions and bigger tips. Charlie—the guy you talked to—was pretty ticked off at me." She gave a rueful little laugh. "To tell the truth, I'm surprised he talked to you at all."

"He knew where you were?" Evan felt sick. Why had he allowed himself to be fobbed off so easily? he wondered. Why hadn't he called back? If only he'd—

"Don't," Sunny said, brushing her fingertips against his arm. It was the first physical contact she'd made with him in nearly eighteen years. As insubstantial as the touch was, it seared Evan to the bone.

"Sunny," he whispered, covering her hand with his own. He felt her fingers tremble. Heard her breath shatter somewhere between lung and lip. Saw her lovely eyes shimmer with a swirl of elemental emotions. The desire he'd never truly put aside—certainly never fully satisfied—reasserted itself with shocking suddenness.

He wanted her. Lord help him. After all this time, he still wanted her. *Needed* her. It was as though—

"Don't, Evan," Sunny repeated, slowly pulling her hand free. It wasn't really rejection. More a wordless assertion that she wasn't ready to contend with what she—or he!—was feeling. "Please. *D-don't.*"

He nodded, lowering his hand to his side. His hand was shaking. He could feel the galloping throb of his pulse in his fingertips. A scalding sense of shame filled him. She was right, of course. Things were complicated enough without adding sex to the mix. The last time they'd surrendered to physical attraction, it had been a disaster.

"I'm sorry," he apologized, yet again.

"No need," Sunny responded softly.

There was an awkward pause. The air in the living room seemed curiously charged, as though there'd been an invisible lightning strike. Beneath his clothing, the fine hairs on Evan's arms prickled.

"That number I told you I rang," he finally said. "The first Kincaid listing from directory assistance. The one where I never got an answer. Was it—?"

"No." Sunny shook her head. "I'm not even sure who you were calling. Those Kincaids—whoever they were—weren't family."

He digested this, shifting his stance once again. Then, very cautiously, he said, "What about the…uh…"

"The drunk you talked to?" Sunny's voice could have etched glass. "That was my daddy."

Her drawl returned, full force, on the last two words. *Mah dayuh-dee,* they came out.

"I didn't know," Evan said after several moments.

But even as the assertion was leaving his lips, he wondered whether it was entirely true. Hadn't he...suspected? Hadn't hearing that slurred male voice cursing him on the other end of the line made him speculate about Sunny's reluctance to discuss her family?

"I didn't want you to," she retorted, jutting her jaw. A flush of color appeared in her cheeks—anger, painfully infused with embarrassment. "I know you weren't close to your father. But the couple of times you mentioned him to me, you at least sounded like you *respected* him. What was he? A multimillionaire CEO? A pillar of the Chicago community? If I told you about my d-daddy, probably the best I could say is that I think he truly loved my mama and he never hit me. He—he was an alcoholic, Evan. He got falling down drunk two or three times a week. And when he was sober enough to work, he was a mechanic. I was ashamed of him. He's been dead three years, and I'm *still* ashamed of him!"

"Sunny—"

"Maybe you're goin' to say I had no need to be," she swept on, her Southern accent intensifying. "That who and what he was didn't reflect on me that summer on St. Simons. Doesn't reflect on me now. Maybe you're even goin' to tell me it wouldn't have mattered to you if I'd filled you in on every sorry detail about my life when I wasn't with you. And maybe—m-maybe you'd be tellin' the truth. *But it mattered to me!* It m-mattered s-s-so much I thought I'd d-die if you—if y-you—"

She broke down. Clearly hating her weakness, she whirled away from him. Her shoulders were shaking. Her breath was ratcheting in and out in uneven, wretched-sounding snatches.

Evan didn't really think about what he did next. It wasn't a matter of should he or shouldn't he. There simply was no way he could stand by and let Maddy Malone—much less Sunny Kincaid—weep her heart out without trying to comfort her.

Taking her by the arms, he forced her to turn around. Then he gathered her close, settling her firmly against his chest and tucking her head beneath his chin.

"Sh-h-h-h-h," he soothed, rubbing her back. "Sh-h-h-h-h, sweetheart. It's all right."

Resistance to his ministrations kept her body rigid for over a minute. Then, abruptly, she yielded, sagging into his embrace with a wrenching sob. Evan tightened his arms, biting the inside of his cheek to short-circuit his own impulse toward tears. He continued shushing and stroking, desperately wishing that there were more he could do to help.

How long Sunny wept, he was never sure. It probably wasn't that long. She might go down in the face of overwhelming emotion, but she was too strong—too proud—to stay down for long.

Her sobbing eased gradually, finally halting all together. She made an odd sound that was part hiccup, part sigh, then rubbed her forehead against the front of his shirt. He could feel the warmth of her skin through the tear-dampened fabric.

His awareness of her altered. Intensified. He became conscious of the tease of her silky hair beneath his chin. Of the soft press of her breasts against his chest. Her scent—a mix of natural feminine musk and soap—tantalized his nostrils.

"It's all right, sweetheart," he murmured, clamping down on his instinctive reaction to this sensory stimulation. "Everything's all right."

After a few moments Sunny began to ease away from him. Although his body clamored for him to do exactly the opposite, Evan loosened his hold and let her go. She took a slightly unsteady step back, then lifted her head and looked at him.

Evan knew that there were women who could cry prettily. His ex-wife had been one of them. While he'd been vulnerable to her picturesque weeping early in their marriage, he'd become completely inured to it long before their divorce.

Tears did *not* become Sunny by any objective standard. They left her eyes swollen; her skin, blotched. Yet the genuineness of the emotion that they signaled affected Evan to the core.

"Wh-why—" Sunny snuffled, wiping beneath her nose with the back of one hand "—why did she d-do it?"

It took him a second or two to understand to whom she was referring. "Barbara, you mean?" he asked, tensing.

"Y-yes."

What could he say? He was disgusted beyond words by his ex-wife's actions. What she'd done to him—well, he'd been complicit in his own deception. If not in the immediate aftermath of the summer on St. Simons, then certainly later on. He'd accepted her attractive surface because it had been easier to do so than to delve beneath. In many ways he'd gotten what he'd deserved.

But Sunny...

What Barbara had done to her was unforgivable. The calculated cruelty of it sickened him.

"I'm not sure I really know," he answered honestly.

"She must have loved you...a lot."

Evan caught his breath at this assertion. It was difficult for him to think back. That Barbara's main feeling toward him these days was a combination of contempt and resentment, he was certain. Precisely what she'd felt nearly eighteen years ago, or on their wedding day, he wasn't sure.

Perhaps she *had* "loved" him, in her own way. At least for a time. The problem was, he seriously doubted that her definition of love coincided with Sunny's in any meaningful way.

"She wanted me," he said finally. "But not *me*...me. She wanted social position. Money. I was a means to an end."

"Did you love her?"

"I...I don't...know."

"You *married* her."

Evan stared at Sunny, wondering whether she realized how revealing the way she'd inflected the previous sentence had been. He knew from Chris that she'd had a tragically short but evidently happy marriage to an Atlanta cop. It was plain that the notion of marrying without love was repugnant to her. It also seemed she assumed that he must share this attitude.

This apparent faith in his emotional integrity was astonishing, all things considered.

"I...cared...for Barbara," he said, gesturing awkwardly. "We had a lot in common. Knew the same people. Spoke the same language. Shared the same experiences. We were...comfortable together. Barbara was the kind of woman my family—most of my friends, my business colleagues—expected me to pick as a wife. And she was...*there*. Not throwing herself at me, exactly. That wasn't her style. But she let me know I was a priority for her." He sighed, forking a hand back through his hair, feeling more and more appalled by the relationship he was describing. "I suppose it got to be an ego thing for me. She knew it. She fed it. And I— well, I pretty much swallowed it whole."

Evan saw something close to pity in the depths of Sunny's tear-reddened eyes as he finished speaking. He wondered whether she was thinking of her own marriage.

"I see," she said eventually, her voice very quiet.

Maybe she did. Maybe she didn't. Evan didn't know for certain. But in a blinding flash of revelation, he suddenly grasped a core truth about his decision to ask Barbara Wilcox to become his wife.

This truth impacted him like an elbow to the solar plexus. The feeling was strangely familiar. He'd played basketball in prep school, and his guarding style had been up close and aggressive. A few of his opponents had taken definite exception.

Dear Lord, he thought, struggling to keep his equilibrium. *Why hadn't he realized? Why hadn't he—?*

Maybe he had, only he'd lacked the guts to face up to it.

"She wasn't you," he blurted out, then cursed himself as he saw Sunny flinch and take another step back. His careless choice of words had caused him to hurt her. Again.

He started to reach out for her but aborted the gesture because he feared she'd reject his touch—or worse.

"No, please, Sunny," he pleaded hastily. "I didn't mean it like that! I…I tried to forget you after that summer on St. Simons. Only I couldn't. I'd see a girl with reddish-brown hair, I'd hear a laugh like yours, and it would all come back to me. But nothing—*nothing!*— about Barbara reminded me of you. And when you get down to the nitty-gritty, that has a lot to do with why

I married her. Whatever wrongs Barbara may have done me...*I used her.* I used her as a buffer against my memories of you.''

Sunny closed her eyes, seeming to need to sink deep within herself to absorb and accept what he'd just told her. Her posture relaxed a little, and the tension in her fine-bone features eased. After several moments, she exhaled on a long, slow sigh. Her eyelids fluttered open again.

''I'm sorry,'' she said. But it wasn't an apology. It was an expression of compassion. Evan knew then that despite its tragic end, her marriage had been a good and loving one. He felt a terrible pang of jealousy in reaction to this realization, then found himself succumbing to a bittersweet sense of gladness. Sunny had been happy. That was important to him.

''So am I,'' he answered.

The impulse to reach out reasserted itself. This time he gave in to it. Cautiously he lifted his right hand to her face. He brushed his fingertips lightly against the curve of her cheek. She quivered at the contact, but didn't try to elude it. He smiled, just a little, and used the pad of his thumb to blot up a lingering tear.

''Evan...'' she whispered, her eyes darkening to a mix of moss-green and hammered-pewter. Her chin angled up a few degrees.

''We can't go back,'' he said gently, forcing himself to lower his hand. ''But now that we know the truth about what happened on St. Simons, I'd like to try to go on. To get to know you again. To be...friends.''

''You think we could?'' Her tone was guarded.

''We could give it our best shot.''

Sunny studied him gravely for a second or two. Then she began to smile. Watching the slow curving of her lips—the sudden indentation of her dimples—was like seeing the sun come out after a storm. He felt himself smile back.

"I'd like that," she told him simply.

There was a pause. Although Evan had the distinct impression that Sunny wouldn't object if he touched her again—even gathered her into another embrace—he held back. He didn't want to rush things. Friends, he'd said. They were going to be *friends*.

"So, what do we do now?" Sunny finally asked, scrubbing her cheeks with her palms.

Evan considered, darting a glance toward the doorway that led to the hall of the house. He wondered wryly whether Chris and Lucy had remained within earshot after they'd left the living room. The issue of privacy aside, it didn't much matter. If either or both of them *had* been listening in, it seemed unlikely that they'd heard anything they didn't already know or had been able to guess.

"Well, I suppose we could tell our host and hostess they won't need plan B," he said.

"Plan B?"

"Tying us up and sticking us in a supply closet until we straighten things out."

Sunny blinked, apparently bewildered by this scenario. Then comprehension blossomed on her face. A moment later Evan Blake heard Sunny Kincaid laugh for the first time in nearly eighteen years.

Chapter 6

Maddy had a very restless night following her remarkable reunion with Evan. When she finally dozed off after hours of tossing and turning, her dreams were anything but soothing. Several of them were erotic in the extreme, jacking up both her pulse and respiration rates and leaving her full of yearning.

She managed to battle her overheated subconscious into submission by about four-thirty. Unfortunately, the piercing wail of a car alarm jerked her awake after less than two hours of sleep. Groaning, Maddy flopped over and stuck her fingers in her ears.

While this expedient served pretty well for the following sixty minutes or so, it was no buffer against the sudden shrill of her bedside phone shortly after seven-thirty. Eyes closed, Maddy groped for the receiver. She knocked over her alarm clock and a stack of law books before she retrieved it.

"H'lo," she muttered.

"Maddy?"

The voice was deep, drawling and almost as familiar to Maddy as her own. "Darrell?" she asked, prying her eyes open.

"Got it in one."

Darrell Parker was Maddy's supervisor. He was as tough as they came, yet he'd never become hardened at heart. He'd been a rock for her after Keith's murder. He'd also been a major supporter of her decision to go to law school. But only after he'd secured her pledge that she would become a prosecutor.

"Is somethin' wrong?" she asked, sitting up.

"Depends on your perspective. I know it's early and you're on vacation. But I thought you'd want to know one of your clients violated himself."

She tensed, her mind racing through possibilities. "Who?"

"Piece of work named Brown. Wilson Glenn Brown. Aka—"

"Wild Will, Willie the G-Man and Blast-off." The guy had been out of prison, what? A month? "Is he dead?"

Day-uhd, she pronounced it. Although she'd worked to soften her accent, it tended to return under stress.

"Uh-uh. Suspect ran a red light and took off when a patrol car tried to pull him over. He smashed into a median on I-85. The car's totaled. He's busted up, but he'll live."

"Anyone else hurt?"

"Nope."

"Thank God. I suppose the car was stolen?"

"Oh, yeah. Hot-wired, not 'jacked. Robbery likes Brown for a liquor store heist earlier in the evening, too."

Maddy rubbed her forehead. "Three strikes—he's gone."

"Probably so. Anyway, just wanted to give you a heads-up."

"I truly appreciate it, Darrell. You take care."

"Always do. Enjoy the rest of your time off, y'hear?"

Maddy sighed as she hung up the phone, then leaned back against the headboard of her bed. She closed her eyes, attempting to summon up Wilson G. Brown's mug shot. Instead, Evan's image appeared behind her lids. Shaken, she reopened her eyes.

Grateful though she was to know the truth about what had happened nearly eighteen years ago, it was hard to cope with the sudden upending of so much she'd believed for so long. Even more difficult was dealing with the tidal wave of emotions that Evan's unexpected reappearance in her life had unleashed.

Friends, he'd said last night. Let's try to be...*friends.* And she'd agreed.

But was friendship what either of them really wanted? she wondered. How did "being friends" fit with the desire she'd seen in Evan's sky-blue eyes? And how could she reconcile "being friends" with the potent sense of connection she'd felt when he'd held her as she'd wept? Or with the searing rush of need she'd experienced when he'd caressed the curve of her cheek?

Maddy shifted her position. She was unsettlingly conscious of the feel of the sheet against her naked legs. She was also aware of the stiffening of her nipples beneath the wash-worn T-shirt she wore instead of a nightgown or pajamas.

The bed in which she was sprawled was not the one which she'd shared with Keith during their marriage.

She'd found herself unable to sleep in that bed following her husband's murder. She'd ended up giving it away and purchasing another.

She slumped down until she was lying against a mashed-up pillow. Then she yawned, trying to ignore the aching throb between her thighs. Friends, she instructed herself. She and Evan were going to be...

She drifted off. She was just on the verge of falling back to sleep when the roar of a lawnmower yanked her back to consciousness. Her eyes popped open.

She glared balefully at the bedroom's plastered ceiling for several seconds then kicked off the sheet and got up. She knew from experience that the racket from next door would go on for at least ninety minutes.

She padded into the bathroom, muttering under her breath. A glance at the mirror that hung over the sink gave her a shock. She looked awful! Puffy-eyed. Pasty-skinned. If Evan could see—

No! she told herself sharply, turning away from her reflection. *Don't even think about it!*

Maddy stripped off her loose-fitting sleep shirt and stepped into the shower. She was just beginning to relax under the steaming spray when her temperamental water heater decided that enough was enough, and the gushing warmth turned icy cold.

She was still shivering when she stomped out to retrieve the morning paper from the front steps about five minutes later. Her hair was clinging damply to her skull. Beneath the terry cloth robe she'd put on, her body was covered with goose bumps.

To say her mood was not improved by the subsequent discovery that she'd run out of coffee was to understate the case. After muttering to herself for a moment or two, Maddy stalked over to her refrigerator, yanked open the door and extracted a can of Coca-Cola. So what if it wasn't the nutritionists' breakfast beverage of choice? She needed her morning dose of caffeine!

A split second after she popped the tab on the Coke, the kitchen phone rang. Maddy started at the sound, spilling several ounces of soda on the front of her robe.

"Damn!" She plunked the can down on the counter, next to the newspaper. The phone sounded again. "All right, all right," she said irritably, crossing to the wall where it hung. She snatched up the receiver on the third ring and snapped, *"What?"*

No answer.

Maddy rolled her eyes. If this turned out to be a prank call—or, worse, one of those stupid computerized telemarketing ploys—she was going to be seriously ticked off.

"Anybody there?" she tried again.

"Maddy?"

She recognized the cultured baritone instantly. Her breath snagged in her throat. Her knees got a bit wobbly. "E-Evan?"

"Yes." He sounded pleased that she'd identified him. "I hope I didn't wake you."

"Oh, no." She pressed her hand to her chest, feeling the *ba-boom, ba-boom* of her heart through the soda-dampened fabric. "That happened hours ago. My getting woken up, I mean."

"That's a relief. I know a lot of people like to sleep in on weekends. I told myself I had to wait till after nine to call."

Maddy glanced at her kitchen clock. The time was nine-oh-one. A fizz of pleasure bubbled away some of her crankiness.

"I appreciate that." Friendly, she reminded herself

firmly. Keep this friendly. "But I'm usually a pretty early riser."

"Me, too, most of the time."

"Oh, really?"

"Uh-huh."

There was an awkward pause. Maddy shifted her weight and fidgeted with the phone cord. So much for friendly conversation, she thought. Maybe they could discuss the weather next.

"I, uh, called to make sure you were okay," Evan finally declared. "After last night."

"I'm fine," she answered quickly. And she was. Still a little shaken, maybe. But essentially fine. "Are you?"

"Better than I was."

Another pause. Maddy fought down the urge to ask Evan to elaborate on his last comment.

"You're *sure* you're okay?" he pressed. "You sounded a little, uh, distracted when you answered the phone."

A startled laugh tickled up her throat in response to his oh-so-tactful choice of words. Maddy knew how she'd sounded.

"'Distracted'?" she echoed, allowing herself a small snicker. "Is that a code phrase for meaner than a junkyard dog?"

"Well..."

"I've had a few problems this morning. Ran out of hot water while I was taking a shower. Discovered I didn't have any coffee in the house. Dumped a Coke down my front—"

"Coca-Cola? I know it's the hometown drink, but Coca-Cola before nine in the morning?"

"A girl's got to have her caffeine, Evan."

"Ah." A chuckle. "I see. Well, I've got a serious latte habit myself."

"Hooked on lattes, hmm?" Probably paid a couple bucks a cup for it, too. Specialty coffees were one of those trendy indulgences that Maddy didn't get. Couldn't afford, either. "Next thing you know, you'll be doing the hard stuff. Popping roasted coffee beans. Mainlining espresso."

Evan laughed. After a brief hesitation, she found herself joining in. It felt good. No. More than that. It felt *right*.

Eventually their shared laughter dissipated into a companionable silence. Maddy leaned back against the kitchen wall. She could feel herself smiling. Not some little corner-curl smile, either. This was close to a flat-out grin.

"I'm sorry things haven't been going your way this morning," Evan said after a bit.

"That's life," she answered easily. "But my problems are small pototoes compared to a lot of people's." She flashed back on the conversation she'd had with Darrell Parker and snorted. "Wild Will Brown's, for example."

"Who?"

Maddy held back for a beat then asked, "You know what I do for a living, right?"

"You're a parole officer. And Chris said something about you going to law school at night."

It seemed to Maddy that Evan sounded more approving of the latter than the former. No big surprise. Most folks reacted the same way. Still, it nettled her. She was proud of her current position. So what if discharging her duties meant that she tended to associate with crumb bums rather than with the crème de la crème? That was no reason for the man on the other end of the line to look down his—

"Maddy?"

She blinked, forcing herself to take a steadying breath. What Evan had said about her was absolutely true, she reminded herself. She *was* a parole officer and she *was* going to law school at night. As for the way in which he'd said it…well, maybe she was being a little thin-skinned.

"Wilson Glenn Brown—aka Wild Will—is a parolee of mine," she explained, combing her fingers through her nearly dried hair. She'd gotten it styled the day before yesterday. "He got arrested overnight after he smashed up a stolen car. He's also the prime suspect in a liquor story robbery."

"How does that affect you?"

The question surprised her. So, too, the concern she sensed lurking behind it. "You mean, do I get in trouble if one of my so-called 'clients' screws up?"

"Yes."

"No. Not really."

"But you're upset by it."

A denial rose to her lips. Maddy swallowed it an instant later when she realized that Evan was right. For all her flippancy, she *was* upset. No, she didn't think that everybody whose records landed on her desk could be rehabilitated. She'd had that idealistic notion knocked out of her—quite literally—by an ex-con named Samuels. Nonetheless, she kept pulling for her parolees to make it on the outside. And when they didn't…

"Yeah," she acknowledged quietly. "It bothers me. Not that I'm surprised. I made Brown for a likely recidivist as soon as I read his jacket." She frowned, scuffing a toe against the kitchen floor. "Maybe he was living down to my expectations."

"Hey." There was an edge to Evan's voice. "Being bothered by what happened is okay, Sunny. It wouldn't be like you not to give a damn. But don't go assuming blame you don't deserve."

Maddy bit her lip, shaken by his apparently unpremeditated use of her old nickname. His categorical assertion about what "wouldn't be like" her was disconcerting, too. After nearly eighteen years apart, how could Evan Blake claim to know anything about her character? Until less than twenty-four hours ago, he'd basically believed her to be a fickle little slut!

"Anyway," Evan went on, his tone softening. "I'll bet for every Wild Will you've got, there's a Dick Spivey."

Maddy sighed. Then, reluctantly, she started to laugh. She couldn't help it. "Actually, no. He's one of a kind."

"Do I hear an unspoken 'Thank God' at the end of that?"

She laughed again. "Depends on the day."

There was yet another break in the conversational flow. A quick glance at the kitchen clock made Maddy catch her breath. She'd been chatting with Evan for more than a half hour!

"Maddy?"

"Mmm?" She twisted the tie belt on her robe.

"I realize this is last minute, but if you don't have any other plans…well, I was hoping we could get together today. Have lunch. Or dinner. Or a drink. Maybe go to a movie."

Maddy swallowed, conscious of a sudden speed-up in her pulse. Her knees started to feel a little rocky again. Her gaze strayed toward the newspaper she'd brought in. One of the below-the-fold headlines on the front page caught her attention.

"How do you feel about baseball?" she asked impulsively.

Silence from the other end. Then, carefully, "Baseball?"

"Yeah."

"As a native Chicagoan, I have to say I believe the Cubs will win the World Series sometime during the next millennium."

"Wishful thinking. Anyway, you're in Braves territory."

"The Braves? Too bad they choked during the playoffs."

"We didn't choke! We peaked too early in the season."

"Uh-huh. Right. It was Choke City, babe."

Maddy huffed indignantly because she knew it was expected. But inwardly, she was relishing the back-and-forth. She and Evan had done a lot of teasing on St. Simons once she'd accepted the idea that someone like him really, truly, enjoyed spending time with someone like her. The ease with which they'd slipped back into the bantering pattern both surprised and pleased her.

"So?" her caller prompted after a few seconds.

"So, what?"

"So, do you think we might get together today? Or do you draw the line at socializing with Cubs' fans?"

"Why, Mr. Blake, I've been known to be polite to people wearin' *Yankees'* caps on occasion," she returned, putting on a Dixie belle drawl. Then she reverted to her normal voice. "And as for our getting together...well, it's looking like a gorgeous Saturday outside, and the front page of the paper just reminded me the Braves are playing at home. Maybe we could take in the game. It starts a little after one."

"Fine by me," Evan said immediately. "Tell you what. I've got a couple of errands to run this morning. Why don't I pick up a pair of tickets while I'm out, then swing by your place about noon? No point in taking two cars. And maybe we can get a bite to eat after the game. What do you think?"

Maddy found herself thinking a number of things. Among them, that after nearly five years of being on her own, she wasn't particularly comfortable with the guy-takes-charge routine.

Which wasn't to imply she felt that the man on the other end of the phone line was being overbearing. She didn't. Evan had embraced her suggestion about the baseball game with enthusiasm. And he certainly wasn't forcing his logistical ideas on her. Nonetheless...

She had the definite impression that he was accustomed to running the show. To having things go his way.

He'd given off a similar vibe on St. Simons, she mused. Despite his relative youth, there'd been a cool aura of assurance about him. While he'd been infinitely less arrogant than most of his friends, he'd been endowed with a special kind of self-confidence. Rich-kid confidence, she'd decided at the time, envying the innate sense of security it seemed to imply.

"Sounds like a plan," she replied. "With one proviso. This is Dutch treat. You pay your way. I pay mine."

"Sure," Evan agreed after a tiny pause. "No problem."

* * *

"I should've worn my lucky shirt," Maddy grumped about eight hours later. "We might've won if I'd worn my lucky shirt."

Realizing that discretion was the better part of valor when dealing with a woman whose favorite team had just gone down in ignominious defeat, Evan suppressed a smile. Inwardly, though, he was grinning.

He'd had a terrific time at the game. Not because the Braves had lost. He felt bad about that, actually. But not so bad that he hadn't enjoyed watching Sunny watch them get skunked.

He'd been entranced by her. She'd been totally caught up in the game—yelping with excitement whenever the Braves pulled off anything approaching a decent play, groaning in dismay when they flubbed. She been as unselfconscious as a child in her responses.

Except, of course, for the joltingly adult moment when she'd reacted to the Braves' first and only base hit of the game by flinging her arms around him. Surprised, he'd done the natural thing and returned the embrace. In the space of a single heartbeat, what had been an essentially friendly hug had become fraught with electricity. Sexual awareness had arced from him to her and back again in a powerful, pulsating loop.

They'd broken apart a moment later, gazing at each other with undisguised shock. Which one of them had been more shaken was impossible to say.

"Sunny, I—" he'd begun hoarsely.

"Evan, I—" she'd said simultaneously.

At that point, the Braves' clean-up batter had been called "out" on a questionable pitch, ending the inning and leaving his teammate stranded on first. The stadium had erupted in boos and shouts. Seizing on the distraction, Sunny had pivoted away from him and joined in the noisy protest. He'd stared at her for a second or two more, then followed suit. They'd spent the rest of the game pretending what had happened...hadn't.

"Not to knock the home team," he said mildly, picking up the pitcher of beer they were sharing and topping off her glass. "But I think the Braves needed more than your lucky shirt today."

"I suppose." Maddy sighed heavily and shook her head. "Bad enough they lost, six-zilch. But they played lousy ball doing it! Did you *see* that unforced error in the top of the fifth?"

"Mmm," Evan responded neutrally, continuing to discipline his expression. If truth be told, he'd missed the mistake in question. He'd been too busy studying Sunny, trying to catalogue the changes wrought by the passage of nearly eighteen years. He'd been struck by how gently the hand of time had touched her. Even in the unforgiving glare of direct afternoon sunlight, she'd looked a decade younger than her actual years.

"And then there was that—"

"Hey, Maddy," a gravelly voice interrupted. Its source was a burly, middle-aged white guy wearing a Braves cap.

One of the many things Evan had discovered during the course of the past few hours was that Madison "Maddy" Malone was a very popular lady. She'd been hailed with obvious affection by at least a half dozen people at the ball game. She'd been the recipient of several hollered greetings in the stadium parking lot, too. She'd also gotten the VIP treatment at the barbecue joint where they were eating.

"Hey, George!" Sunny smiled, dimples flashing. "Where's your wife?"

"She's waitin' on me out in the car. You go to the game?"

"Uh-huh. I was hopin' to convert Evan here to rootin' for the Braves. He's a Cubs fan. Just moved to Atlanta from Chicago. Evan, George Roberts. George, Evan Blake."

"Hi," Evan said politely, extending his hand.

The older man shook it. He then gave Evan an assessing once-over. Evan endured the scrutiny without resentment. He'd been similarly checked out by the people to whom Sun—uh, Maddy had introduced him at the ballpark.

"I've seen you before," George announced after a moment, his eyes narrowing. "Tues—no, Monday. You were with Lucy Falco's husband. I seem to recall he's from Chicago, too."

"That's right." Evan was taken aback. "You have quite a memory, Mr. Roberts."

"George," the older man corrected, unbending a bit. "I was a street cop for twenty years. My legs were shot to hell—pardon the language, Maddy—by the time I put in my retirement papers, but my mind stayed sharp."

"George is in charge of day shift security for the building where Gulliver's Travels is located," Sunny explained.

"Ah." Evan nodded.

"Well, I gotta run," George declared after a moment. "Nice seein' y'all. Sure wish you'd wore that lucky shirt of yours today, Maddy. Might've kept the Braves from puttin' on such a pitiful performance."

Sunny laughed and waggled her fingers. "Bye, George. Give my best to Marilee."

"I sure will."

"Good to meet you, George," Evan added.

"You, too, Evan."

Sunny turned her head as she tracked the older man's exit. The movement emphasized the graceful line of her throat. It also revealed a tempting glimpse of the back of her neck.

Evan had never given much thought to Sunny's nape during their time together on St. Simons. Eyeing it now, he found himself wondering whether the skin he was seeing was as creamy smooth as it looked.

And then there were Sunny's ears. Maybe it had something to do with the way they were framed by her pertly styled hair, but Evan found them intensely alluring, too. He could imagine himself whispering secrets in them. Or nibbling on—

The realization that Sunny was speaking to him penetrated his semierotic reverie. Evan shifted in his seat, berating himself for his lack of control. Friends, he emphasized. He'd told her he wanted them to be *friends*.

"I'm afraid I missed what you just said," he admitted.

"I asked if somethin' was wrong."

"No." Evan picked up his glass of beer and took a drink. "Everything's fine, Su—uh, Maddy." Thinking of her as Maddy was damned near impossible for him. But he'd decided he needed to make an effort to use that name when he spoke aloud. The incident with the spontaneous embrace aside, he'd done pretty well at the ball game. "Why would you think—"

"Because of the way you keep starin' at me."

Busted. Well, he deserved to be.

"Sorry," he apologized. "I didn't mean to be rude. It's just that—uh—"

"I'm not the girl you remember?"

Evan frowned, uncertain of her tone. From a lot of

other women—including his ex-wife—he would have interpreted the question as a cue to start complimenting her on her youthful appearance. But coming from Sunny...

Finally he said, "I think we've both changed."

His companion cocked her head to one side, seeming to consider this assertion very carefully. Her eyes drifted away for a few moments, her manner oddly abstracted. But when she brought her gaze back to his, her expression was direct.

"I recognized you right away, Evan," she told him quietly. "The second I saw you at Gulliver's Travels, I knew who you were."

"I knew you, too." He paused for a moment, remembering the surge of response he'd felt. Then he smiled, a little ruefully. "Although I will admit your hair was a bit of a shock."

Sunny patted at her casually cropped tresses with a self-conscious gesture. "I...I suppose it would be."

"When did you cut it?"

"About five years ago." She lowered her hand. Evan noticed that it was less steady than it had been on the way up. "It was...because of my husband."

He hesitated, whipsawed by what was becoming a familiar pair of very contradictory emotions. Half of him wanted to know everything about the man Sunny had married. The other half...

"He didn't like it long?"

"No." The response was quick, but followed by a grimace. "I mean, yes. Keith did. Like my hair long, that is. Loved it, as a matter of fact."

"Then why—?"

Sunny eyed him silently for several seconds before asking, "How much did Chris tell you about me? Besides mentioning I was a parole officer and going to law school?''

"Not a lot." It was the truth. His friend had been very circumspect. "I don't want you to get the impression he gossiped about you behind your back. After we, uh, ran into each other at Gulliver's Travels on Monday, I asked him some basic questions about you. He gave me some basic answers. That's all.''

"So, you know my husband was a cop, who was killed in the line of duty.''

"Look, if you don't want to talk about this—''

"No." Sunny straightened her spine and cocked her chin. "It's all right, Evan. You told me about you and Barbara. I think I should tell you about me and Keith.''

"Only if you're…sure.''

"I am." She took a deep breath, meeting his gaze evenly. "Keith and I had been married for almost seven years when he was murdered. I…I guess you could say I went a little crazy when I got the news. Chopping off my hair was part of it.''

Her mouth quivered for a moment, then firmed up. "I'm still not sure exactly why I did it. A friend of mine, who's really religious, said I was followin' the Bible. You know, those passages about showing grief by ripping your clothes and shaving your head? And maybe there's an element of truth to that. But lookin' back, I think it had more to do with the fact that Keith loved my hair bein' long. I mean, there was a part of me that was so damned *mad* at him for gettin' himself killed! If he'd been there, I would have yelled at him. Hit him, even. But h-he wasn't. So I grabbed a pair of shears and I started whackin' away at my hair. Because I knew K-Keith would hate it. Which was fine by me. Because right then, during those first few minutes after

I heard that 'sorry for your loss' notification, I hated him. He'd hurt me by dyin' and I—" she paused, her throat working "—I wanted to hurt him back as hard as I could."

"Oh, Sunny…"

His companion picked up a paper napkin and wiped her nose. Her gray-green eyes were dry, but suspiciously bright. "Not very nice, huh?"

"There's nothing 'nice' about losing someone you love," Evan answered, suddenly reliving the anger he'd experienced at his father's death. Never mind that they hadn't been close. He'd still cared about the man. He'd cared, and he'd felt betrayed by his sudden passing. How much worse must it have been for the woman sitting opposite him?

"No," Sunny agreed after a second or two, discarding the now-crumpled napkin. "There sure isn't."

"What was he like?"

The question clearly surprised her. And why not? Even Evan was startled to hear it come out of his mouth.

"K-Keith?"

He nodded, trying to gauge her expression.

Sunny nibbled her lower lip for a few moments, seemingly lost in thought. Finally she refocused and said, "Keith was…different…from you."

Evan caught his breath. Deep down, he'd been braced for just such a response. Still, it hurt. "I see."

"No. I don't think you do." To his great astonishment, Sunny leaned forward and placed her right hand on top of his left one. Her fingers tightened around his. He experienced an odd jolt of response—from wrist, to elbow, to shoulder—at the contact. "I'm not sayin' that as some kind of—of *payback* for what you told me about why you got together with Barbara. I won't claim it didn't sting, hearing you say how much the two of you had in common. But the other part, about how there wasn't a single thing about her that reminded you of me…''

She paused, her hazel eyes darkening with emotion. A tinge of hot pink crept up into her cheeks.

"I felt sad for you, Evan," she finally continued, withdrawing her hand. The physical disengagement was slow. Almost reluctant. He forced himself not to try to prolong it. "Genuinely sad. But I felt kind of *proud* for me, too. Proud that *I'd* married someone for what he was, not what he wasn't. Only later, when I got home, I started thinking.''

She paused again, her lips curving into a bittersweet smile. "I realized that in a lot of ways, Keith Malone was about as far from you as I could get. He was a good ol' Southern boy with a community college degree in police science. The first and only time he left Georgia was on our honeymoon. He was barely five-ten. Stocky build. Dark brown hair. Dark brown eyes. He was a kind, decent man. A first-class cop, too. But nobody'd ever think to put him in a Ralph Lauren ad, if you know what I mean.''

Evan remained silent for ten, perhaps fifteen seconds, struggling to absorb what he'd just heard. It was ridiculous to be jealous of a dead man, but he knew he was. At the same time, he felt a strange sense of gratitude toward Keith Malone. It was plain that while he'd lived, he'd made Sun—Maddy—happy.

Eventually, unable to help himself, he asked, "Did he know about us?"

The color in Sunny's cheeks flared, then ebbed away. "Keith realized he wasn't my first. Aside from that…''

She made a gesture. "If he'd asked, I would've told him. But he never did."

There was a long pause. Then Evan said, "You miss him."

"Every day." The admission was touching in its simplicity. It moved Evan far more profoundly than a more elaborate avowal of grief would have. "But I also understand he's gone. I've mourned. Now, I'm tryin' to move on."

Their conversation flowed into less personal channels after that. The change of tone was gradual. It was also mutually adopted. When he reflected upon it later, Evan realized that both he and Sunny had begun retreating into their respective emotional corners at the same time.

Which wasn't to say that they'd disconnected from each other. Quite the contrary. Beneath the casual chit-chat, Evan had felt the throb of a very complicated kind of intimacy.

He'd just finished telling Sunny about his new job— he'd been hired to be the chief fund-raiser for the Atlanta-based philanthropic foundation where Chris Banks worked as executive legal counsel—when a waitress presented their check. He automatically picked it up and reached for his wallet.

"Evan."

He took a moment to calculate the appropriate tip, then glanced across the table. "Yes?"

Sunny stared at him, brows arched.

"What?" he asked, puzzled by her accusatory expression.

She redirected her gaze. Very pointedly.

The tab, Evan realized a split second later. Oh, geez! He'd agreed they were going to go Dutch, hadn't he?

Well, no. Not *agreed*. Sunny had delivered an ulti-
matum. He'd acquiesced. And he'd been perfectly willing to let her reimburse him for the cost of her baseball
ticket. He'd gone along with her shelling out for parking, too. But now…

His ex-wife had expected him to pay for everything—including his own birthday, anniversary and
Christmas gifts. The handful of women he'd dated in
the wake of his divorce had been similarly inclined in
their fiscal expectations. While he hadn't minded picking up the tab for any of them—he had the money, he
also harbored some old-fashioned ideas about gender
relations—he'd sometimes felt as though he was being
treated like a human ATM.

Given this background, he should have found
Sunny's show of economic independence refreshing.
Endearing, even. And to a certain extent, he did. But he
also found it…irritating.

He understood her being wary of him. It had been
less than a day since they'd discovered the truth about
the betrayal of their summer romance. What was
twenty-four hours measured against nearly eighteen
years of hurt? Still. Was it really necessary for her to
make such a fuss about him treating her to a meal?
What did she think? He was trying to buy her with
barbecue?

She'd never insisted on splitting the bill back on St.
Simons, he reflected. Not that he'd lavished a lot of cash
on her. And maybe, just maybe, he'd felt a little guilty
about that. Hence his purchase of the gold bangle. He'd
desperately wanted to offer Sunny tangible proof of his
feelings for her.

He still wanted to, he realized. But…how?

"Evan?"

"Let me get this one, Maddy. Next time it's all yours."

Next time...

The words sang through Maddy's brain like an anthem. She knew that it was unwise—or worse—to get so excited over two little syllables, but she couldn't stop herself. Evan wanted to see her again!

Of course, he'd talked about there being a "next time" once before. Nearly eighteen years ago, in his family's boathouse on St. Simons. What if—

No, Maddy told herself fiercely. She was not going to fall into that trap. Speculating about what might have been was pointless. What had happened, had happened. It couldn't be undone. What mattered now was...now.

She glanced left, studying Evan's chiseled profile as he turned his car onto the street where she lived. It was difficult for her to tell what he was thinking. It had always been difficult. Even at seventeen, Evan had been remarkably self-contained. That was one of many reasons he'd intrigued her. And when he'd begun to open up...

"I've never talked to a girl the way I talk to you," he'd confessed one night as they'd ambled along the beach. He'd just finished describing his dreams for the future, and he'd clearly been embarrassed by his volubility.

"I'm glad," she'd answered, meaning it.

"You make me feel..." He'd halted. She had, too. He'd looked away for a moment, gazing out at the moonlit ocean. When he'd looked back, there'd been a yearning expression in his deep blue eyes. Lifting his hands, he'd cupped her face and said, "I think I'm in love with you, Sunny Kincaid."

"And I think I'm in love with you, Evan Blake," she'd whispered in return, trembling at his touch.

A week later, they'd met in the boathouse and surrendered to the urges of their adolescent bodies. A day after that—

"Here we are," Evan announced, pulling up in front of her house. He put his car into park and turned off the engine.

Maddy watched as he got out, came around to the passenger's side and opened the door for her. "Thanks," she said.

"You're welcome," he returned.

They walked to her front door without speaking. Maddy had already debated the issue of whether she should ask Evan in. She'd decided against it. Despite their history together, their relationship was still too...new.

"So," she said as they reached their destination.

"So," her companion returned.

"I had a great time, Evan."

"Even though the Braves lost?" His tone was teasing. The look in his eyes was not.

Maddy smiled, trying to ignore a sudden fluttering in her stomach. "You can't have everything."

"Probably not," Evan agreed, a hint of huskiness entering his voice. "But that doesn't stop people from wanting it."

"Do—" her breath snagged, then escaped in a rush "—you?"

He'd taken possession of her hands, she realized with a shock a moment later. Without her registering what he was doing, Evan had clasped her hands in his. He was massaging her inner wrists, feathering the sensitive skin with the pads of his thumbs.

"Do I...what?" he asked.

Maddy scrambled to retain her grip on the thread of their conversation. Her body was thrumming. She felt far warmer than she should on a pleasant May night.

"W-want everything," she finally managed.

"Sometimes. But right now, all I really want is...this."

This was a kiss. Only Evan didn't have to take it. Maddy gave it freely. Even as he was angling his head down, she was angling hers up. Because in her heart of hearts, at this crystalline moment in time, a kiss was all she really wanted, too.

Their lips touched. Once. Twice. Three times. The first contact was featherlight and fleeting. The second, a heartbeat longer and a little more intense. The third...

Oh. Oh, yes.

She'd thought she'd forgotten his taste, his scent, his *feel.* She hadn't. Her body remembered his as though their last embrace had been a few scant days ago.

And yet there was a dizzying overlay of strangeness to Maddy's realization that she was back in Evan Blake's arms again. Because for all the sensory familiarity the situation evoked, there was no escaping the reality that they'd spent more than seventeen years apart, traveling in very different directions.

I think we've both changed, he'd told her earlier.

He'd been right.

And until she understood exactly how much, in exactly what ways, and exactly why, to let "this" go any further than it already had would be a very dangerous thing.

Whether Evan sensed her sudden misgivings or experienced some of his own, Maddy never found out. It didn't really matter. But in the same moment she started to ease back, so did he.

They stood on her front steps staring at each other for what could have been a long time. Then again, it could have been no more than a few seconds. Maddy was reminded of what had happened in the wake of the foolishly impulsive hug she'd given him at the ballpark.

"Evan—"

"Sunny—"

They started—and stopped—in unison.

Evan cleared his throat. "Maddy," he corrected, his diction precise. "I meant…Maddy."

A breeze stirred, ruffling his hair, sending a lock of it curling onto his forehead. Maddy clenched her fingers, resisting the urge to reach up and brush it back into place. Her heart did a curious little swoon when Evan forked it off his brow.

"It's all right if you call me Sunny," she finally said.

"Even if your friends—?"

"There are different kinds of friends."

"What kind are we?"

"I *think* that's what we're tryin' to find out."

Evan smiled, his gaze caressing her face. "Next time?"

"Next time," the former Sunny Kincaid concurred, and smiled back.

Chapter 7

There were three "next times" during the two weeks that followed. Maddy picked up the tab for the first. She and Evan split the costs for the second and third. They'd planned a fourth—

Ding-dong.

"Just a minute," Maddy called, resisting the urge to fling the wrench she'd been using across the kitchen floor. What had started out as one leaky pipe had turned into a plumbing nightmare. No permanent damage yet, thank heavens. But still a major mess. And yet another indication that her modest home was in need of some serious professional repairs.

She knew people who'd do good work for a reasonable price, of course. Unfortunately, even "reasonable" would mean stretching her current budget beyond the snapping point. And while she supposed she could finagle some kind of installment payment deal, she really hated the idea of being indebted to—

Ding-dong.

"All right, already!" she hollered, heading toward the front of the house. The back of her skull throbbed dully, the legacy of an accidental encounter with the underside of her ancient garbage disposal. "I'm coming!"

Maddy reached the front door and pulled it open. She blinked. Her jaw went slack. It took her several seconds to accept that she was seeing what she thought she was seeing.

Because what she thought she was seeing was Evan Blake.

He looked as though he'd stepped out of the pages of a *GQ* article on classy but casual dressing. Wire-rimmed Ray-Bans. Crisp white polo shirt. Slightly rumpled khakis. Well-polished loafers. No socks. He had a navy sports jacket slung over his left arm. He was also carrying a small bouquet of flowers.

"Wh-what are *you* doing h-here?" she finally croaked.

Evan removed his sunglasses, seemingly unfazed by this ungracious greeting. His eyes were very blue against his lightly tanned face. They crinkled at the outer corners as he offered her a pleasant smile.

"I thought we were supposed to have brunch and see a movie," he said. "The new Spielberg picture."

Have brunch? See the new—

Maddy groaned, suddenly remembering the date they'd made two nights before. She looked down, deeply embarrassed. Then she registered her appearance and felt even more humiliated. Oh, Lord! She looked like something the cat had dragged in after throwing up on it! Bare feet. Stained denim cutoffs that barely covered her rump. A semiwet T-shirt that had faded from screaming scarlet to an ugly shade of rust.

And no bra. Very obviously—thanks to the dampness of the T-shirt—no bra.

Maddy brought her arms up, crossing them in front of her. She could feel the budding thrust of her nipples. She could also feel her cheeks turning fire-engine red with mortification.

"Wrong day?" Evan suggested mildly. Where he'd been looking while she'd been staring at the ground, Maddy didn't know. But he was behaving like the perfect gentleman now, his gaze firmly fixed on the bridge of her nose.

"No." She pulled a face, then gave a rueful little laugh. "Right day. Right time. I'm just running behind this morning." Or was it afternoon already? "A few...housekeeping problems."

"Can I help?"

Her first impulse was to say thanks, but no thanks. She was accustomed to managing on her own. Plus, her place was in shambles. Bad enough that Evan had caught her looking like a bum. She didn't want him thinking that she lived in a pigsty, too.

And yet...

There was no denying that she could use some assistance. Heck. Just having company would be nice! As for her less-than-fancy life-style—well, she was what she was, and she lived how she lived. Had she not tried to hide the full truth about herself nearly eighteen years ago on St. Simons, things might have gone much differently.

"You know anything about plumbing?" she asked, gesturing Evan inside.

"I flushed a cherry bomb down a toilet at prep school

once," he admitted, giving her the bouquet along with a quicksilver grin.

"Practically a pro." Maddy giggled. Then she treated herself to a sniff of the delicately fragrant blossoms she'd just been handed. "You can supervise."

Dusk in Atlanta's Inman Park neighborhood.

"Oh. Oh...Evan."

"Here?"

"Just a little—yes. *Yes!* Right there."

"Harder?"

"No. That's..."

"Good?"

"Mmm. Definitely...g-good."

Evan Blake stroked his thumbs slowly—very, very slowly—up the arch of the former Sunny Kincaid's left foot. She gave a small wriggle of pleasure, making a sound that was midway between a sigh and a purr.

They were relaxing on the handkerchief-size patio in Sunny's tree-studded backyard. She was supine on a slightly rickety chaise longue. He was straddling the end of the piece of lawn furniture, massaging her feet.

After a few more languid strokes, Evan switched his attention to Sunny's toes. And very pretty toes they were, too, he reflected.

If he hadn't been feeling so content, he might have been concerned about his finding his companion's tootsies so appealing. Then again, maybe not. It wasn't as though Sunny's feet were the only portion of her anatomy that attracted him.

There were her long, lithe legs.

Her slim hips and sassy derriere. Plus her small, but beautifully shaped breasts.

Her slender, oh-so-competent hands drew him, too.

There were her ears, as well. Mustn't forget them.

Or the nape of her neck which was—he'd been delighted to discover—as creamy smooth as it looked.

And her mouth. Lord, yes. Her mouth. He could spend hours meditating about the allure of Sunny's sweetly ripe, dimple-framed lips. Never mind the pleasure to be had in succumbing to—

Whoa! Evan stopped himself. Too far, too fast. He'd made up his mind after the post-ball-game kiss they'd shared that he needed to go slowly with his one-time summer love.

He and Sunny—no, he and Maddy Malone—had a chance to create something special and lasting. He believed that with every fiber of his being. He also believed that physical intimacy could enhance that "something" a hundredfold.

But only if the timing was right.

Only if both of them were equally ready and willing.

Sex had been part of what had screwed things up for them on St. Simons. He couldn't—*wouldn't!*—let that happen again.

He'd stay celibate to prevent it, if he had to.

Suppressing a sigh of frustration, Evan put down Sunny's left foot and took up her right. He rubbed his knuckles against the sole.

"Mmm…" she breathed, her eyelids fluttering down.

He and Chris had ended up talking about the problematic situation a couple days ago, after their weekly handball game. Although he'd won in straight sets, he'd been in no mood to do the gracious victor routine. His opponent had noticed.

"Problems?" Chris had asked.

"No," he'd snapped, shucking off his sweat-sodden tank top and tossing it into his gym bag. "Why?"

"Aside from the fact that you nearly took my head off with a cross-court slam?"

He'd raked a hand through his damp hair. "Your wife pushing you for more secrets about me?"

Evan had regretted the question as soon as he'd finished asking it. The implication had been unworthy of his long friendship with Chris. Insulting to Lucy, too.

"Chris—" he'd begun, genuinely ashamed of himself.

"It's okay." His friend had waved off the attempted apology. "Given what I said when I was grilling you about your relationship with Maddy, I don't blame you for thinking along those lines. But just for the record, there *are* a few things I don't 'share' with my wife. Among them, the details of my best buddy's love life. Or—" a crooked smile "—his lack of one."

Evan had given a humorless chuckle and rubbed the back of his neck. He'd felt a headache coming on. "That obvious, huh?"

"Well, I don't think people are pointing you out on the street and snickering. But you definitely seem... torqued up."

"Gee, thanks."

"Correct me if I'm wrong. But I thought you and Maddy were seeing a lot of each other."

"We are." He'd toed off his left athletic shoe.

"And?"

He'd toed off his right athletic shoe. "And, nothing."

"Nothing?"

The incredulity in Chris's voice had made Evan flush. He'd glanced around, relieved to find that they were alone in the locker room.

"Not 'nothing' nothing." He'd peeled off his socks.

Balling them up, he'd chucked them into his gym bag with his shirt. "Just not...you know."

There'd been a long pause. His friend hadn't pressed. Just waited. Finally, his voice tight, Evan had confessed, "I want Sunny, Chris. More than ever. But I'm...worried."

Actually, scared spitless was closer to the mark. But he wasn't ready to bare his soul quite that far. Not even to Chris.

"Because of what happened on St. Simons?"

"Partly." He'd rubbed his palms against his thighs. "It's not just wondering whether I'll be able to make that night up to her. I've got to think about competing with her dead husband, too." He'd stopped, remembering Sunny's expression as she'd spoken about Keith Malone. After a long moment, he'd looked at his friend. "She loved him. She really, truly loved him."

"Past tense, Ev."

"What?"

"Past tense," Chris had repeated. "All of it. The Fourth of July fizzle. Maddy's marriage. I'm not saying they don't matter. But if you let yourself get so hung up on what happened—"

"Evan?"

Sunny's voice pulled him back into the present. Which was as it should be. The present was the period upon which he was supposed to be focusing, according to his good pal.

"What is it?"

"Are you...okay?"

"Yeah." He nodded. "Just fine."

Her expression was skeptical, but she didn't push. Shifting topics and position she said, "I appreciate the foot massage."

"I may be a failure as a plumber, but I can be—" he smiled, sliding his palms upward "—handy to have around."

Sunny gave a throaty little laugh. The sound made Evan's body tighten. "Amen to that, Mr. Blake."

He kneaded his way from her calves to the backs of her knees. There he paused, recalling something from an interlude on St. Simons.

"Still ticklish?" he inquired, teasing with his fingertips.

"Why don't you f-find out—" Sunny's voice was hushed and a note or two higher than it had been "—for y-yourself."

He did.

She was.

"I...I'm sorry about the garbage disposal," Sunny eventually said. Although her voice had returned to its normal register, she sounded a bit breathless. Nearly a minute of effervescent giggling had also left her looking a bit flushed.

Evan went back to massaging her lower legs. His hostess had traded the skimpy cutoffs she'd been wearing when he'd arrived for a more modest pair of white duck shorts. Still, he wasn't sure how far he trusted himself when it came to touching her naked thighs.

"No need to apologize," he replied. "After all, *I'm* the one who reversed the hoses when we reattached it."

"I should have made sure it was empty before I turned it on."

"It could've been worse." He chuckled. "You know, I had no idea those things had such a spew range."

"I'm afraid that shirt of yours is ruined."

Evan glanced down at himself. Sunny had ordered him into the shower after his unexpected dousing with a flume of liquified garbage. She'd also insisted on washing and ironing his soiled clothes. While he and his khakis had come clean, the front of his white Polo shirt was stained with a large, multicolored splotch.

"I've got others," he answered, shrugging.

"I'd like to pay to replace it."

He grinned. "Only if you'll let me pay to repaint your kitchen."

Sunny sat up so abruptly the chaise teetered. "That's ridiculous!"

"Why?" Evan was amused by her vehement reaction. He was intrigued by the emerald flash in her eyes, too. "We've already agreed the disposal blowup was my fault. The walls got the worst of it. I should take responsibility for fixing them."

"I sponged everything off. There's no need to repaint."

"Then there's no need for you to replace my shirt. As I said, I've got plenty of others."

Sunny mulled this over for a few seconds, clearly having a problem with his attitude. Finally, however, she gave in.

"All right," she assented, leaning back against the chaise.

There was a pause. Evan resumed his massage, enjoying the feel of sleek skin over long, smooth muscles.

Somewhere in the distance, a car horn honked and a dog howled. Somewhat closer, an exasperated mother called for her children to come in to sup-per...*immediately.*

Evan glanced up. The sky was cloudless, tinted a twilight color between blue-gray and violet. He could just discern the silvery outline of a crescent moon.

A breeze rustled through the trees. He thought he felt

Sunny shiver. He recalled having heard someone mention that Atlanta was having a cooler-than-usual spring.

"Do you want my jacket?" he asked. His blazer had been spared contamination by the disposal disgorgement. He'd brought it with him when they'd come out to the patio. It was draped over the back of the chaise.

"No." Sunny shook her head. "I'm fine."

"You sure?" He scooted up a few inches, ignoring a creaky groan of protest from the chaise.

"Positive." She expelled a breath and brushed at her hair. "I was just thinkin' about having to hire a plumber."

"Is that a big deal?"

"I live on a budget. I didn't have a plumber figured in this month. Or next month. Or the month after that."

Evan weighed the implications of this statement. He also thought about the condition of Sunny's home. While it was a cozy, comfortable place, it was rather rundown. Suspicion stirred.

"Your husband's death," he began, picking his words carefully. He didn't want to give the impression that he was criticizing the late Keith Malone. Or that he was finding fault with the way she lived. "It left you—uh—I mean, you've had financial...difficulties?"

Sunny sat up again. She opened her mouth to say something, then apparently changed her mind and snapped it shut. Her eyes flicked down, then right, then finally settled on his face.

"Keith had everything in order when he was killed," she said firmly. "He made certain I'd be taken care of. *Good* care. But about six months after he d-died, my daddy took ill. Cancer. He was in and out of hospitals for more than a year. Needed all kinds of medical treatments. Only he didn't have any insurance."

"You...paid the bills." He wasn't surprised.

"They ate up most of what Keith had left me. By the time he finally passed away, I was pretty deep in debt."

The tilt of Sunny's chin warned Evan against offering sympathy or commendation. He shifted a bit closer to her, but stayed silent.

"It took me a couple years to pay everything off," she concluded evenly. "But I did. I'm all square now. And even if it means squeezin' nickels till Thomas Jefferson yells 'Uncle Sam,' I am *never* going back in the hole again."

Now why did you have to go and tell him all that? Maddy demanded of herself as soon as she'd finished speaking. *Wasn't it enough, you pouring out the pathetic truth about your dead mama and your drunken daddy that night at Lucy and Chris's? Did you have to ruin a perfectly nice Sunday afternoon by paintin' yourself as some kind of ex-borderline pauper turned skinflint?*

Evan couldn't understand. He just *couldn't*. No man who could dismiss the ruin of what she knew must be a fifty- or sixty-dollar designer-label shirt the way he had could ever understand!

And that remark he'd made about paying to have her kitchen repainted? She'd bet he'd thought that was funny. But if she'd taken him up on the idea, he probably would have flipped open his black calfskin wallet and pulled out enough cash to hire a crew of interior design experts. Wouldn't have blinked twice about it.

She could imagine what was going through his head right now. He probably figured she was looking for pity. Or worse—much, much worse—that she was trying to soften him up for a loan.

"Sunny—"

"I don't want your money, Evan," she told him sharply.

He stiffened, plainly taken aback. After several uncomfortable seconds he said, "I never thought you did."

Maddy chewed her lip, realizing that she'd offended him. For all his calm, quiet dignity, she could see the hurt in his eyes.

"I don't want you feelin' sorry for me, either," she added.

Evan inhaled a long, slow breath. Then he moved up the chaise longue, obliterating most of the distance between them.

"I wouldn't dare," he answered, taking her hands in his. She resisted for an instant, then gave in. Their fingers interlaced. His steady, sky-colored gaze moved from her eyes...to her lips...and back to her eyes.

Maddy swallowed, her body starting to tingle as though she'd been transfused with champagne. Her pulse snarled briefly, then stuttered into double time. She felt her nipples peak against the semisheer fabric of the lace-trimmed bra she'd donned when she'd changed out of the actively unattractive T-shirt and cut-offs she'd been wearing when he'd shown up at her front door.

"E-Evan?" she murmured shakily.

"Sunny..."

She leaned forward a little. He leaned forward a lot.

Their lips met. Mated. Their breaths mingled. The taste of Evan flooded Maddy's tongue. She angled her head left. He angled his right and deepened the kiss. She freed her hands from his and lifted them, clutching at his strong shoulders.

She felt his palms stroke up her rib cage, trembling as his thumbs came to rest just beneath the outer curves of her breasts. She arched into the embrace, tightening her grip on him. After a moment he began to ease her back...back...

Two things happened almost simultaneously.

First, the chaise longue collapsed beneath them.

Second, the cell phone Evan had automatically tucked in his sports jacket as he'd left his condo went off.

The caller was his mother.

Chapter 8

Lucy Banks was shocked. So shocked, she actually
stopped stirring the pasta sauce she was preparing for
herself and Maddy.

"His mother *what?*" she asked, her voice shredding
on the final word.

Maddy reached into the vegetable bin of the Banks's
refrigerator and extracted a head of romaine lettuce. She
understood her friend's reaction all too well. She'd had
a similar response five days ago.

"Told him his ex-wife is getting married again," she
answered, bumping the refrigerator door closed with her
hip.

"She actually thought he'd be interested?"

Maddy shrugged, crossing to the sink. "I'm not sure
about 'interested,'" she said honestly. She'd only heard
one side of the brief conversation between Evan and his
mother. And that side—Evan's—had basically con-

sisted of polite monosyllables. "But she obviously thought he should know."

Lucy huffed, shook her head and returned to her cooking.

Maddy rinsed and dried the romaine, then began to tear the crisp green leaves into bite-size pieces. That she'd been given anything to do was quite a compliment. She knew that Lucy was extremely territorial when it came to her kitchen. She'd already gotten an earful of complaints about the caterers who'd be coming in to help with the Fourth of July cookout the Bankses were giving for their friends and business associates.

Chris and Evan currently were out of town—the former in Washington, the latter in New York—on foundation business. Lucy had suggested that Maddy join her for what she'd blithely described as a "Girls' Night In."

What it really was, was an act of charity, Maddy thought. A tactfully disguised act of charity, to be sure. But still, an act of charity.

Evan had invited her to attend a benefit ball with him the following weekend. She'd no sooner said yes than she'd begun to regret it. Being with Evan at a baseball game—or at the Banks's pending picnic—was one thing. But accompanying him to some ultraelegant, thousand-dollar-a-couple party?

Her anxiety about the so-called "gala" had grown into something close to panicky despair when she'd realized that she didn't know what to wear. What *not* to wear, yes. But when it came to deciding what qualified as appropriate attire in Atlanta's swankiest social circles, she was clueless.

Desperate, she'd applied to Lucy for advice. After indicating that she was aware of the ball but would be missing it because of a family obligation back in Chicago, her friend had promptly offered to lend her something.

"Oh, I don't think—" she'd immediately demurred.

"At least check through my closet," the vivacious brunette had insisted. "I do a lot of socializing because of *Gulliver's Travels*, so I have a ton of dressy stuff. You're more than welcome to borrow an outfit. Or two. Or three. All I ask is that you don't look too gorgeous. I really hate people who look better in my clothes than I do."

Confronted with this kind of generosity—and painfully aware of her very limited means—Maddy had agreed to take a look through her friend's wardrobe.

"I guess Mrs. Blake's call really broke the mood, hmm?" Lucy inquired, adding a dash of salt to her copper cooking pot.

Maddy smiled ruefully, remembering how a tender embrace had suddenly deteriorated into a slapstick tangle of arms and legs.

"Actually, I think having the chaise fall apart did that," she said dryly. "The call was the final coup de grace."

"Mmm." Lucy tasted the pasta sauce, frowned thoughtfully, then reached for a pinch of freshly grated parmesan cheese. "You two must have been pretty carried away."

"Well..." Maddy looked down, flushing a bit. She grimaced a moment later when she realized that she'd ripped up enough romaine to feed six people. *Get a grip,* she ordered herself.

"Have you done it with him yet?"

Maddy brought her head up with a jerk. *"Lucy!"*

"I'm not asking for specifics." The response was demure, but followed by a saucy wink. "Although if you feel compelled to reveal all the juicy details, I won't stick my fingers in my ears to avoid hearing them."

"There are no juicy details."

"You don't think two people making out in public so passionately they collapse a piece of furniture is…juicy?"

Maddy felt the heat in her cheeks intensify. "The chaise was old," she said. "And we weren't out in public. We were in my backyard."

"In broad daylight."

"It was dusk. Almost dark," she said, quibbling.

Lucy sampled the pasta sauce again. After a moment she added a bit more cheese. Then she returned her attention to Maddy. "In other words, you haven't. Done it with Evan, I mean. Except for that one time when you were kids."

Maddy slumped against the counter with a sigh of surrender. Evasive tactics obviously weren't going to work. Time to 'fess up. "In other words, yes."

"Do you want to make love with him again?"

"We're still getting to know each other, Lucy. It's barely been a month." The longest month of her life in some ways. The shortest, in many others.

"So?" Lucy waved her wooden sauce spoon. "I knew I wanted to jump Chris within a couple minutes of catching him checking out my chest. Which isn't to say I owned up to it right away. Being a nice Catholic virgin, I had to wrestle with a certain amount of guilt. Impure thoughts and all that."

"But in the end, you…did?" Maddy was genuinely curious. Lucy and Chris seemed so different. Yet they fit together so well. She envied their relationship. Wondered at it, too.

"Jump him?"

"Yeah."

Lucy tilted her head to one side, her glossy brown hair rippling around her striking face. "I think we pretty much jumped each other simultaneously," she said, her dark eyes sparking with what obviously were pleasurable memories. "But I was kind of aggressive during the foreplay portion of the evening. I mean, Chris had some WASPy hang-ups about—" She broke off, homing in on Maddy like a laser. "Oh, no," she groaned. "Don't tell me! Evan's being *noble*. He's so hot for you I'm surprised he hasn't spontaneously combusted, but he's trying to play it cool so—"

"Do you really think so?" Maddy blurted out.

"Do I really think so, what?"

"You really think—" she swallowed, rubbing her palms against the cotton skirt she was wearing; her heart was hammering. "Evan w-wants me?"

Lucy stared, her eyes going huge with astonishment. "For God's sake, Maddy," she choked out. *"Don't you?"*

"I-I'm not sure." It was a relief to finally admit to the gnawing uncertainty with which she'd been living. But it also left her feeling frighteningly vulnerable. "He seems to enjoy my company. We've had some wonderful times together. And we've—well, things *have* gotten pretty intense on a couple of occasions. But Evan hasn't—I mean, he—he doesn't turn off, exactly, Lucy. But he seems to pull back. I get these, uh, *mixed signals* from him, you know? As though he isn't really sure how he feels. As though he's—he's—"

"Scared."

"S-scared?"

Lucy nodded. The up-down movement was very definite.

"Scared of what?" Of her? Of himself? Of...them?

"Failure."

Maddy shook her head, totally bewildered. "I don't understand."

"Evan's worried about pleasing you in bed, Maddy," Lucy declared, turning off the burner she'd been using and setting down the wooden spoon. "He blames himself for your first time being lousy, and he's afraid a return engagement won't be any better."

"He told you this?"

"Of course not."

"He told...Chris?"

"I have no idea." A grimace. "If he did, Chris wouldn't tell me. Buddy bonding and all that. Buddies don't tell their wives or girlfriends about their buddies' love lives. Only, for heaven's sake, don't ever let a guy know you know that. It'll upset him like you wouldn't believe."

"Then how—"

"Men are really sensitive when it comes to sex, Maddy," Lucy continued bluntly. "Now, I'm not setting myself up as an expert because of any vast personal experience. Chris was my first. And even though I had a couple of romances during the ten years after our divorce, I didn't sleep around. But I grew up with a widowed father, three unmarried brothers, four uncles and ten male cousins. I could qualify for a Ph.D. the masculine psyche! Not that it's all that complicated. The stuff you hear about women being fragile? Puh-leeze. The male ego is like an eggshell. Apply a little too much performance pressure, it cracks like Humpty-Dumpty."

"You think that's what I've done?" Maddy shifted uneasily. Had she seemed too needy around Evan? she asked herself. Been too obvious in her eagerness to be with him?

"Not at all." The response was quick and unequivocal. "I think Evan's pressuring himself. He's tuned in to you in a major way, Maddy. Think about it. He realized your first time wasn't very good, right? A lot of guys wouldn't have noticed. Or cared if they did. I have a friend named Tina back in Chicago who says that's why it's so easy to get away with faking it in bed. Because guys aren't paying attention to anything but themselves. Tina also says that the old joke about guys thinking the ideal girl is one who puts out then turns into a sausage pizza, isn't such a joke. But, anyway. I'll bet you Evan's spent nearly eighteen years lugging around this feeling he failed you sexually. Then, just a month ago, he found out he'd been tricked into thinking you were some heartless little slut, when you weren't. Add that he's plainly nuts to be with you now and—" a broad gesture "—well, it's no *wonder* you're getting mixed vibes."

Maddy took nearly a minute to sort through what she'd just heard. It made sense, she conceded. Although the notion of Evan Blake being insecure about anything was difficult for her to wrap her mind around. He exuded self-confidence. Not arrogance. Rather, the kind of bred-in-the-bone assurance that came with knowing he had a guaranteed place in the world.

"So what am I supposed to do?" she finally asked.

"Do you want him?"

Maddy's pulse stuttered. She felt herself flush again. "What do you think?"

"I think, yeah," her friend replied. "And not just on

a chaise longue. I think you're as gone on him as he is on you.''

Maddy caught her breath.

I think I'm in love with you, Sunny Kincaid, a handsome, blue-eyed boy had told her on a moonlit beach nearly eighteen years ago.

And I think I'm in love with you, Evan Blake, she'd replied.

Her response had been a lie. Because she hadn't *thought*. She'd *known*. She'd loved Evan Blake.

She still did.

That the love she now felt was different from the love she'd felt back on St. Simons was inevitable. The passage of time—the pain she'd suffered—had changed her. It was Maddy Malone who now loved Evan Blake.

"Maddy?" Lucy prompted, a hint of concern in her voice.

Maddy drew herself up and flashed her friend a smile. "Let's eat," she said decisively. "Then let's go through your closet and see what you've got."

Sunny had changed, Evan reflected as he finished knotting his black bow tie. Ever since his return from his business trip to New York, she'd been...different.

The precise nature of this change was difficult to describe. She seemed, well, the closest he could come to articulating it was to say that she seemed to know something he didn't. Something about *him*.

But what could it be?

That he'd missed her like hell during his time away? He knew that.

That he desired her so much he could taste it? He knew that, too.

That he was deeply, devotedly in love with her?

Evan shook his head and reached for the jacket of his tuxedo. Okay. So he'd taken a while to face up to it. But he knew *that* about himself, as well.

How ever many of his personal secrets to which Sunny might be privy, there definitely was one thing about him of which she could not be aware. And that one thing was that he planned to ask her to marry him this evening, after the ball. And after he did—and assuming, please, God, that she accepted—he intended to make love to her with all the tenderness at his command.

Be my wife, Sunny Kincaid, he thought. *Make a life with me, Madison Malone.*

Evan donned the dinner jacket, then buttoned it up. His gaze strayed to the small velvet box sitting on top of his bedroom bureau.

He hoped with all his heart that she liked the ring. It was a Blake family heirloom. Barbara had never worn it. He'd never even shown it to her. From the moment they'd started discussing marriage, she'd made it clear what kind of engagement ring she wanted. An old-fashioned gold band with a trio of modest, rose-cut diamonds had not fit the bill.

Strange thing, Evan reflected, adjusting his cuffs. While they weren't a matched set by any means, the engagement ring he planned to offer Maddy Malone was similar in style to the delicate gold bangle he'd intended to give Sunny Kincaid. Yet as far as he could recall, he'd been ignorant of the ring's existence at the time he'd purchased the bracelet.

He checked his watch, calculating the time it would take to drive from Buckhead to Inman Park. Ten minutes, he decided. He'd leave in—

Brring-brr-ing.

Evan went rigid. His mind jumped back to the previous Tuesday when Sunny had called to cancel their dinner date while he'd been en route to pick her up. Please, he prayed. No parolee problems tonight!

Brring-brr-ing.

He crossed to the phone in four swift strides and scooped up the cordless receiver. "Hello?"

"Evan?"

He recognized the breathy contralto voice instantly. Icy fingers fisted in his gut. He came within a nanosecond of disconnecting. Upbringing—for better or worse—trumped impulse.

"What do you want, Barbara?" he asked flatly.

A brittle laugh came through the line. "Do I have to 'want' anything, darling?"

He'd married her, Evan thought with a sudden flash of self-loathing. God help him, he'd married her! How could he have been so blind to what she was?

"No, you don't *have* to," he returned. "But you always do."

"That's rather unpleasant, Evan."

"You think so?"

There was an exasperated huff on the other end. "Fine. Be that way. I'm calling because I have some news. I thought it would be better if you heard it from me personally."

"If it's that you're marrying Paul Johnson, I already know."

"You've...you've been keeping tabs on me?"

Something in Barbara's voice made Evan's skin crawl. An edge of eagerness. She wanted him to care, he realized. To care and to be hurt by her coming marriage because of it.

"Hardly. My mother phoned with the news under the

misguided impression that I'd give a damn. What can I say except the groom-to-be has my sincere condolences.''

"You bastard!"

"*I know what you did, Barbara.*" The words erupted out of his mouth in a cold, compressed voice that he scarcely recognized as his own.

"D-did?" His ex-wife echoed after several seconds. The query held a quaver of fear.

"Nearly eighteen years ago on St. Simons Island to a girl called Sunny Kincaid."

"Oh, *that!*" Barbara sounded almost giddy with relief. Evan spent a second or two wondering what she'd thought he'd discovered about her. Then he decided he didn't care. "Good God. Don't tell me you tracked down your summer sweetie after all these years and compared notes."

"We met by accident."

Barbara tittered nastily. "Let me guess. She sashayed up to your table and asked how you wanted your burger done."

Evan made no response.

"I did you a favor, you know."

"A…favor?" He remembered the anguish he'd seen in Sunny's eyes when he'd recounted his version of what had happened on St. Simons. He felt sick.

"She was *trash*, Evan! You obviously knew she wasn't appropriate. Why else did you sneak around with her? You and she—God! It's worse than that pair-up between Chris Banks and Lola What's-Her-Name, the pizza waitress. And you know what a disaster that was. Their marriage lasted less than a year!"

Evan took a deep breath, shutting his mind to the first few sentences of his ex-wife's diatribe.

"Her name was Lucy, Barbara," he said very evenly. "Lucia Annette Falco. And just to bring you up-to-date, she's the manager of a very successful travel agency here in Atlanta. That's where I ran into Sunny. Sunny's a friend of hers. A friend of her husband's, too. Which is an interesting coincidence, since Lucy's husband is *my* good buddy, Chris Banks."

"W-what?"

"You hadn't heard? Lucy and Chris remarried in January. They found out what you did to Sunny before I did. Chris is probably too much of a gentleman to rat you out to your fiancé, even though he and Paul were pretty tight in law school. But Lucy's part Sicilian and she—"

Click.

Maddy stood in front of the mirror that hung on the back of her bathroom door and scrutinized her reflection. She was clad in an elegant sluice of amber silk ornamented with a provocative shimmer of beads and embroidery. A matching stole was loosely draped around her dramatically bared shoulders. Strappy gold sandals peeped from beneath the gown's fluid hem.

"This is the one," Lucy had decreed after she'd taken the deceptively simple garment out of a plastic dress bag and slipped it on over Maddy's head. "Maybe a little nip and tuck in the bust. Otherwise, it's perfect.

"I'm not sure…" Maddy had murmured, stunned by the image staring back at her from the cheval glass in her friend's bedroom.

"I am," Lucy had responded smugly, making a minute adjustment to the gown's spaghetti straps. "This is…*you.*"

Only it wasn't, Maddy mused, checking her eye

makeup for smudges. It was no more her than the sexily tousled salon hairstyle she was sporting. Or the antique gold drops that dangled from her earlobes.

She'd initially assumed the earrings were costume jewelry. An offhand comment from Lucy had disabused her of this notion.

"They're real gold?" she'd gasped, pulling them off. "Lucy, I can't borrow real gold jewelry from you!"

"Why not? You're borrowing a real dress."

"Which I'm still terrified is going to get something spilled all over it."

"For heaven's sake, Maddy. Evan's taking you to a black tie gala, not a food fight."

She'd shaken her head. "What if I lose them?"

"You won't. But even if you do, I've got insurance." Lucy had smiled. "Or, as you Southerners say, *insur-ance.*"

Maddy nibbled on her lightly glossed lower lip, vac-illating between excitement and anxiety. Evan was in-viting her into his world tonight. She wanted to make him proud. She wanted to—

Ding-dong.

She jolted, her heart starting to thud. *This is a mis-take,* she thought frantically. *I can't do this.*

The doorbell sounded again.

Maddy sucked in a deep breath, her pride reasserting itself. *Yes, you can,* she told herself, smoothing a palm down the front of her borrowed finery. *You can do any-thing you set your mind to.*

She flicked off the bathroom light and headed to the front door. While she didn't rush, she didn't dawdle, either. She was aware of the subtle caress of silk against skin as she moved.

She had a greeting prepared by the time she opened

the door. Gracious, but not gushy. She didn't want to babble like a girl going to her first prom. Unfortunately, the sight of Evan in his impeccably tailored evening wear seemed to blow several critical circuits in her brain. Her rehearsed salutation fled.

"Wow," she breathed.

Her escort seemed just as startled as she was. Then he started to smile. The slow curving of his lips fused another bunch of her synapses.

"I think that's my line," he responded after a moment. His compelling gaze stroked down her body and back up to her face.

"W-what?"

"I'm the one who's supposed to be saying wow. You look—" another top-to-toe appraisal "—absolutely beautiful."

Maddy blinked. Her mind was mush. And her body was starting to melt like a chocolate bar in a microwave. "This—this isn't my dress," she announced. It suddenly seemed very important that the urbanely handsome man standing before her understand this fact.

"Really?" A quirked brow. "Could have fooled me."

"It's Lucy's. The, uh, earrings are hers, too."

Evan seemed amused. "What about the shoes?"

Was he making fun of her? Maddy wondered. The possibility stung. "N-no," she answered, tilting her chin. "They're mine. I...I bought them on sale."

Evan took a step forward. Then he leaned in close. "And the perfume?" he inquired in a husky whisper, his warm breath teasing her ear.

Perfume? Maddy thought blankly. What per—

"Oh, God!" she cried. "I forgot to put on any perfume!"

Evan caught her upper arm as she started to whirl away from the door to rectify her oversight. His firm but gentle touch sent a shudder of response running through her. She looked at him, trying to remember how to breathe.

"No need, Sunny." He lifted his free hand and traced the curve of her cheek with exquisite care. "You're perfect as is."

Chapter 9

For the first hour or so of the gala, Maddy *felt* perfect. She felt as though she…well, not belonged, exactly. She doubted that she'd ever truly feel as though she "belonged" to the high-society milieu that was Evan's as a birthright. But she *did* find herself relaxing into the belief that she could fit into it, at least for one glittering night.

The first blow to her burgeoning self-confidence came during the dessert course of the benefit's lavish dinner. It was a small thing, really. But the fact that its source was Evan left her vulnerable to everything that followed.

"And what do you do to occupy your time, little lady?" the silver-haired man seated to her right inquired after delivering a lengthy monologue on his own business dealings. His name was Spalding Rutherford. Maddy had seen his photograph in the *Atlanta Journal-Constitution* several times.

His question caught her with a bite of raspberry tart in her mouth. But before she had a chance to chew and swallow, Evan—who was seated to her left—inserted himself in the conversation.

"Maddy's going to law school," he said smoothly.

Going to law school. That was all. No mention of the work which had, in a sense, led to their reunion.

"Law school?" Rutherford turned to his wife, a well-preserved ash blonde in black satin and pearls. "Did you hear that, Janelle? Law school."

"Our middle boy, Chase, is a lawyer," Janelle informed everyone at the table with a complacent smile. "He's with my daddy's firm in Baton Rouge."

"Whereabouts are you attendin'?" someone else at the table—a magnolia-skinned redhead who'd mentioned that she'd recently opened a decorating business—inquired.

Maddy cleared her mouth, slanting a glance at Evan. She flashed back on the phone conversation they'd had the morning after they'd learned the truth about what had happened in the aftermath of their Fourth of July liaison on St. Simons. She remembered the tone she'd thought she'd heard when he'd confirmed his knowledge of what she did for a living.

"I'm taking night classes here in Atlanta," she replied.

"You mean you're only goin' part-time?"

"I have a day job." Maddy picked up her napkin and dabbed at her mouth. Glancing around, it suddenly dawned on her that she appeared to be the only woman who'd finished her dessert. "As a parole officer."

There was a startled silence. Maddy saw several of her tablemates exchange looks. No one rushed forward to volunteer that he or she had a son, daughter, father or second cousin three times removed who shared her career path.

"So, you work with…criminals?" Janelle Rutherford asked.

"Just like your daddy." Her husband chuckled at his own wit. "Jane's daddy's defended some of the biggest criminals in the state of Louisiana," he explained. "Two ex-congressmen. One ex-governor. Probably a half dozen—"

"That isn't funny, Spalding. Every single one of those people was acquitted."

"Of course they were, honey." Another chuckle. "That's why your daddy bills four hundred dollars an hour!"

"Since all of my 'clients' have pleaded out or been found guilty of *something,* I suppose you could call them criminals," Maddy interpolated. "A lot of them are repeat offenders. Hard-core. Frankly, more than a few probably should be locked up for life. But some are simply people who've made mistakes and paid the price for it. They're tryin' to do the right thing and get their lives back on track."

"Still." The redhead shivered, placing an elegantly manicured hand on her escort's forearm. He gave her fingers an absent, there-there pat. "I can't imagine what it would be like, dealin' with that kind of… individual…every day."

Maddy smiled briefly. She didn't suppose the other woman could. Then again, *she* couldn't imagine dealing with people who were willing to spend tens of thousands of dollars to have twenty-five coats of lacquer applied to their dining room walls.

"It's not every day," she corrected. "I usually get weekends off."

"Which is when she has to deal with individuals like us," Evan immediately picked up.

There was a fractional pause. Then everybody at the table started to laugh, including Maddy. But inside, she felt as though a line had just been drawn, straight through her heart.

Us, the man she loved had joked. Individuals like...us.

The former Sunny Kincaid understood that Evan Blake's *us* didn't include her.

"Excuse me," a feminine voice cooed about an hour later.

Maddy, who was temporarily on her own while Evan went to get them some champagne, summoned up what she hoped was a pleasant smile and pivoted around. Her head was starting to throb. Likewise, her high-heel-encased feet.

The source of the syrupy interruption was a lushly beautiful blonde decked out in ice-blue chiffon and diamonds. Maddy had absolutely no idea who she was.

"Yes?" she responded.

"The man you're with," the blonde said. "Would he happen to be Evan Blake?"

Several rude retorts—among them, "Why?" and "Who wants to know?"—rose to Maddy's lips. She forced herself to swallow them.

"Yes," she answered politely. "He is."

"I knew it." The blonde laughed delightedly. "I just knew it! I'm Sherrie Norman, by the way."

"I'm...Maddy Malone."

"Short for Madeline?"

"Madison."

"Oh, how darlin'! My name's short for Charmaine,

if you can believe it. Anyway. I thought I recognized your—ah—ah—"

"Friend."

"Friend? Really?" Sherrie's glossy pink lips curved into a voluptuously pleased smile. Maddy found herself thinking about cats, cream and defeathered canaries. "Well, the thing is, I knew this girl back in college. And she had a silver-framed picture of him—your *friend,* Evan Blake—on her dorm room desk."

"Oh?" A greasy chill swam through Maddy's stomach.

"She was stuck on him like glue." The blonde sidled a bit closer and lowered her voice. "Just between you and me, I didn't care for her much. But I *will* confess I thought her taste in men was just fine. Not that I ever said a word, you understand. She gave the impression that it would be highly unwise to come between her and her Evan. I mean, she once mentioned something about taking care of this other girl who tried to go after him. Some waitress, I think she was. Barbara—that was her name, Barbara—maintained Evan didn't take the girl seriously. He had some fun with her, I suppose. You know how good-looking men are. Still, Barbara said this girl was definitely from the wrong side of the tracks. You know, the type who'd do just about anything to catch herself a rich—"

"Sorry I took so long," Evan apologized, materializing by Maddy's side with two flutes of champagne. "I was sidetracked by someone from the—oh, excuse me." He smiled apologetically, dipping his head. "I didn't mean to interrupt."

Such perfect manners, Maddy thought numbly, taking one of the glasses. The steadiness of her hand astonished her.

It wasn't the regurgitation of Barbara Wilcox's venom that hurt her. She was immune to that, to a large degree. Rather, it was the realization that Barbara's characterization of her would likely be shared by many people in Evan's circle. Even now.

"Sherrie, Evan Blake," she said quietly. "Evan, this is Sherrie Norman."

"Pleased to meet you, Mr. Blake." Sherrie beamed and batted her lashes. "I was just telling your friend Madeline that I believe you and I have an acquaintance in common..."

Evan didn't flinch when the beautiful blonde invoked the name of his ex-wife. In fact, he finessed the reference so suavely that Sherrie Norman felt free to elaborate on all the other things they probably had in common.

As it turned out, she and Evan *did* know a number of the same people. They'd also skied on the same slopes in Aspen, snorkeled off the same island resort in the Caribbean, and dined at the same "charming" restaurant in the Napa Valley.

The former Sunny Kincaid stood and listened to their chummy tête-à-tête, occasionally contributing a smile or a nod. And all the while, she felt herself retreating further and further...

Back to "her" side of the tracks.

An hour later the throbbing in Maddy's head had escalated into a full-scale pounding. The balls of her feet felt as though they were being stabbed by hundreds of tiny knives. The smile muscles in her face seemed to be paralyzed. Unfortunately she couldn't tell whether they were locked into the "lips up" or the "lips down" position.

"Will you excuse me for a few minutes?" she asked Evan as the song they'd been dancing to came to an end. Well, actually, *he'd* been fox-trotting. She'd simply been moving in time to the music and trying to follow his lead. "I need to powder my nose."

"Why?" Evan teased, easing his hold on her with flattering reluctance. His hand slid along her spine, lingering briefly in the small of her back. The warmth of his palm seeped through the fine fabric of her gown. "Your...nose...looks perfect to me."

"That's very nice of you to say." She tried to ignore the thrill that cascaded through her as her partner let his gaze drift downward—from her nose to her lips, from her lips to her partially bared breasts. "But I still need to go."

"I'll be here when you get back," he promised, looking her directly in the eyes.

Maddy made her way to the ladies' room with her head held high. She was profoundly grateful to find the lavishly appointed facility empty. Slipping into one of the stalls, she shut the door and slumped down on the commode. Inhaling shakily, she buried her face in her palms.

She'd been wrong, she thought bleakly. There were some things she simply couldn't do. And being with Evan in this kind of situation seemed to be one of them.

Which made her wonder about being with him in *any* situation.

Evan Blake fit into "her" world very easily. He'd proven that repeatedly. But try as she might, she knew that she could never fit into his. And at some level—at that "Maddy's going to law school" level—he obviously knew it, too.

She sat in her hunched-over position for a minute,

maybe two. Finally she forced herself to straighten up. She had to see this through, she told herself. To finish out the evening and then—

Maddy froze as she heard the ladies' room door open. A rustle of fabric and the click-click-click of high heels signaled the arrival of at least two people.

"...little obvious, honey?" a vaguely familiar female voice inquired.

"Hush, Nadine. If you didn't have Richard all wrapped up, you'd've been after him with a harpoon."

Maddy put her hand to her lips as she realized to whom she was listening. "Nadine" was the redhead from the dinner table. The other woman was Sherrie Norman.

"A *harpoon?* What a tacky thing to say."

"Oh, you know what I mean. Tell me you didn't get a tingle from Evan Blake."

"Well...maybe." The response was coy. "Just a little."

"He rang *my* bell clear across the ballroom."

There was a pause. Maddy kept very still, barely allowing herself to breathe. She listened to the gush of a water faucet being turned on. After ten seconds or so, the water stopped.

"You sat with him at dinner, didn't you?"

"Mmm-hmm." Nadine sounded preoccupied.

"What about his...date?"

A bitchy little laugh. "The prison guard, you mean?" Maddy sat bolt upright.

"What?"

"Oh, Sherrie!" More laughter. "If you could see your face right now! You look like you swallowed a porcupine!"

"She's a *prison guard?*"

Nadine took a few seconds to get her hilarity under control.

"Well, no," she eventually admitted in a rather disdainful tone. "But close to it. She's a parole officer. Can you believe it? Evan spun some tale about her going to law school. Only when I asked her where, she said she was takin' night classes. Part-time. If you ask me, she's probably doin' one of those legal-aid secretary correspondence courses you see advertised on TV."

"What would someone like Evan Blake be doing with someone like that?"

"What do you *think,* honey?"

Another pause. Maddy clenched and unclenched her hands.

"Sherrie?"

"What do I think?" the blonde repeated coolly. "I think the man's havin' fun with another...'waitress.' I also think anything *she* can do, *I* can do much better."

"Are you all right, Sunny?" Evan asked shortly before midnight, stealing a glance at the woman sitting to his right.

"I'm fine. Just a little...tired."

"Mmm." He returned his gaze to the road and flicked on the turn signal. He gave a rueful chuckle. "I should have warned you that these so-called galas can be hard work."

"You should have warned me about a lot of things."

"What?" He wheeled the car left, onto the tree-lined street where Sunny's home was located. Was she accusing him of something?

Out of the corner of his eye, he saw his companion lift her chin. "You should have told me people were going to ask whose dress I was wearing."

"Whose dress...?" he echoed blankly, pulling into her driveway. Then he realized. "Oh. Lord. You mean the designer."

"That's right." Sunny undid her seat belt as he turned off the car's engine. "Some woman came up to me at one point, checked me out from head to toe and said, 'Calvin, right?' And I said—um, no, Lucy Falco. She looked a little upset for a second, then bobbed her head and said, "Oh, yes. Milan. *Fabulous.*"

Evan chuckled again. "She'll probably be at Neiman-Marcus first thing tomorrow trying to buy a Falco original."

Unbuckling his own safety harness, he got out of the car and walked around to the passenger's side. The night was soft and still. A balmy air carried the gentle scent of flowers.

He opened Sunny's door and handed her out. She gave him a small, off-center smile of thanks. Evan was tempted to lean in and brush his mouth over hers, but he restrained himself. There was something in her eyes...

They walked to her front door. She invited him in. He immediately accepted. She offered to make him some coffee. He agreed to that, too.

They chatted their way around a variety of subjects. It seemed to Evan that the conversation grew more awkward the longer it went on. Topics were haphazardly introduced, then clumsily abandoned. Sentences petered off into silence with greater and greater frequency.

It was in the midst of one of these silences that he decided he couldn't wait any longer. It was time to declare himself.

"Sunny—"

"Evan—"

Their voices collided. Were immediately cut off.

"Have you noticed how often we seem to do that?" he asked wryly after a brief pause. "Please. Ladies first."

There was another pause. An inchoate sense of anxiety jittered through him as he watched Sunny draw herself up and level her shoulders. The supple movements made her gown ripple over her slender body. Beading winked out an alluring message. Desire intertwined with disquiet.

"This isn't going to work, Evan," she finally stated. Her voice was steady. So was her gaze.

He stared at her, stunned. Whatever he'd expected her to say, this wasn't it. "I don't...understand."

"You and me. We...we're too different. Our being together isn't going to work."

"No." He shook his head, denying her assertions. All of them. Categorically.

"Yes."

"How can you say that?"

"How can I not? It's the...t-truth."

"The *truth?*" His voice spiked. He shoved his hands into his trousers and felt the velvet box that contained the engagement ring he'd spent most of the evening dreaming about slipping on her finger. He yanked his hands free. "For God's sake, Sunny. The truth is—"

"You're ashamed of me."

Evan gaped. But even as he began to formulate a rejection of Sunny's shocking charge, his memory replayed a fragment of the conversation he'd had earlier in the evening with his ex-wife.

"I did you a favor, you know," Barbara had claimed.

"A...favor?" he'd countered.

"She was *trash*, Evan! You obviously knew she

wasn't appropriate. Why else did you sneak around with her?"

He caught his breath, feeling as though he'd taken a kick to the gut. His memory skipped further back, to the heart-to-heart he'd had with Chris following the scene in Gulliver's Travels.

"Okay," he'd conceded to his best friend. "Okay. I'll admit it. I had some doubts about whether she'd fit in with my friends. I mean, they made—we *all* made jokes about the full-time islanders. Stupid, snotty jokes…"

But that had been nearly eighteen years ago! he told himself fiercely. The idea that he was ashamed of Sunny in any way, shape or form now—

"I am not ashamed of you," he said, fighting to keep his temper in check.

"Then why did you lie about me?"

"Lie?"

"At dinner tonight. You told everybody I was going to law school."

"But you *are* going to law school!"

"Nights. Part-time. I'm a parole officer, Evan. I work with *criminals!*"

"Given that you stood me up for a date last Tuesday because one of your 'clients' got busted for possession with intent to distribute, you think I'm not aware of that?" he fired back.

"What I *think* is that you don't want any of your fancy friends to be aware of it!"

"Those people are not my friends, fancy or otherwise. I barely know them."

"You could've fooled me. You have so much in common with them. Like skiing and snorkling and sipping witty little—"

He uttered an oath. "Are you talking about Sherrie Norman?"

"Remembered her name, did you?"

The possibility that Sunny's strange behavior might be rooted in jealousy streaked through Evan's consciousness like a flare, igniting a volatile mix of surprise and male satisfaction. He doused the reaction a moment later, hoping it hadn't shown on his face. Instinct told him that this was *not* the moment to accuse the woman he loved of being overly possessive.

"I remember a lot of people's names," he pointed out. "As for my conversation with Ms. Norman, what did you want me to do? Tell her to shut up? So we spent a few minutes talking about some people we know and some places we've been. It was no big deal."

"Maybe not to you. But what about me, Evan? I don't know any of those people. I've never been to any of those places."

Evan took a deep breath. Expelled it in a hiss. "Let me get this straight," he said tautly. "First, I made the mistake of telling a table of semistrangers about your future aspirations rather than your current occupation. Then I committed the unpardonable sin of having a polite discussion with a woman I'd just met. And based on those two egregious acts, you've decided you and I shouldn't be together anymore?"

Sunny flushed. "Do not take that condescending tone with me, Evan Blake."

She had a point and Evan knew it. Even to his own ears, his remarks had sounded pretty damned patronizing. But still—

"I'll stop condescending, if you'll start making sense."

The color in Sunny's cheeks grew more vivid. Her eyes flashed a dark and dangerous green.

"Sense?" she spat out. "Fine. Let's talk about sense. No. Let's talk about *sensitivity*. As in, havin' some! When you asked me to go to this ball tonight, did you spend one solitary second considerin' that the prospect would send me into a panic about what I should wear? About how I'd afford the 'proper attire' once I finally figured out what it was? Did you think of me sweatin' about the possibility of makin' a total fool of myself? Of...of embarrassin' y-you?"

Evan blinked. No, he realized with a pang. He hadn't. Even knowing what he did about Sunny's financial situation—and about her stiff-necked pride—he hadn't considered any of those things.

But what if he had? he questioned a moment later. Attending tonight's benefit was something the foundation expected him to do, especially since Chris was out of town. How would Sunny have reacted if he'd decided to go solo? Or...supposing he'd gone ahead and asked her to accompany him, then suggested that he might help her underwrite the cost of a gown?

Oh, yes, he thought sardonically. He could envision what kind of response *that* little scenario would have prompted! And it wouldn't have involved a thank-you note on engraved stationery!

"I'm sorry," he said. One of them needed to be reasonable. He guessed the task fell to him. "Maybe I was...insensitive. But whatever you went through before the gala, Sunny, it turned out all right, didn't it? You looked—you *look*—beautiful."

"This isn't me, Evan!"

"Of course it's you."

"No, it's not! I'm tricked out in somebody else's clothes. Somebody else's jewelry—"

To hell with reasonableness, Evan abruptly decided, and closed the distance between them.

"Do you honestly believe any of that matters to me?" he demanded harshly, catching her by the shoulders.

Sunny flinched from his touch. *Flinched* from it. And he felt a shudder run through her at the same time. For one awful instant he remembered the way she'd jolted beneath him when he'd taken her virginity.

"Let go of me," she said, her voice high and tight.

"Wh-what?"

"Let…go…of…me."

Evan opened his hands. They were shaking. So was his voice when he invoked his one-time lover's name.

Sunny took a step back. The physical space she opened between them wasn't very great. But the psychological gap…

He could think of only one way to bridge the chasm, to bring her back to him. Taking a deep breath, he uttered the words he'd had locked inside his heart for nearly eighteen years.

"I love you, Sunny."

Her lips trembled for an instant, then parted on a sudden exhalation. There was a sheen in her hazel eyes. After a moment she replied, very evenly, "I've heard that before."

Evan stared at her, unable to speak. Unwilling to believe that he'd heard what he'd just heard.

"I think you'd better leave, Evan."

"But—" He had to force the word up his throat and out his mouth.

"Please. Just…*go*."

Chapter 10

While tears were not unknown in the place where Maddy worked, parole officers were seldom the ones who shed them. This fact had a lot to do with why she chose to keep her swollen eyes hidden behind dark glasses when she arrived for work on Monday morning.

"Hey, Maddy," the receptionist greeted her.

"Hey, Simone," Maddy responded, keeping her head down as she scribbled her signature in the logbook.

"You got a cold, girl? You sound all snuffly."

"Allergies."

"Sorry to hear that. I had allergies real bad last year. There's somebody waiting on you already. A Ms. Dora-Jean Purvis Spivey Spivey Spivey. She sounded all snuffly, too. But in her case—"

"Where is she?" Maddy interrupted, alarmed. She'd unplugged her phone after Evan had left and kept it unplugged until this morning. What if Dick had needed help and been unable to reach her? What if she'd failed at the job she'd thrown in Evan's face so angrily Saturday night?

"I put her and her bag in your office. I hope that was—"

Maddy was already dashing down the hall.

"You're…what?" she heard herself say in a shattered voice several minutes later.

"I'm leavin' Dick because there's no place for me in his life now that he's a rich man," Dora-Jean Purvis Spivey Spivey Spivey declared moistly, blotting her smudged eyes with a wad of tissue.

Something deep inside Maddy recoiled at the other woman's words. "Okay," she said carefully, blinking against the sudden sting of tears. "Let me see if I've got this straight. Friday, Dick proposed to you and you said yes."

Dora-Jean nodded and sniffled. Then she gave Maddy an odd look and asked, "Ms. Malone, are you *sure* you don't want a few of my tissues? You're gettin' all watery-eyed—"

"I'm fine! It's just…allergies."

"But—"

"*Please*, Dora-Jean. Let's just get through this, all right? Friday, you and Dick got engaged. And Saturday—" she swallowed "—Dick became the sole winner of the latest Georgia state lottery."

"Eleven point three million dollars after taxes. At least, that's what Mr. Blake estimated."

"Mr. B-Blake? Dick's spoken with E-Evan Blake?"

"Uh-huh. Right after he won, he tried to call Ms. Falco and her husband—seein' that Ms. Falco's his employer, and her husband's still sort of his lawyer. Only they weren't home. So Dick left a message sayin' he had somethin' really important to tell them and would they please call him back. Then he tried to call you, only you weren't home, either. Then he wanted to call the prison where Tom and Butch are. Only he realized the guards probably wouldn't let 'em come to the phone. So, he sat around, burstin' at the seams with his big news and tellin' me all the wonderful things we were goin' to do with his money.''

"How did Evan Blake get involved?"

Dora-Jean wiped her nose. "Ms. Falco finally called Dick back on Sunday. She was real stunned by his news. Then her husband got on the line. He told Dick to call his friend Mr. Blake right then and there, because he—Mr. Blake—is some kind of expert at managin' other people's finances. Dick wasn't too sure at first. He said somethin' about havin' the impression you didn't trust Mr. Blake. But I guess Ms. Falco's husband soothed his mind. Because as soon as he got off with him, Dick—"

At this juncture, the door to Maddy's office swung open and Dick Spivey marched in.

"Ms. Malone, I apologize for burstin' in here like this," he began earnestly. "I know this isn't my regular day. And I don't want you to think I'm breakin' my parole obligations by missin'—"

Dick stopped, looking around as though he'd suddenly realized that something wasn't quite right. Finally he focused on Dora-Jean. She was staring at him with tear-filled eyes, pressing her tissue-stuffed hands to her abundant bust.

"D-darlin'?" he said. "Wh-what are you doin' here?"

Dora-Jean stood up. "I'm leavin' you, Dick. I gave

Ms. Malone my engagement ring. And a letter of explanation.''

"Why?"

"Because I knew I could trust Ms. Malone to—"

"Not that 'why'!" Dick took a step forward. "Why are you leavin' me, Dora-Jean?"

"You know w-why." The blonde's chin wobbled.

"No, I don't. I've pretty much figured out why you left me the other two times. But *now?* Just give me one good reason—"

"I can give you eleven-point-three million good reasons! You're a rich man now, Dick Spivey! Or you will be, once you present your winnin' ticket. You can have anythin' you want. A fancy house with a Jacuzzi. A brand new pickup truck. An entire set of Elvis CDs and videos. And you can go anywhere you want—"

"Not while I'm on parole." Dick darted an anxious glance at Maddy. "Not unless I get special—"

"Oh, you know what I mean!" The former Mrs. Spivey gulped several times, then began to weep. "You're movin' into the life-styles of the rich and famous, and there's no way I can follow along. You were so sweet over the weekend, talkin' about our gilt-edged future in the lap of luxury. But with every word, my heart got heavier. Because I knew, Dick. *I knew I could never fit in.''*

Maddy closed her eyes. Her throat was dry. Her temples were pounding. She felt as though she were being squeezed to death by a vise.

"I thought you loved me, Dora-Jean," she heard Dick Spivey say in a soft, almost solemn, voice.

"I—" a hiccupping sob "—d-d-do."

"And I love you, darlin'. So how can you think

there's anywhere we could be together where you wouldn't fit in?''

There was a long pause. Maddy opened her eyes and discovered that Dick had crossed to Dora-Jean and taken her in his arms. She wiped beneath her nose with the back of her left hand, trying not to sniffle.

I love you, Sunny, Evan had told her. Despite all the abuse she'd heaped on him, he'd responded with a declaration from his heart. And she...

She'd sent him away. She'd hurt the man she loved, then she'd told him to go!

"What about p-people thinkin' I'm m-marryin' you for y-your money?" Dora-Jean asked shakily, stroking Dick's skinny chest.

"Anyone who thinks that doesn't know you very well," Georgia's newest multimillionaire stated. "Which makes them *ignorant.* Call me stupid, Dora-Jean, but I don't pay attention to ignorant people. And neither should you!"

"I hope you didn't mind my telling Dick Spivey to call you, Ev," Chris said, settling into one of the chairs positioned in front of Evan's desk. "But he was in desperate need of financial counsel. And since you're the best..."

"Adequate to the occasion." Evan massaged the back of his neck and glanced at the clock on the wall. Twenty-three past eleven, it proclaimed. Roughly thirty-five hours had elapsed since he'd lost his first and only love for the second time. "And no problem about Mr. Spivey. I'm glad to help, any way I can."

"What does Maddy think about her multimillionaire parolee?"

Evan's body tightened. He forced himself to look at

his friend. Chris wasn't angling for information, he decided after a moment. His question had been a straightforward one.

"I don't know," he answered honestly. "I haven't spoken to her since Saturday night."

Chris frowned. "You two went to the benefit, right?"

"Right."

"And...?"

Evan shook his head, his eyes straying to the top drawer of his desk. He'd placed two items inside that drawer when he'd arrived at work. The first was a small velvet box containing a family heirloom. The second was a simple gold bangle wrapped in tissue paper. Why he'd brought them with him, he had no idea. A desire to torture himself, maybe.

"And I blew it, Chris." He met his friend's gaze again. "I started the evening with an engagement ring in my pocket. I ended it the same way."

"You were going to ask Maddy to marry you?"

"That was the plan."

"*Was* the plan? Meaning, you didn't?"

"I never got the chance. Sunny did a preemptive strike. Told me our being together wasn't going to work because we're too different. Accused me of being...ashamed...of her."

"Said she didn't think she'd fit with your side of the aisle."

Evan surged out of his chair. "Damn you!" he exploded, slamming a fist against the top of the desk. "If you're suggesting for one second that just because Sunny's background—"

"Whoa! Whoa!" Chris held up both hands. "Simmer down, Ev. I'm not suggesting anything of the kind. Madison Malone is a remarkable woman. In fact, if you were in a rational mood, I'd probably make some crack about her being too good for you. But since you're obviously borderline nuts at the moment, I won't. The thing is, Maddy reminds me of Lucy in a lot of ways. And without spilling too many family secrets, part of the reason Lucy and I crashed and burned the first time around was that she felt...socially insecure.''

"Lucy?" Outrage gave way to astonishment. Evan sank back into his chair. His atypical surrender to temper had left him feeling a little rocky.

"I had the same reaction," Chris admitted with a rueful smile. "I couldn't imagine anyone as smart and gutsy and beautiful as Lucy being insecure about *any-thing*. But she was. And my boneheaded inability to understand that led to some problems. Which led to some more problems. Which eventually led to me doing something so monumentally stupid it makes me sick to think about it."

"What...what did you do?"

"I arranged for Lucy to walk in on me kissing another woman."

Evan couldn't hide his shock. "Oh, geez, Chris!"

"I wasn't trying to drive her away. I was trying to make her jealous."

"J-jealous?"

"Lucy's insecurity had made her pull back from me. I thought she'd stopped caring. But even when I realized she hadn't, even when I started to grasp what a terrible mistake I'd made, I didn't go after her. I let things...stew. And when I finally *did* reach out, I didn't put up much of a fight after the first rebuff."

"But you found your way back to each other in the end," Evan reminded him after a long silence. "You're together again."

"Yeah." Chris nodded, seeming lost in thought. Eventually he refocused and said, "You and Maddy— *Sunny*—found your way back to each other, too, Evan. Now, I don't know what happened between you Saturday night. Or what precipitated it. But I have to ask— whatever went wrong, whatever was said—does it negate the feelings that made you put an engagement ring in your pocket?"

"Is it true?" Simone the receptionist asked, big-eyed with excitement. "Dick Spivey won the big jackpot?"

"It's true," Maddy answered, signing herself out for the rest of the day with an unsteady hand. She had no idea whether what she intended to do would repair the damage she'd inflicted, but she knew she had to try it.

"Well, damn! Who says crime doesn't pay?"

"Playing the lottery isn't a crime."

"Huh. Tell that to my granddaddy, the Baptist minister."

"I know your granddaddy, Simone," Supervisor Darrell Parker drawled, plunking down a stack of reports. "I wouldn't try to tell him *anything*." He glanced at Maddy, cocking a brow. "It's barely eleven-thirty. You takin' an early lunch?"

Maddy met her boss's questioning gaze steadily. "I have some personal business I need to take care of, Darrell. I've cleared my afternoon appointments. My paperwork's squared. Can somebody cover for me if something unscheduled comes up?"

"And why would 'somebody' want to do that?"

"Aside from the fact that she's covered for every sorry somebody in this place more times than any of them has fingers?" Simone asked sweetly.

"Yeah," Darrell growled. "Aside from that."

"Because—" Maddy took a deep breath "—it would mean a lot to me."

The older man regarded her narrowly. "This 'personal business' isn't goin' to sidetrack you from law school, is it?"

Maddy shook her head, no longer trusting her voice.

"Well, then...scat."

She did. And as she did, she heard Simone call out a prediction that taking care of her "personal business" might be just the thing to cure her "allergies."

The minute hand on the clock on Evan's office wall clicked to twelve, straight up. A split second later he cursed and cast aside the IRS memorandum he'd been pretending to read.

He'd realized the answer to Chris's question as soon as he'd heard it. No. *Nothing* that had happened Saturday night had negated his desire to make Madison Malone his wife.

Hard on the heels of this fundamental truth had come the understanding that translating his desire into reality wasn't going to be as easy as he'd initially thought it would be. He'd made a lot of unilateral assumptions. Taken a great deal for granted. Lord. When he thought of the arrogance implicit in his marriage-proposal-followed-by-lovemaking scenario!

Hence his decision not to go haring off after Sunny as soon as Chris left his office. He'd needed to pull himself together. To get himself completely under control. The only way to make things right was to—

"The hell with it!" Evan exclaimed, yanking open the top drawer of his desk. He plucked out the ring box and the tissue-wrapped bracelet. Standing up, he stuffed the former into the right pocket of his jacket and the latter into the left. Then he headed for the door to his office.

He was just reaching for the knob when the door swung inward. He stumbled back a step to avoid being smacked in the face. He opened his mouth to tell the interloper that whatever his or her business was, it would have to wait.

And then he saw who the interloper was.

"S-Sunny?"

"Evan? Oh…Evan!"

Exactly how she made the transition from standing in the doorway of Evan's office to lying on his office sofa, Maddy was never entirely certain. Her recollection of the process was always rather…blurred.

She remembered apologizing over and over and being assured that all was forgiven and understood.

She also remembered being apologized *to*, and offering unreserved absolution in response.

She remembered a fair amount of kissing, caressing and loosening of clothes, too…

"Evan," she moaned against her one-time lover's clever, questing lips. "Oh…Evan."

There was a teasing nibble at the right corner of her mouth. It was followed by a hungrier nip at the left corner. Desire sparked. Pleasure sizzled.

"I love you, Sunny," Evan said hoarsely, winnowing his fingers through her short hair as though he intended to inventory every single reddish-brown strand. He traced the outer curves of her ears, triggering a silvery rush of arousal through her nervous system. "I love you so much."

"I love you, too," she promised, tugging off his expensive silk tie and flinging it aside. She began to unfasten the buttons of his pale blue Oxford cloth shirt. It was not an easy task, given the shakiness of her hands. "I love you...more than anything."

The hand Evan slid down her front was unsteady, too. But she felt the power of it burn through the fabric of the peach-colored top she had on and gloried in it. She wriggled, trying to help, as that same hand began to tug that same peach-colored top upward.

The stroke of skin against skin produced a delicious kind of shock. Maddy inhaled sharply. Evan's scent—clean, crisp, with just a hint of spice—filled her nostrils and hazed her brain. Her head spun. She squirmed, vaguely conscious of the rub of the sofa's upholstery against the backs of her thighs.

"Yes," she whispered, her pulse hopping like a speed-crazed rabbit. Her fingers throbbed with it. Her toes tingled. "Oh, yes..."

There was pleading in her voice. And persuasion. Likewise, a giddy sort of passion. Evan responded to all of them. The ambivalence she'd described to Lucy was gone, like smoke before a strong wind. He groaned uninhibitedly as she licked the hollow at the base of his throat. She would have sworn that he was as caught up in the moment as she.

But then something started to change. Subtly, at first. Then with increasing obviousness. What had been an intuitive rhythm—a perfect balance of give and take—began to tumble out of sync.

Wha...? she wondered, clutching at what had seemed

like the only stable element in a maelstrom of very elemental sensations.

"Maddy." Evan sounded desperate. And a little dazed. He shifted awkwardly, apparently trying to ease away from her. His fumbling movements induced an unsettling sense of déjà vu. "Sweetheart, please. We need to...stop."

"*S-stop?*" Maddy's green-gray eyes were enormous with shock. Except for her kiss-reddened lips, her face was pale. Despite his efforts to ignore it, Evan found the contrast incredibly provocative.

"At least...slow down," he temporized after a moment, struggling to keep his voice on an even keel. It was difficult for him to gauge to what degree he succeeded in his effort, given that he could scarcely hear himself speak through the thunderous pounding of his heart.

"But—*why?*"

He raked a hand through his hair, grappling with the fact that he'd been on the verge of taking Sunny on the sofa of his office. With the door unlocked. With the blinds on the windows only partially drawn. That she'd been ready and willing—as eager as he for consummation—was no excuse.

He'd fallen on her like a starving dog on a bone nearly eighteen years ago. He'd promised himself that he would never, ever, do that again. He'd come perilously close to breaking that pledge.

"I...I need to ask you something." He staggered to his feet. His knees felt like jelly. This was in stark contrast to another portion of his anatomy, higher up. It was pressing against the zipper of his trousers like a steel rod.

"Whatever it is," Sunny returned. "My answer is yes."

Evan smiled crookedly. "I hope so," he told her. "But just—just give me a minute, okay?"

Actually, he only needed a few seconds to locate his suit jacket and empty its pockets. Then he returned to Sunny. She'd sat up and restored her clothes a bit. There was a hint of petulance to the set of her mouth, but there was faith—and love—in her eyes.

Evan seated himself next to her. Very carefully, he unwrapped the gold bangle and offered it on his outstretched palm.

"This is something I planned to give to you nearly eighteen years ago," he said. "I found it the day Chris and Lucy helped me unpack. The same day I found your photograph. It's...yours."

The woman Evan Blake loved took his modest offering with trembling fingers. She slipped the bracelet on her left wrist, then traced the delicately etched design with something close to reverence. "You...you got this for m-me?"

"For Sunny Kincaid. And this—" he snapped open the small velvet box and held it out "—is for Maddy Malone."

"Oh." It was a gasp. "Oh."

"Will you marry me?"

Hazel eyes met blue ones. For a breathless instant time stood still. Then:

"Yes." It was another gasp. "Oh, Evan...*yes!*"

Somehow, the ring got out of the box and onto the proper finger. There was a wild flurry of hugs and kisses, laughter and tears. Temptation beckoned, stirring Evan's blood, singing through his brain. But he reined

himself in before desire shoved him back to the brink
he'd teetered on a short time ago.

"Now what?"

Had his own body not been aching with it, Evan
might have found Sunny's very obvious frustration
funny. He did, however, find himself feeling rather flat-
tered by it. He was only human, after all. And very,
very male.

He cleared his throat. Considered the possibility that
the woman in his arms was going to respond to what
he was about to say by accusing him of insanity. Also
contemplated the notion that this accusation might be
on the mark. Then he cleared his throat for a second
time.

"I think we should wait," he said simply.

"Wait?"

"For our...honeymoon."

Sunny blinked rapidly several times. Then something
new entered her eyes. Something warm. Something very
womanly. Something that once again made Evan feel
as though she might understand him better than he understood himself.

"Why?" she asked softly, stroking his chest with her
newly be-ringed left hand.

Slowly, carefully, he cupped her face. "Because
we're not a pair of inexperienced kids fumbling through
their first time. Because we're adults, who've been with
other people. Who've learned a lot about life during the
past eighteen years. What happened between us in the
boathouse wasn't wrong. But it was a mistake. For all
we felt for each other, we weren't ready for that kind
of commitment. I know I hurt you that night. I can't
undo that. But you and I—we can make our second time

a first, Sunny. By waiting till we've pledged ourselves before God, our friends and whomever else wants to look and listen.''

Sunny turned her face left, then right, kissing each of his palms in turn. Had he been standing, the touch of her lips would have dropped him to his knees.

"I have one question," she said.

"What?"

"Do you think we can be married by the Fourth?"

Chapter 11

In the end Evan Blake and the former Sunny Kincaid didn't simply marry "by" the Fourth of July. They married *on* it. The ceremony was performed by one of Maddy's law school professors, who just happened to be a justice of the peace. Their exchange of vows and rings was witnessed by Chris and Lucy Banks, two people who knew a great deal about the blessings of rediscovered love.

The addition of several dozen guests—among them, Maddy's boss, Darrell Parker, and Evan's mother—plus some eleventh-hour renegotiating with the caterers, transformed the Banks's Independence Day cookout into a wedding reception. The joyousness of the occasion impressed everyone present, including one of the most junior attendees....

"Sorry I took so long," Maddy apologized to her husband of barely five hours. She'd gone upstairs about forty-five minutes before to freshen her makeup after the cake-cutting ceremony and found herself waylaid by her new mother-in-law.

Although her style was as cool and tart as a lemon sorbet, Dianne Blake had conveyed that she approved of her son's second marriage and sincerely hoped to get to know his new bride better. Her unexpected words had touched Maddy deeply. So deeply that after the other woman had left to return to the festivities, she'd started to cry.

Lucy had shown up a minute or so later, trailed by Tiffany Tarrington Toulouse-Huffmeister and the soon-to-be re-Spiveyed Dora-Jean Purvis Spivey Spivey Spivey. There'd been a few seconds of intensely feminine alarm, but they'd been defused by Maddy's fervent assurance that she was shedding tears of happiness. This admission had precipitated an emotional exchange of hugs which had soon dissolved into an old-fashioned sobfest. It was a reaction that all involved agreed no man would possibly understand.

By the time Maddy had dried her eyes, she'd felt revived. Reenergized. As light as a soap bubble. She'd also discovered that she had to redo her face and hair. Hence, her rather lengthy absence from the party.

"The wait was worth it," Evan answered, slipping an arm around her waist and brushing a kiss against her cheek. While Maddy succeeded in not melting into his embrace *too* obviously, she couldn't keep her pulse from accelerating in response to his touch. She loved him so much! And she wanted him so badly she ached with it. While she cherished his idea that they wait to consummate the renewal of their relationship until after their marriage, the enforced celibacy had been difficult.

"Let me introduce you to John and Leigh Gulliver and their son, Andy. John, Leigh—my wife, Maddy."

"Gulliver?" Maddy reluctantly turned her attention from her new husband to the compelling looking couple he'd been talking with when she'd returned from her primping. The woman was a willowy blonde with wide-set blue eyes. The man was tall, dark and scarred on one side of his face. He was as intimidating as his wife was lovely. "As in...Gulliver's Travels?"

"Guilty as charged," the man responded with a quick, charismatic smile. The change of expression transformed his hard features. "Pleased to meet you, Maddy."

"Congratulations on your marriage," Leigh Gulliver added warmly.

"Thank you."

"Yeah," the young boy identified as Andy piped up. He appeared to be about five years old. Maddy thought she could see traces of both his parents in his mischievous face. "'Gratulations. And this is a *really* fun wedding conception."

There was a startled silence.

"I think you mean *re*ception, buddy," John Gulliver said after a moment, mussing his son's toffee-colored hair with affection.

"I do?" The youngster bit his lower lip and furrowed his brow. "Then what's a con—"

"Something we'll discuss later," his mother interrupted firmly.

Andy considered this edict with a faintly mutinous expression. Maddy struggled not to laugh. The tightening of Evan's fingers against her waist suggested that he was having a similar problem. She didn't dare look at him to find out.

"Okay," the little boy acquiesced with a put-upon sigh. Then something seemed to occur to him. The incipient poutiness disappeared. Looking up at Maddy with big, bright eyes, he asked, "Do you have handcuffs?"

Maddy nearly choked. "H-handcuffs?"

"Yeah." An enthusiastic nod. "Before you came, Mr. Blake told us how you're sort of like a lady p'liceman. That you have this really cool job as a, uh, uh, well, I forgetted the right name. Some kind of off'sir. But the main thing is, you make bad guys be good after they get done in jail. Isn't that right?"

Maddy glanced at Evan, realizing with a sweet, sharp pang that he must have made a special point to mention her occupation to the Gullivers. He gazed back, wordlessly affirming his pride in her and everything she chose to do. After a tender, tremulous moment, she looked back at Andy. Her heart was very full.

"That's pretty much it," she affirmed, her voice a bit huskier than it had been.

"So, you have handcuffs—right? And p'rolly a gun, too."

"Uh, well…yes, Andy. But not with me."

"I knowed *that*," the youngster asserted. "You don't have 'em 'cuz you just got married to Mr. Blake and you're goin' on your honeymoon thing. Mr. Blake told us that, too. Not about the handcuffs. About the honeymoon thing. I bet you'll have fun. My mommy and daddy had one, and it was good, even if they didn't bring me back a baby like I wished for. Only my 'pinion is, you should wait for the fireworks and leave after."

It took Maddy a moment to untangle the last few sentences. When she did, she felt herself flush. She looked at Evan again. The instant their eyes met, the rest of the world seemed to fall away.

"We're leaving on our honeymoon thing before the fireworks?" she asked throatily.

His mouth curved, but his gaze remained serious. "If you don't mind."

"But I didn't think..." Maddy shifted, acutely conscious of the thud-thud-thudding of her heart. While she couldn't deny that she'd spent a significant chunk of the past few weeks fantasizing about how she and Evan would spend their wedding night, she hadn't given much consideration to the venue. She'd left that up to her husband-to-be. And based on what little he'd said, she'd more or less assumed that he'd arranged for them to initate their marital intimacy in one of the city's luxury hotels. "I mean, I didn't pack..."

Evan pressed a fingertip to her lips. "It's all taken care of, Sunny. Trust me."

She did, of course. With every bit of her being— body, heart and soul—the former Sunny Kincaid trusted the man who'd grown from the boy she'd tumbled into love with eighteen years before. Still. She experienced a flash of panic several hours later when she realized where Evan intended they spend their wedding night.

"The...b-boathouse?" she asked as he guided her along the path that led from his family's St. Simons "cottage" to the beach. "The boathouse where y-you and I..."

"Not exactly," he answered, lacing his fingers with hers.

Her pulse jolted. She was sure he must feel it. "What does that mean?" she managed, her breath threatening to clot in her chest. "Not...exactly?"

"I've had some work done on it."

"Work? What kind of—"

Maddy stopped dead in her tracks as the boathouse loomed into view. Her heart seemed to stop, too, at least for a moment or two.

"Oh," she whispered. Her vision blurred. She blinked rapidly several times, trying to clear it. She wanted to make certain that she was seeing what she thought she was seeing. And if the old cliché about being able to believe one's eyes was true, she was. "Oh...*Evan.*"

What she remembered as a rather ramshackle structure made of weather-silvered wood had been transformed into something out of a fairy tale. The small building had been freshly painted. It had also been garlanded with ivy and flowers and illuminated with what looked like thousands of tiny, twinkling lights.

"I originally wanted candles," Evan said. He was standing a few inches behind her. "But then I got worried about the place catching fire and burning down before we ever got to it."

"I...I don't know what to s-say."

Evan put his hands on her shoulders and turned her to face him, his thumbs massaging with seductive deliberation. Maddy lifted her chin a few degrees, staring up into his deep blue eyes. She saw heat in them. And hunger. And love. Above all, love.

"The only thing I want to go up in flames tonight is us, Sunny," he whispered, his voice velvet soft and utterly adult. The sound of it sent honeyed shivers dancing up and down her spine.

The shivers multiplied and radiated outward when he lowered his head and claimed her mouth. Maddy gave herself up to the caress with a long, languorous sigh, bringing her hands up and tangling her fingers in the hair on the back of his head.

Yes, she thought with absolute assurance. Oh, yes.

The kiss deepened. Darkened. It left Maddy so dizzy with longing that she didn't immediately realize when Evan swept her up into his arms and carried her into the boathouse. That her perspective on the world would spin and shift seemed...almost normal.

The interior of the boathouse was even more enchanting than the outside. A lush, floral-patterned carpet graced the floor. Shimmering swags of fabric veiled the rough-hewn wooden walls. Frosted glass globes glowed softly from each corner, bathing the place with a lambent, romantic light. There were bunches of flowers, casually arranged in baskets, scattered around.

And then there was the bed. It was king-size. Made up with snowy white linen. At least a half dozen lace-trimmed pillows were mounded at one end like dollops of whipped cream.

Maddy staggered slightly as Evan set her down, but managed to steady herself by catching his arm. She felt his muscles bunch and release beneath her clutching fingers.

Somewhere in the back of her sensation-hazed brain she registered the voluptuous tickle of the carpet against her stockinged soles. Her shoes had come off. When, she had no idea.

She looked around, trying to take everything in. She wondered fleetingly how this astonishing metamorphosis had been arranged, then decided that the practical details didn't matter. Better to surrender to the magic of the moment.

To the man who'd created it.

"*Sunny...*" he said.

"*Oh, Evan...*" she replied.

They embraced, moving together like dance partners, swaying in response to music only they could hear. Maddy pressed her lips to the side of Evan's throat, tasting the faintly salty tang of his skin. His pulse throbbed. So did her own.

She inhaled, breathing in the clean, masculine scent of her once-and-soon-to-be-again lover. She slid her palms up his chest and shifted her body, instinctively mating feminine-soft to masculine-hard.

Evan groaned deep in his throat. His hands stroked down her body to clasp her hips. His intention might have been to hold her still. But after a moment he brought her even tighter against him. His fingers flexed once, then began to knead through the soft fabric of her dress.

Maddy turned her face up toward his. Their lips fused in a potent, passionate kiss. Evan groaned again. She absorbed the sound greedily, whimpering with pleasure as it poured into her mouth like wine.

They'd rushed and fumbled eighteen years earlier, each of them desperate with wanting, but neither one of them completely certain of what to do. This time they took it slowly. They savored each step on their erotic journey. Cherished each kiss, each caress, to the fullest.

And they still fumbled, just a little, as they began to undress each other.

"God, S-Sunny," Evan exclaimed on a breathless laugh as he slid his fingers beneath the catch of her bra. "I'm shaking."

"Me—" she struggled with the button on his right shirt cuff, finally managing to undo it "—t-too."

Finally the last article of clothing was slipped off and

cast aside. As it fluttered to rest amid the stylized pastel flowers woven into the carpet, Evan scooped Maddy up in his arms again and carried her over to the bed.

He positioned her against the pristine sheets with great care. After brushing her mouth with his once, twice, three times, he straightened. He moved back a half step so he could gaze down at her newly bared body. The audaciousness of his perusal seared along her nervous system like an electrical current, making her blush and burn.

But she didn't turn away or try to shield herself from his blood-pounding scrutiny. She gazed back at him with her own brand of daring, devouring him with her eyes.

The strong shoulders.

The sleekly muscled chest.

The taut belly.

The arrogant jut of his masculine arousal.

Maddy swallowed hard, moistening her lips with a quick lick of her tongue as desire sizzled through her veins. After a few incendiary seconds, she dragged her eyes back to her husband's face.

"I was too shy to l-look last time," she confessed in answer to the question she read in the depths of his eyes.

Evan's smile flashed like summer lightning, charged with a very male kind of satisfaction. "And this time?"

"I've looked." She extended her left arm, the slender gold bangle that still adorned her wrist gleaming softly. She beckoned, the rose-cut diamonds of her engagement ring catching the light. "Now I want to touch..."

He joined her on the bed, stretching out beside her with predatory grace. They exchanged kisses. Moist. Melting. Openmouthed.

"Last t-time—" she began shakily as her new husband covered her breasts with his palms.

"I looked," he told her, his voice husky with emotion. He nipped at her earlobe, triggering a shudder of pleasure. His thumbs grazed the hard buds of her nipples. "You were beautiful then. But you're even more beautiful now."

Maddy *felt* beautiful. And bold. As appetites escalated, she was the one to accelerate the pace. She touched. Teased. Tempted.

She wanted.

Needed.

Loved.

Finally Evan joined them. The sensation of being filled by him made her gasp with delight. She lifted her hips to accept him more fully, glorying in the stretch of accommodation. He said something on a half-shattered breath and adjusted his position a few critical centimeters. The movement of flesh against flesh was intensely, almost unbearably, arousing.

Maddy was dazed by the power of her own desire. But in the midst of her sensual bedazzlement she became aware that Evan was holding back. She could feel it in the corded tension of his body. Hear it in the uneven rasp of his breathing. See it in the midnight-blue of his heavy-lidded eyes and the clench of his jaw.

"This time—" he whispered "—for y-you."

She lifted a trembling hand and touched his face. "No, my love," she whispered urgently. *"For us."*

The first geysering rush of ecstasy stunned her. The second swept her into gloriously foreign territory. Her body moved of its own accord. Not mindlessly, but in answer to a summons so elemental that it could not be intellectualized.

"Yes," Maddy gasped frantically, clinging to Evan. He was both the cause of and the one safe haven in the storm of pleasure that had taken possession of her. "Oh…Evan. Oh. *Yes!*"

She reached what she thought must be the peak and shattered on it. But there was more. Much, much more.

And in the end, the best of it was shared—utterly, absolutely—with the man she loved.

Making love with Madison Blake for the first time was such a transcendent event that Evan was almost tempted to call it an out-of-body experience.

Almost. But not quite. Because the ineffable sense of physical satiation that he experienced in the wake of their initial joining made it abundantly clear that his body had been intimately involved throughout the entire, bliss-inducing process.

How long it took him to gather himself together afterward, he never tried to estimate. But once he recovered the ability to think in a reasonably coherent manner, he was assailed by doubt. Not about Sunny. About himself.

She felt it. Somehow, some way, she felt it. Because as he opened his mouth to utter a question so helplessly revealing in its triteness that he cringed at his inabilty to stop himself from asking it, she lifted her head.

"Are you—" he began huskily.

"Yes, I am," she said immediately, regarding him with eyes that held both womanly warmth and wisdom. The corners of her kiss-swollen lips curved into a smile. A small, but decidedly smug, smile. "And yes, it was."

Evan swallowed, temporarily deprived of speech. Then a great rush of emotion suffused him. The burden he'd carried for eighteen years lightened to the point of being almost impossible to discern. That he would never feel entirely free of it was something he accepted. And he thought the lingering weight on his conscience—no matter how light—was for the best in a way. He never wanted to forget how far he'd had to travel, how much he'd had to learn, to find the happiness he now knew.

Maddy lowered her head to his chest and snuggled close. He relished the tease of her breath against his skin. She shifted a little, the silken strands of her hair tickling beneath his chin.

"I can hear your heart," she announced after a few moments.

Evan smiled, slipping an arm around her. "And I can feel yours," he returned, letting his hand settle on her left breast. The velvety tip pebbled against his palm. His body stirred in response.

"I love you."

"And I love you."

There was a long pause.

"What time is it?" Maddy eventually inquired.

"Time?" Evan's body had progressed from stirring to stiffening. He tried to calculate. "Uh, probably a bit after midnight."

"So it's tomorrow."

"Well..."

His new wife lifted her head again. At the same time, she slid her hand beneath the sheet.

"We finally had our fireworks on the Fourth," the former Sunny Kincaid said. "What do you say to an encore on the fifth?"

* * * * *

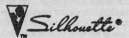

If you enjoyed what you just read,
then we've got an offer you can't resist!

Take 2 bestselling
love stories FREE!
Plus get a FREE surprise gift!

Clip this page and mail it to Silhouette Reader Service™

IN U.S.A.	**IN CANADA**
3010 Walden Ave.	P.O. Box 609
P.O. Box 1867	Fort Erie, Ontario
Buffalo, N.Y. 14240-1867	L2A 5X3

YES! Please send me 2 free Silhouette Intimate Moments® novels and my free surprise gift. Then send me 6 brand-new novels every month, which I will receive months before they're available in stores. In the U.S.A., bill me at the bargain price of $3.57 plus 25¢ delivery per book and applicable sales tax, if any*. In Canada, bill me at the bargain price of $3.96 plus 25¢ delivery per book and applicable taxes**. That's the complete price and a savings of over 10% off the cover prices—what a great deal! I understand that accepting the 2 free books and gift places me under no obligation ever to buy any books. I can always return a shipment and cancel at any time. Even if I never buy another book from Silhouette, the 2 free books and gift are mine to keep forever. So why not take us up on our invitation. You'll be glad you did!

245 SEN CNFF
345 SEN CNFG

Name	(PLEASE PRINT)	
Address	Apt.#	
City	State/Prov.	Zip/Postal Code

* Terms and prices subject to change without notice. Sales tax applicable in N.Y.
** Canadian residents will be charged applicable provincial taxes and GST.
  All orders subject to approval. Offer limited to one per household.
  ® are registered trademarks of Harlequin Enterprises Limited.

INMOM99   ©1998 Harlequin Enterprises Limited

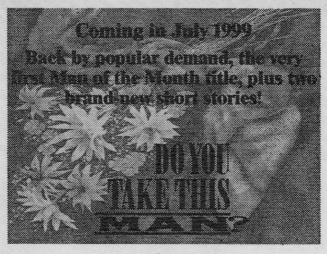
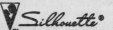

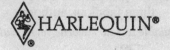

**The combination of physical attraction
and danger can be explosive!**

Coming in July 1999
three steamy romances together in one book

HOT PURSUIT

by bestselling authors

JOAN JOHNSTON

ANNE STUART

MALLORY RUSH

Joan Johnston—A WOLF IN SHEEP'S CLOTHING

The Hazards and the Alistairs had been feuding for generations, so when Harriet Alistair laid claim to her great-uncle's ranch, Nathan Hazard was at his ornery worst. But then he saw her and figured it was time to turn on the charm, forgive, forget…and seduce?

Anne Stuart—THE SOLDIER & THE BABY

What could possibly bring together a hard-living, bare-chested soldier and a devout novice? At first, it was an innocent baby…and then it was a passion hotter than the simmering jungle they had to escape from.

Mallory Rush—LOVE SLAVE

Rand Slick hired Rachel Tinsdale to infiltrate the dark business of white slavery. It was a risky assignment, Rachel knew. But even more dangerous was her aching desire for her sexy, shadowy client….

Available at your favorite retail outlet.

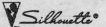